Best wishes

Arlene Hale

ONE MORE BRIDGE TO CROSS

Books by Arlene Hale

WHEN LOVE RETURNS

THE SEASON OF LOVE

THE RUNAWAY HEART

A TIME FOR US

PROMISE OF TOMORROW

GOODBYE TO YESTERDAY

HOME TO THE VALLEY

WHERE THE HEART IS

A GLIMPSE OF PARADISE

ONE MORE BRIDGE TO CROSS

ONE MORE BRIDGE TO CROSS

by Arlene Hale

LITTLE, BROWN AND COMPANY — BOSTON – TORONTO

FIRST EDITION

T08/75

LIBRARY OF CONGRESS CATALOGING IN PUBLICATION DATA

Hale, Arlene.
   One more bridge to cross.

   I. Title.
PZ4.H1618on [PS3515.A262]   813'.5'4   75-2368
ISBN 0-316-33856-7

*Published simultaneously in Canada
by Little, Brown &Company (Canada) Limited*

PRINTED IN THE UNITED STATES OF AMERICA

For
Mary with the sunshine smile

ONE MORE BRIDGE TO CROSS

1

THERE WAS a parade on Fifth Avenue and the resulting traffic jam in midtown Manhattan was monumental. Sara Denning sat impatiently in a cab at the corner of Madison Avenue and 49th Street listening to the meter ticking off the fare, glancing at her watch and knowing that if the police didn't get the traffic moving very soon, she was going to be late. No one in her right mind trying to sell something to the firm of Garrison, Holmes and Ferry would arrive even a minute behind schedule.

"I'm getting out, driver," Sara said. "What's my fare?"

He told her. "It will only be a minute or two —"

She knew better, so she gave him the money, added a tip and climbed out, gripping her portfolio. Everyone was needlessly blowing their horns and shouting angrily as Sara rushed away through the crowded streets. The way people were thronging into Saks Fifth Avenue she thought they must be having some kind of sensational sale. Mentally she clicked off the things her wardrobe lacked; clothes were an important item in her job and also a very costly one. But there was no time to shop.

She walked rapidly uptown, half-skipping, half-running. The portfolio under her arm represented some brutal hours of work when she had been assigned the job of doing the layout for a new product called Whiff for Garrison's company.

"The boss likes you or he wouldn't have given you the assignment," Jerry had told her. "Besides, if anyone can break down Steve Garrison's resistance, it's you."

She had not been as confident as he, but had thrown herself into the project with determination and had drawn out the best she had in her. When Jerry reviewed what she'd done, he thought it was her most successful effort since she had come to work at Waterman's Advertising Agency.

"Great, baby, just great," he'd said.

It was all too obvious his mind was not on her work but other things. Jerry Lydell had been growing more persistent in the last couple of weeks and Sara frankly didn't know what to do about it. Jerry was like the city — busy, exciting, rushing. But she longed to slow down, to take her time with something, to do what she really wanted for a change. She knew she shouldn't complain because her job paid well and was interesting and challenging, but there were uneasy moments when she wanted to pack up her pencils, pens and paints and simply go off to the sea somewhere and stay until she had grown to know its every mood, color and season.

At last, she reached the impressive professional

building that housed the firm of Garrison, Holmes and Ferry and pushed open the glass doors, striding across the polished lobby, past the splashing fountain and a new piece of sculpture done in hammered aluminum that somehow did nothing to stir her imagination, and dashed to make the elevator.

She reached the reception desk fifteen minutes late, was greeted rather coolly and asked to wait. Ten minutes stretched to fifteen, and then nearly half an hour had gone by. She was growing more nervous by the second, but she resisted the urge to open the portfolio and stare at her work one more critical time. She heard a door open at last and glanced up. Hal Hartley! Hal was one of the sharpest artists around and they had clashed head-on more than once. He was a tough competitor and if he was after the Whiff account too . . .

"You may go in now, Miss Denning."

In her dealings with Steve Garrison, Sara had found him to be hardheaded and difficult to please, and now the moment of truth had arrived. Garrison did not like to waste time, so she spared only a moment for the usual pleasantries. Then she put her drawings on the easels spread around his room and she went into detail about each piece of work, talking a bit too fast. Garrison rocked back and forth in his swivel chair, rolling a big cigar between his fingers and now and then rubbing a hand over his balding pate. He didn't give her a clue as to what he thought by even a flicker of an eyelash. When she had finished, she felt breathless.

She had probably sounded too eager, too confident, and leaned too much to a hard sell.

Garrison's cigar lighter flamed on and off. Minutes crawled along like hours. Then he went to peer at each large drawing, examining a detail here, murmuring about another there. It all meant nothing. If there was one thing Garrison loved to do, it was to keep people dangling.

"I'm not sure you've caught the right effect. It seems a bit superficial, but I'll need a day or two for a final decision. If you'll leave the drawings —" Her heart skipped a beat. "Of course. Thank you for your time, Mr. Garrison."

She let herself out, nodded to the receptionist and with the empty portfolio case in her hand, she walked out of the plush offices and down the hall to the elevator, uncertain and spent. How long would she have to wait? How good had Hal Hartley's work been? Sara pressed the button for the elevator, endured a maddening wait and then rode down to the lobby once more.

The air wasn't good today and she knew what this would mean to her brother, Lee. Somehow he would manage to put in his full day's time as a driver for a pharmaceutical supply house, but he would come home, eyes stinging, thin shoulders rounded from the effort of breathing, and he would have a restless night despite the help of an air conditioner. He had not been strong since a childhood disease had weakened his lungs and he was not getting any better, rather probably worse. Their doctor had helped with medication, but he had been suggesting rather strongly that Lee consider a different climate.

Lee did not share the doctor's views.

"I'm not going anywhere," he had told Sara stubbornly. "Listen, I'm all right. I can handle it. Besides, where would I go and what would I do? New York's our home, Sara, and even if it's not the greatest, it's all we have, right?"

It had been hard to put up an argument to that, for their ties *were* here. They had grown up in Queens, where they had gone to school and made friends. Their parents were buried there as well. When it had seemed best, they had left their old home and moved into Manhattan, taking an apartment together and sharing the expenses. So far, it had worked out very well. Lee went his way and she went hers and yet they were together, and when they were both home for weekends, they felt as if they were still a piece of a family.

Half an hour after she left Garrison, Holmes and Ferry, Sara was back in her office near the UN building. As she glanced out to the river, a wave of the will-o'-the-wisp crossed her heart — there was a yacht leaving a dock, bound for heaven only knew where, and she wished she was on it.

Her door opened and Jerry appeared. "How did it go?"

"He'll 'be in touch.'"

Jerry frowned. "You mean he didn't take it on the spot? What's the matter with Garrison? Is he blind or something?"

"Or something," Sara said wryly. "Hal Hartley was there ahead of me, and Garrison didn't think I'd caught the right effect."

Jerry lifted his dark brows at that and came to take a chair beside her desk. He was handsome and very bright and had worked his way up to an important position at the agency, so he knew all the perilous ins and outs of the business.

"Hartley can't hold a candle to your work, Sara. It was some of your best. Relax. It will be okay."

"Will it?" she asked.

"You're just down now. The job's catching up with you, but it will all straighten out soon. Wait and see. Tomorrow Garrison will call and everything will be coming up roses."

"I wish I could believe that."

He reached out and touched her hand. "Hey, forget about Garrison. Concentrate on tonight. We're going out, remember?"

"Jerry, I know I promised but I don't think I'm up to it. I'm a little worried about Lee."

"Your brother's a big boy now and he can take care of himself," Jerry said with an edge in his voice.

Jerry resented her concern for Lee, thinking she was being overly protective.

"Jerry, it's been a bad day, please —"

Jerry set his jaw and stared at her. Then with a curt nod, he got up and moved to the door.

"Okay. But sometimes, Sara, you try my patience no end —"

He left, closing the door noisily and Sara drew a

deep breath. The last thing she needed right now was to have Jerry angry with her. She kept remembering Garrison's last remark to her and she *knew* deep down she had lost the account to Hal Hartley.

The apartment Sara and Lee shared was not fancy but comfortably furnished. The location was more convenient for Lee than Sara. Whoever got home first put the pot on, and usually it was Lee. When Sara reached the door today, she smelled the aroma of fresh coffee.

"Hi!" she called.

Lee came out of the kitchen and gave her a quick look. "How did it go with Garrison?"

"Zero so far. Hartley was there ahead of me and I'm awfully afraid —"

"Stop stewing," Lee said. "I know you'll get it."

"Oh, to be such an optimist," she sighed. "How was your day?"

"Busy. My last delivery was near the warehouse so I checked the truck in a little ahead of schedule and got home early."

Lee was tall and slender with curly blond hair and burning blue eyes. He was attractive in a wiry sort of way but he looked too pale and dark smudges were riding high on his cheekbones. Sara knew from the way he stood, shoulders slightly hunched, that he was tired.

"Why don't you go and read the paper? I'll handle supper."

"I thought you were going out with Jerry."

"Changed my mind."

By the time Sara had prepared a simple meal, Lee had fallen asleep in his chair, the *New York Times* spread across his lap. She touched his shoulder gently.

"Lee —"

"I guess I dozed off," he said with a yawn.

Sara carried the paper to the table with her and while they ate, she studied the ads, reading them with half-hearted interest. They always sounded good, but Sara's investigations usually revealed something sorely wrong, in everything from apartments to rent to new jobs.

"There has to be something better than I have," Sara said.

Lee stared at her with surprise. "You're kidding! Sis, you've come along very well in the last two years you've been with Bob Waterman. Now cheer up! You're just edgy about the Garrison job."

"Would you listen to this!" she said. "Wanted, a young man as a chauffeur for a busy executive. Remote seaside location. Good wages. Private living quarters. References required. Married man preferred."

"That lets me out," Lee said.

Sara folded the paper carefully. "Lee, why don't you answer the ad anyway, just for the heck of it."

Lee stared at her for a moment and then pushed back his plate.

"Why should I do that?"

"The sea would be good for you. You might even

get some color again. The air would be fresh, clean, pure. I know you'd feel better —"

"And what would I do with you?" he asked with a smile. "I thought we were going to stick together, at least until one of us got married."

"I'll go with you!"

"And do what?"

"Paint like crazy. I could take a room in a town nearby. You know I've always wanted to do some serious painting."

"What do we use for money? A job like that might not pay as well as you think. Besides, it sounds too good to be true."

"We'll squeak by. I have a nest egg saved. Besides, Waterman might let me free-lance for the firm. Who says I have to sit in the office behind a desk to do my best work?"

"Sara, you were never one to go off half-cocked! What's wrong with you?"

"I don't know, Lee. Did you ever get so restless you could scream? And Jerry's getting impatient with me."

Lee lifted his brows. "I thought you liked Jerry very much."

"Like, not love. There is a difference."

Sara tore the ad out of the paper and tucked it under the sugar bowl for quick reference. "Just in case," she said.

"Sara, I have a good job and jobs don't grow on trees. It's not hard work. It's something I can handle and I don't want to throw away a good thing."

Lee was right, of course. They couldn't just go running off whenever they felt like it, and the job sounded so attractive that by now, there had no doubt been a dozen people to answer it. The job was more than likely already filled.

For the next two days, there was no word from Garrison. For the same length of time, the chauffeur ad continued to run in the paper.

It was Friday afternoon, nearly four o'clock, when Bob Waterman got the word and came to Sara's office. When she saw his face, her heart sank.

"We lost the Whiff account," he said. "Garrison turned it down cold."

Sara's disappointment was a deep, sharp thrust that brought bitter tears to her eyes.

"It was a good presentation, Sara. One of the best we've ever sent to Garrison. But who knows how that man thinks —"

"Hartley edged me out?"

Waterman nodded. "That's my guess."

Sara opened her desk drawer and took out her purse. It was not closing time but, under the circumstances, she knew she couldn't just sit here and wallow in her defeat.

Jerry came out of his office just in time to see her duck out the door and called after her, but she didn't stop.

She caught the bus for home and sat very rigidly in her seat, staring out the window, seeing the traffic, hearing the noise, swallowing at the lump in her throat and hating the city and nearly everyone in it. Her mood grew darker and darker so that by the time she reached the apartment, she was only too glad to go inside and lock the door behind her.

It seemed quiet and empty without Lee and, to work off her frustration, she decided to make an especially nice supper for him. But that didn't go well either. She made silly mistakes and broke one of the last pieces that was left of a set of her mother's china she had kept.

She was near tears when her eyes fell on the clipping under the sugar bowl. It was a blind ad with no name, address or phone number, just a number to write to at the newspaper. When Lee's key rattled in the lock, she went to meet him at the door and waved the clipping under his nose.

"Lee, won't you consider answering this? I want out of New York and I'm going, one way or another. I want you to come with me and this could be the solution —"

"You lost the Whiff account?" he asked.

"Yes."

"Tough luck, Sara. But you can't win them all, you know. Now about this newspaper ad, I've been thinking about it." He broke off with a grin. "I already answered it. We should hear something next week."

2

Saturday morning Sara was enjoying extra hours of sleep when she was awakened by the phone. Lee answered it and there was something about the tone of his voice that made her quickly pull on a robe and open the door of her bedroom. Lee saw her and covered the mouthpiece of the phone for a moment.

"It's in answer to my letter — the newspaper ad —"

Sara went to stand beside him.

"Yes, we could come today. I'll leave within the hour," Lee was saying.

Sara couldn't believe it was happening. Lee talked a little longer, said goodbye and hung up, his blue eyes lighted with enthusiasm.

"Have you got a New Jersey road map, Sara?"

"There should be one in the desk. You mean you're actually going for an interview — today?"

"It seems a little unusual, but I take it this is not a run-of-the-mill kind of job. We're to see a man named Chadwick and he lives in a place called Windmere which is located near the town of Vincent."

Sara found the New Jersey road map and they pored over it, searching out the best route.

"I told Chadwick that you would be coming along. He wants to meet you as well."

"Isn't that a little strange?"

Lee lifted his shoulders. "Just a careful man, I suppose. He wants to see what kind of terrible company I keep."

She laughed at that, her heart lightened by her brother's cheerful mood. The outing would be good for both of them, even if the job didn't pan out.

They ate a hurried breakfast, dressed for the drive down the New Jersey coast and were soon off.

"Now, Sara, I don't want you to get your hopes up," Lee cautioned. "It may not work out at all —"

But Sara couldn't help being excited. She wanted Lee to have the job if it was anything at all and would get him out of the city and the bad air. As for herself — she thought of the sea with a kind of wistful sigh. To have a few days, a few weeks, a few months even, all to herself, to *be* herself, to do and think as she pleased for that heavenly time, was something she wanted with every inch of her being.

When they reached Vincent, Lee stopped at a gas station. A tall young man, thirty or so, came out, wiping his hands on an oily rag.

"Yes, sir, what can I do for you?"

Lee leaned his head out the window. "Could you direct us to a place called Windmere?"

He stared at them for a moment.

"It's about eight miles from here but I'd better draw you a map. The road twists and turns and there are a dozen ways to get lost."

Lee got out of the car and watched and listened as the map was drawn.

"I'm not sure I can find it even now," Lee said.

"It's the way Chadwick wants it. Private. I'd bet my last dollar you're after the chauffeur's job," the attendant said.

Lee nodded. "Possibly. You know about it?"

"Not much. I knew the last driver. He lasted two weeks. The one before that didn't stay ten days. I wish you luck, mister."

"Some particular reason why they don't stay?"

"I don't like telling tales out of school to strangers but some funny things have happened out there —"

"Like what?" Lee asked.

The attendant shook his head. "No more. I shouldn't have said what I did."

"You make it sound almost ominous."

"Maybe you like remote places; I don't. They give me the creeps."

Sara heard them talking together while the gas tank was filled and she wondered more and more about the place called Windmere, a touch of apprehension brushing across her thoughts.

Lee came back to the car and got behind the wheel.

"That's Mark Williams. He owns the place and seems a decent sort."

"I heard what he said about Windmere."

"Local scuttlebutt. Probably doesn't mean a thing and besides, we've come this far, we won't turn tail until we look things over for ourselves."

"It sounded almost too good to be true when I read about it in the paper; maybe it is —"

Lee started the car again and they made the first

turn, Sara following the crude map Mark had drawn for them. The farther they drove, the more aware she was that the countryside was becoming less and less populated. Finally, they had nearly run out of houses altogether and she began to appreciate how perfect it was here. After busy, crowded New York, what more could they ask?

The last half-mile was down a winding lane and there the sand dunes rose up with clumps of scrub brush dotting their crests. Occasionally there was a patch of thick trees and then all at once they had reached a gate.

"Closed," Lee said. "Williams didn't tell me about this."

"There must be a button to press or something —"

"Yes, I think I see it."

Lee got out of the car, pressed a button and waited. A speaker suddenly came to life and Sara jumped at the unexpected sound of a woman's voice.

"Who's there, please?"

"Lee Denning. From New York. I'm expected."

The speaker went dead, there was a click and the gate swung open. They drove through and Sara glanced back to see it swinging shut, controlled electrically from the house.

"You'd almost think we were going to a thieves' hideout or something. Talk about private —" Lee said.

Sara laughed. "Well, private is private. Sometimes I'd like to put up an electric gate and keep everyone out of my life, too."

The road was wider now, the grounds to either side

well kept, although part of it was given over to tall pines, and here and there an explosive flower bed rose unexpectedly with a burst of color.

"Fenced in," Lee murmured.

She too had noted the fence, back amid the trees, almost unobtrusive, but nonetheless, very much there.

"The man's a maniac for privacy," Lee said.

All at once, just as they had come upon the gate, they came upon the house — a three-story affair rising up out of a cliff. It was white clapboard and had two tall brick turrets at either end of the main body of the house. Then a couple of wings branched out, like afterthoughts. Still, it was attractively built — perhaps unique was a better word — and it smelled of money with a capital M. Lee brought the car to a halt at the front door.

"This is going to be a wild-goose chase, Sara. We sure don't belong here. Well, here goes nothing. How do I look?"

"The wind's ruffled your hair. I'll loan you my comb."

A few minutes later, inspecting each other carefully, exchanging rather foolish grins, they went up to the massive front door and raised the old-fashioned knocker that surprised them by setting off a loud buzzer inside.

The door was opened by a maid. She scarcely glanced at them. "Mr. Chadwick is waiting for you in the den."

They followed the broad back of the plump little woman and in a moment were ushered into a large room lined with books, filled with leather furniture and a desk that partially faced an open window. Sara caught an enticing glimpse of the blue sea and the dipping white sails of a boat, buoyant in the wind.

The man behind the desk got to his feet. He was tall and slender, with silvery gray hair, a smooth face and a clipped white mustache. He looked very dignified and Sara found herself being appraised with the expert air of a man who dealt every day with people and bent them to his wishes.

"I'm Eldridge R. Chadwick, III. I'm glad you could come today on such short notice, Mr. Denning. And this is your sister Sara?"

"Yes, sir, it is."

They exchanged polite nods and Chadwick motioned them into chairs. There were the usual questions and Lee answered them quickly and honestly. Then abruptly, Chadwick was addressing himself to Sara.

"And what do you do, Miss Denning?"

She explained about her position with Waterman's Advertising.

"I know the firm. You're resigning?"

"I'd like to, very much."

"And do what?"

Sara lifted her chin. "Paint what I please. Walk by the sea. Channel my ambitions into something more personal. Frankly, I'd rather do more with my life than entice someone to buy a certain toothpaste or a particular brand of soap powder."

He thought about that for a moment and a terse

smile touched his lips. "You sound a great deal like my daughter, Marcia." Then he turned back to Lee. "The job pays two hundred a week, I furnish uniforms and there is a small cottage adjacent to the house where you and your sister may live. You can take your meals in the kitchen or in your own cottage as you prefer. You'll be expected to drive me to Vincent to catch the seven-thirty train in the morning and meet the eight o'clock every night. Weekends I'll need your services occasionally on Saturday. Sunday is your day off. You'll be expected to keep all the cars in good working condition and ready to roll at a moment's notice. Is that clear?"

Lee swallowed. "Yes, sir, it is."

"I made a few phone calls after receiving your letter and your references are quite good. I'd like you to start immediately. If there are loose ends to tie up in New York, send your sister back to do it."

Lee blinked and shot Sara a quick glance.

"Well?" Chadwick prompted.

"Could we have a moment to talk alone, sir?" Lee asked.

"Step out to the patio, walk down the beach if you like. Come back in half an hour."

Lee got to his feet and Sara followed him to the door Chadwick had pointed out. They walked across a flagstone terrace and then down a flight of stone steps.

"Whew!" Lee said.

"What do you think?"

"He comes on a little strong. Does it seem to you

that he's in a tearing hurry to hire me? Why all the rush?"

"The man needs a chauffeur."

They began walking down the beach, the sand underfoot a satiny softness, and a gull came winging overhead to give them a quick look and then went on after learning they had nothing to feed him.

"My word, this is beautiful!" Sara said.

They paused to stare out to the sea and in this particular spot, it was breathtakingly lovely. The coast made a U shape and while the cliff on which the Chadwick house stood had an almost imposing look, the mansion was at the same time like a centrally located castle in command of all the other houses around, of which there were precious few.

"It might be lonely as the devil here, Sis," Lee said. "There's a house out on the point at the end of the U and another at the other end and not much else in between but the Chadwick place."

"Ah, the peace and quiet! Imagine watching the sun come up in a place like this."

"You want me to take the job, don't you?"

"What have you got to lose?"

"We know nothing about Chadwick, but I have a hunch he already knows a great deal about us."

"He's obviously an important man. It's no crime to have money and a place like this, Lee."

"You remember how it was when we were kids? We were always suspicious of people who had things better than us. We always felt as if we were in another class, another world really."

She linked her arm through his, feeling his sharp bones, aware of the poor thinness of his body. She wanted this for him. The air was delightful here.

"Would you mind being at beck and call at all hours?"

"It doesn't sound as if there would be much else to do. I could handle it without half trying."

"Then take it! I have a feeling about it, Lee."

He drew a deep breath and looked back over his shoulder to the house on the top of the cliff and he pursed his lips.

"Well, I suppose I can go back to New York if it doesn't work out. I could always drive a cab. I'll phone my boss and tell him I won't be back."

"Let's go and tell Chadwick."

The events that happened after that took place within less than an hour. The maid, who introduced herself as Elsa, showed them the cottage and Sara found it more pleasant than she had dared hope.

"It was a guest house originally, so they tell me. I haven't been here long myself. Now, it's been turned into the chauffeur's quarters. Quite fancy, really," Elsa said.

It was near the wing that housed the garage and was almost hidden in pine trees but it, too, had a view of the ocean and Sara began anticipating the thought of waking up to that sight every morning.

Lee was supplied with uniforms that were a little too large for him, but which Elsa assured would be altered to fit him. Next they were given lunch on the spacious patio.

Then Sara was sent on her way back to New York to resign from her job, close their apartment, and put the belongings they wouldn't be needing into storage. There would be friends to get in touch with for a hurried goodbye.

Lee rode with her as far as the gate. "Are you sure you can handle all of this alone?"

"Just watch me and see."

"Take care."

"Oh, Lee, it's going to work out, I know it! The whole thing is just — well, I can't believe it's happening."

He smiled at that and climbed out of the car to press a button on the inner side of the gate. It swung open and she drove through, waving to him. In her rearview mirror, she saw the gate close behind her and Lee standing behind it. For a brief and uneasy moment, she knew what it might be like to see her brother behind bars in a jail. Then she banished the thought. Windmere was hardly a prison, but a very exclusive home of a man who could obviously afford it.

It took Sara longer to drive back than it had taken Lee to drive down. Her thoughts were in a whirlwind and there was so much to do she scarcely knew where to start first. But she knew that she wanted to get back to Windmere as fast as she could.

Sunday she phoned Jerry and when he heard her

intentions, he was so startled that he hung up on her after shouting, "I'm coming right over and talk some sense into your head!"

When he arrived, he grasped both her hands and pulled her down on the couch beside him.

"Now listen, Sara, you can't go off like this on some wild scheme. You can't leave, you can't!"

"It's already decided. I'll phone Waterman in the morning and tell him the news."

Jerry shook his head with disbelief. "Sara, you know how I feel about you. You must know that. Think what this will do to us!"

"Jerry — dear Jerry — I know and perhaps that's why I must leave. I wish I could say that I had truly fallen in love with you; it would solve everything — I mean — well, I'm saying this very badly, aren't I?"

Jerry took his hands away. An ashen look came to his face.

"Jerry, you're so nice and I like you so much, but —"

"Let's not labor the point. I know a brush-off when I hear it!"

"Don't be angry. You have to understand this is what I really want."

"Another bridge to cross? Everything's a bridge with you — did you ever stop to think where this bridge is leading you?"

"To freedom, I hope. Self-expression. A time to search my soul."

"E. R. Chadwick for crying out loud! Do you know who he is?"

"No."

"He's a big man on Wall Street. An eccentric millionaire, possibly a billionaire. It seems like there was some kind of family scandal a few months back, but I can't remember what it was now."

"You should see Windmere. It takes your breath. The view is out of this world."

"And that's where you'll be, Sara. Out of this world. I've heard about Windmere — Chadwick guards it like a bastille."

"Wish us luck, Jerry? Can't you do that much?"

Jerry's face was frozen with anger and hurt. "I don't want you to go. I'm not going to let you forget me and I'm not going to give up that easily, Sara!"

"Jerry, I have no intentions of forgetting you."

He drew a deep breath. "I hope I can believe that."

"You can."

She put her arms around him and lifted her lips to accept his kiss. She was going to miss him. For a heartbeat or two, she almost regretted her decision to leave him and go to Windmere. But it was something she had to do and the summer would be gone before both of them knew it. She told him as much and he managed a smile.

"It will be a very *long* summer for me —"

"I'm sorry you're so unhappy about this, Jerry. I don't like leaving with a cloud between us."

When they had said their last goodbye and he had gone, Sara was very much aware of his unhappiness and it dampened her enthusiasm. She was certain he would understand eventually why she felt she had to go. Some weekend, she would invite him to Windmere and then he would see for himself what a lovely place it was and if she could do some really good work there —

She'd cross that bridge when she reached it. At the thought she smiled, remembering what Jerry had said about her bridges. Then she purposely turned her mind to Windmere, where Lee was waiting.

3

It took Sara three hectic days to get things in order so she could leave, and during that time, Jerry's attitude didn't change. She had phoned all their friends about her plans and saved her last day for Diane Franklin, her best friend. They met for lunch, and over their salads Diane gave her a studied look.

"I have to admire you," Diane admitted. "It takes nerve to just pull up roots and take off like this."

"Jerry thinks I'm crazy."

"He'll come around, Sara."

"I hope so. I hate hurting him and I keep hoping he'll understand, but he doesn't."

"You were lucky to fall into something like Windmere! But you're the busy, busy, busy sort. Are you sure you'll be content there in such a secluded place?"

"It's a dream come true, Diane. You should see the view! The beach! I can spend six months doing nothing but painting the sea. You have to promise to come visit me soon."

"I'll take a vacation in a few weeks. Perhaps then —"

Sara and Diane had been friends for a long time. It would seem odd not to be able to reach out for the phone and hear Diane's voice. They had always aired their gripes to each other, helped each other solve their problems, gone on shopping binges together and were nearly as close as sisters.

"You're the only thing I hate to leave in New York," Sara said.

"But you're only a short drive away and we can telephone —"

"Sure."

"Let's not get all misty, Sara. This was to be a celebration lunch, remember. I almost wish I could go with you."

Later, they said goodbye and Sara left her friend on the busy New York sidewalk and caught a cab back to her apartment. The car was loaded and waiting. She turned in the key to the building manager and didn't go back for a last look. She and Lee were leaving that behind.

Sara had no problems finding her way back to Vincent, but from there to Windmere was another story. She made two wrong turns before she finally got on the right route and reached the imposing iron gate. She got out to press the button and heard Elsa's voice.

"It's Sara Denning."

"Lee's been worried about you."

The gate clicked and began to swing open. She drove through and saw the gate close behind her once again, shutting her in. She followed the winding lane back to the house and spied Lee waiting for her at the corner of the garage, motioning for her to drive the car toward their cottage.

"You can park it under the trees," he said.

Once the car was taken care of, Lee helped her with the luggage.

"How did it go?"

"All's well. How's it been here?"

"Unbelievable! I could get lazy on a job like this."

"Oh, I'm so glad you like it! There've been no problems?"

"Chadwick isn't the friendliest person at seven in the morning, but he's decent enough. The household staff have been pleasant, if a bit distant. Elsa said they're giving us three weeks at the outside edge."

"I hope no one is betting on that," Sara said.

"How did Waterman take the news?"

"He blew his stack, but I finally got him to consider giving me some free-lance work. I'm not sure he will and if he doesn't, I won't worry about it."

"And Jerry?"

"The less said the better. But he's heard of Chadwick. It seems he's a very big and important man."

"I already had that figured out."

"You mentioned the staff. Who's here besides Elsa?"

"The cook-housekeeper, Mrs. Goddard. Sam's the gardener but he doesn't live here and he only works a few days a week."

"And the Chadwicks?"

"There's the daughter, Marcia, and Chadwick's brother lives here too but I haven't met him yet."

"Jerry said there had been a family scandal a few weeks ago. Do you know anything about it?"

Lee shook his head and began hanging his things away in a large closet. "No."

Sara went to the window and saw that the sun was dropping low in the sky. The view made her gasp. It was such an expanse of beauty, reaching as far as the eye could see in either direction. Whitecaps dotted the blue water and she could smell the salt of the ocean.

"I can't believe this is for real! Lee, I want to go for a walk as the sun goes down. Could you come with me?"

"Can't right now. It will soon be time to meet Chadwick's train. Give me a rain check —"

"The packing can wait," she decided. "But the sunset won't —"

"Don't get lost —" Lee called after her.

She left the cottage and crossed the fenced-in patio decorated with small white tables and chairs. Pots of flowers gave the place a bit of color and a fragrant scent. It offered an excellent vantage point of the cove and seeing it, Sara hurried down the stone steps that led to the ocean. On impulse she stopped to take off her shoes and nylons and went barefoot onto the beach. She walked out to the edge of the water and strolled along the wet sand, the tide rippling across her toes and then whispering away from her with its special music. There was so much to see here and she wanted to see it all, but she knew she couldn't tonight. Tomorrow it would be different and she would walk around the U shaped cove as far as the house on the point. She paused now to study it. In its own way, it was as impressive as Windmere.

"You like my place?"

She started at the unexpected sound of a male voice and turned around to find a man, broad of shoulder, wearing swimming trunks with a white towel twisted around his waist. He was deeply tanned and his dark hair was wet from a recent dip in the ocean. He looked so healthy that after the pale, necktied and suited men of New York, he came as something of a shock.

"I live in that house you're staring at," he said with a smile. His teeth were very white and straight.

"It looks very interesting."

"You're new here, aren't you? Visiting the Chadwicks perhaps?"

"Not exactly."

He quirked a dark brow at that and she saw how firm his lips were above the jutt of his chin. There was a blunt honesty about him that was appealing.

"If you're not visiting, you must be a new member of the personnel there, or could it be we have a trespasser?"

"My brother is Chadwick's new chauffeur. I'm staying with him. Now, does that mean I'm permitted to stay?"

"Welcome to our beach, our cove and our ocean," he said, making a low, laughing bow. Then he thrust out a brown, broad hand. "I'm Tom Barclay."

"Sara Denning."

His fingers closed around hers for a moment and she felt their strength and warmth.

"I should warn you. You're liable to find me popping up everywhere around here. I'm a photographer and I'm doing a series of studies of the sea. I hope one day to publish them in a book."

"That sounds intriguing."

"I've been wanting to do this for years. I run a portrait studio in Cleveland but my one big dream was to come to a place like this."

"Do you mean you just closed up shop and came here?"

He nodded. "For the summer anyway."

"Then I'm not as crazy as all my friends think! I've more or less done the same thing. How did you manage to find a dream house like that?"

"Sheer luck. A friend of a friend of a friend, you might say. I've leased it for the summer. The family that owns it has gone to Europe for a long holiday and I'm sort of a combination caretaker and renter."

"It looks lovely."

"You said you had done the same thing as me — what did you mean?"

She smiled. "I'm a commercial artist by profession — making all those ads for toothpaste or baby food or a new shampoo — whatever. But I've come here to do some serious painting."

He fell in step beside her as she continued to walk along the water's edge, the sun sliding down quickly in the sky, bathing the water with a rainbow of color.

"Then we have something in common, haven't we?"

he asked. "I use a camera, you use a paintbrush."

"I'll do your house one day if you have no objection."

"None at all."

"I hope to paint dozens of pictures of the sea, of all the area around here."

"Can you spend the entire summer doing that?"

"Can you shoot that much film on one subject?"

He laughed at that. "Touché. I must say, I think I make the Chadwicks nervous, but until they string up a fence and close their share of the beach, I intend to walk here."

"Are they like that?" Sara asked with a frown.

"They're an exclusive bunch. Do you know, I've yet to meet them formally. I've spoken to Marcia on the beach and I've met Eldridge face to face in town but he barely acknowledged me. As for Ryan —"

He broke off and she saw a tenseness in his face.

"Who's Ryan?"

"The son. Eldridge R. Chadwick IV. The R stands for Ryan. You haven't met him?"

"No. I've met no one. I just arrived from New York a few minutes ago. I've only seen Chadwick, Senior, and Elsa."

"I doubt that Ryan's home. He's out somewhere on one of his wild —"

He broke off and paused for a moment. From somewhere he produced a package of cigarettes and held them out to her.

"No. I don't smoke," she said.

He struck a match, cupped his hands around it and

held it to the cigarette. The evening breeze had started and it lifted his hair and billowed the towel around his waist behind him.

In the bright stab of light, she saw that his eyes were narrowed, thoughtful, and that his jaw had become harder.

"It's getting late. I should get back," Sara said.

"You must come and pay me a visit soon at Widow's Point."

"Is that what they call it?"

"Yes. It seems in the old days some ships crashed here and men were lost. There's an old lighthouse down the coast but I think it should have been here on the point."

"I haven't seen the lighthouse! Where is it exactly? Can I reach it by following the beach?"

"A bit tricky, but possible. I'll show you one day soon, if you like."

"Yes, I'd like that very much."

"Material for your canvas?" he asked.

"Possibly."

"And my camera. Ah, Sara, I think this is going to be a very interesting summer. Goodnight. Take care."

He gave her a smile that was warm and friendly and then with a wave he was gone, walking swiftly, his long strides lost in the sand. She watched him go, a very attractive stranger, until the white towel and tiny glow of his cigarette were only blurs in the growing twilight. She thought about Tom Barclay for a moment with a stirring of interest.

She lingered longer on the beach than she had intended, and suddenly the sun was gone and twilight had turned to darkness, stealing away the last hint of color out of the sky.

She was glad a light burned at the bottom of the stone steps, showing her the way. She snatched up her shoes and nylons where she'd left them and climbed to the top. There she paused to catch her breath and take one last absorbing look at the cove and the sea. The house on Widow's Point stood like a gray lump on the rocks, and the garish yard light that marked it was like a tiny green beacon.

Suddenly, she realized she was not alone. She saw a dark figure standing at the patio railing on the cliff's edge, staring mournfully out to sea. Then the man sensed her presence and turned away sharply, furtively, as if he had no right to be there. He disappeared into the shadows without a sound. Sara started to call out to him, not knowing just why she felt impelled to speak with him.

The cottage was empty. Lee had taken the limousine and had gone to meet Chadwick. It seemed strange here and she began turning on the lights to chase away the shadows. She hoped Lee would not be long. The sea was to her back, the gate blocked the drive. Despite the fresh air blowing the curtains at the window, she felt hemmed in. It was just a touch of her crazy claustrophobia or the trip down, the tiresome duty of closing the apartment and handling all the details alone.

Tomorrow the sun would be shining. She would take the paints out of the box where they had lain too long and she would start working. She would begin the pursuit of her idealistic dreams and even if the Chadwicks were a bit odd, probably snobbish, what did it matter? Still, she wondered about the strange, sad man at the railing.

4

Lᴇᴇ ᴡᴀs ʟᴀᴛᴇ in returning to the cottage but when he came, well after nine o'clock, his arms were full of grocery bags.

"I decided to stock our cupboards. I'd rather eat here, unless you'd prefer we took our meals at the house."

"No. I'm glad you've brought something. I'm starving! Was the train late?"

"Yes. I drove in early and bought these things before I met the boss. Did you have your walk?"

"Yes and I met Tom Barclay."

Lee glanced at her curiously. "Who's Tom Barclay?"

"He lives at Widow's Point in that house out there on the left side of the cove. You haven't seen him around?"

"No. But leave it to you!" Lee laughed. "Ten minutes at the place and already you've made friends."

Sara helped put the groceries away and frowned. "I saw someone else as I came back up the steps. Just a glimpse really. A tall, thin man — he acted so strangely. Who could that have been?"

"There's no one here that would answer that description. Maybe it was one of the neighbors from the house on the other side of the cove. Hanson I believe is their name. I haven't seen anyone from there though. Fact is, I haven't seen anyone but the boss and the servants."

"You look very dashing in your uniform, Lee."

He tossed the jacket aside and loosened his black tie. "I feel a little like an idiot," he said. "But every job has its drawbacks and I suppose it's not going to kill me to go around looking so pompous."

"Oh, I hope you'll be happy here, Lee! I know I twisted your arm about answering the ad —"

"I think it's going to work out just fine."

They had always worked well together and in a few short minutes, the kitchen was in order, the coffee was made and a platter of sandwiches had been prepared. They decided to carry the food outside and make use of the patio, which was now illuminated by floodlights and empty. The sea breeze brushed across their faces and Sara ate hungrily.

"You know, Lee, you look better already. Do I imagine it?"

Lee shook his head. "No. The air is unbelievable here. I've been sleeping like a log and I feel better too. So, your little seed is already bearing fruit."

She began to feel relaxed, at peace. The coffee tasted especially good and there were all the bright tomorrows stretching out ahead of her, waiting to be grasped in her eager hands. She would spend a few days just looking around, picking out the scenes she especially wanted to capture on canvas, and then she would start work. Each day she would spend at least four hours and perhaps more at her easel. After that length of time, she'd always found that the quality began to go. She became less an artist and more of a dauber.

"I've rented a post office box in Vincent. There's no mail delivery out here," Lee was saying. "I have a key for you; remind me to give it to you. I stopped in at Mark Williams's station again. If you want gas, I wish you'd buy it from him. He seems like a nice guy and he could use the business, I think."

"Okay, I'll remember."

"Otherwise, my dear sister, you're on your own."

"What about a phone?"

"We can use the extension in the kitchen or order our own. I think we should get our own, don't you?"

"Definitely. I want to stay out of the way of the Chadwicks as much as possible, Lee. They were good enough to let me come here with you, so I should be as unobtrusive as I can."

"Good girl. Will you mind?"

"From what Tom Barclay says, I think we've landed in a bunch of high-toned snobs and you know my feelings about that sort!"

"You should see the cars, Sara. I never thought I'd be driving a Cadillac limousine, but I am! And there's a Lincoln convertible that Marcia uses and a small import car they told me belonged to the son, Ryan. Chadwick's brother has the only clunker in the lot, and it's still better than what we drive."

When she had finished eating, Lee would not rest

until he had taken Sara to the garage and showed her the expensive and elaborate cars. They were polished to a high shine and she could see Lee's typical neatness everywhere in the spacious garage.

"It was a mess in here, I don't mind telling you. But I'm getting things organized now. Chadwick would like me to handle all the minor repairs, if I can, so I wondered about tools. I found a big box full of them — anything a good mechanic could ever want."

After she had seen all Lee wanted to show her, Sara stifled a yawn. "The air's getting to me. I think I'll go to bed."

"I'll come inside in a little while. I think I'll watch the moon come up on the water."

Sara was asleep the moment her head hit the pillow. Her slumber was deep and sweet.

When she awakened the next morning, the sun was shining in her face and she smelled coffee. Lee had already gone but had left a note behind for her.

"Unexpected turn of events," it read. "Chadwick wants me to drive him to Philadelphia for the day. It will be late when we get back. Keep out of mischief, Lee."

She smiled at the last line. Lee was only a year older but he liked to remind her now and then that he was the man of the house.

Sara had just scrambled herself some eggs and had finished frying bacon when she heard a knock at the door. Startled, she went to answer it, wondering who could be wanting to see her. Tom Barclay? Or perhaps Elsa —

The girl standing beyond the screen door was taller than Sara's five foot four inches and had blond hair that streamed down below her shoulders. She was very pretty with clear eyes, a soft mouth and a smoothly tanned skin.

"Hi. You're Sara?"

"Yes."

"I'm Marcia Chadwick. Elsa told me you came in late yesterday evening. Look, do you mind if I come in?"

"Of course not!"

Marcia came in with a restless movement and looked around the room, not really seeing any of it. A bracelet dangled on her arm and she was wearing sandals, shorts and a halter that showed her tanned back. She looked young, and Sara guessed her to be not much more than eighteen.

"Something smells good," Marcia said.

"I was about to have some breakfast. Would you like to join me?"

Marcia shook her head quickly. "I've had my usual cup of coffee. Is it all right if I sit here while you eat?"

"Of course."

What on earth did the girl want? Sara dished up the eggs and bacon and poured a cup of coffee for Marcia as well.

"Thank you," Marcia said. "Elsa told me you were an artist, that you were young and I thought, thank God someone interesting has finally come to Windmere."

Sara laughed. "Well, I'm not certain about that, but I do paint. What about you, any hobbies?"

Marcia shrugged her shoulders. "None to speak of."

"With all that surf out there, I bet you're a good swimmer."

"I get absolutely sick of this place!"

"Oh, dear! And I find it positively beautiful."

Tears welled up in Marcia's eyes and Sara looked away embarrassed. The girl seemed very unhappy but she didn't know what to do about it or what to say.

"We all have our bad days, Marcia," Sara said. "Is there anything I can do —"

Marcia shook her head quickly and dabbed at her eyes. "I don't know what's the matter with me, blubbering to strangers —"

Sara handed her a box of tissues from the kitchen counter. "A good cry never hurt any woman," she said. "It has a way of clearing out all the debris of the soul."

Marcia managed a weak smile. "I'm just in a mood. Everything's in such a mess around here and it's depressing. Ever since it happened, everyone goes around with long faces and pretends it *didn't* happen. But it did!"

"Marcia, I have no idea what you're talking about," Sara pointed out.

"Just as well," Marcia said quickly.

Marcia got up to pace around the room again restlessly, peering out the window and then asking for a cigarette.

"I don't have any."

"It's all right. Fact is, I don't really like to smoke. It's just something I do to occupy my time. Are you going down to the beach after a while?"

"Probably."

"Could I join you?"

"If you like. It's your beach, not mine."

"I just want to talk to someone — you know — girl talk, silly things —"

"Fine. But I'll have to warn you that when I'm working, I like solitude. In fact, it's essential —"

Marcia stared at her and then nodded. "Okay. I like that. You're not afraid to speak up to me. I'm glad."

"So, we have a clear understanding from the beginning," Sara said. "Let me fill your cup again. Or have you changed your mind and decided on some bacon and eggs after all?"

"Well, maybe just a little —"

Sara gave Marcia an ample helping and put the plate in front of her. She tasted them almost dubiously and then decided they were good. She ate hungrily and laughed while she was doing so.

"This is fun, having breakfast with you, Sara. I don't even know how to scramble an egg. Mrs. Goddard always does that, you know."

"You could learn," Sara pointed out. "I'll teach you if you like."

"How is it that you know how?"

"Self-preservation," Sara said with an amused smile. "I either learned or starved."

"Sara, have you ever been in love?"

Sara began to realize that she would never be able

to second-guess what might next come out of this girl's mouth.

"Yes."

"So have I! But I just broke up with Larry. He was so impossible — now —"

"And now, you wish you hadn't. So, that explains the tears. Don't worry, Marcia. Someone else will come along."

"How soon will you go down to the beach?"

"Half an hour. I'll wait for you at the steps."

"Okay."

Then Marcia Chadwick was gone as quickly as she had arrived, leaving behind the impression of silky hair, violet eyes, a jangly bracelet and a restlessness that pulled her first in one direction and then in another.

Half an hour later, Sara was at the top of the steps, waiting for Marcia. After ten minutes had gone by and Marcia had not appeared, Sara assumed there had been a change in plans. With the will-o'-the-wisp girl like that, it wasn't entirely unexpected.

Sara went down the steps alone, leaving her shoes below as she had done before. She had tied back her dark hair with a bright scarf, pulled on a sleeveless blouse and a comfortable pair of shorts. She put on a large pair of sun glasses. The sun caressed her with a welcome warmth and she found the sea even more enchanting this morning than she had last night.

She walked aimlessly, stopping often to simply stand and stare at the sky and the water. She collected a pocketful of shells, fell in love with a gull that circled her, squawking for food, and suddenly discovered that she had come farther than she had intended. The house on Widow's Point was just a few steps away.

"Hello!"

Tom Barclay had seen her as he came out to a terrace just above her head.

"Come join me. I'll fix you something long, tall and cold."

"That sounds too delicious to pass up."

She found the way leading to the house, and Tom came to offer his hand for the last couple of steps, tugging her up beside him.

"I'm glad you came," Tom said. "It's been a kind of off morning for me."

"There must be something in the air," she said, thinking of Marcia Chadwick.

The terrace was flagstone. Comfortable lawn chairs, well padded, set facing the ocean, and Sara caught sight of a freighter — or perhaps it was only a fishing boat — on the horizon.

"What a spectacular view! I believe it's better than the one at Chadwick's."

"It serves my purpose very well. Come in. Let me show you the house."

It was a rambling place built of sturdy stones, and unlike the turret effect of the Chadwick house, this one seemed more content to hug the earth.

"Even the worst winds won't blow this house down," Tom said. "And it's incredibly cool and breezy, even on the hottest days. I promised you a drink. What would you like?"

"A soft drink, fruit juice — something like that."

"Iced tea?"

"Sounds wonderful."

They went inside and here Sara found a very comfortable living room with a fireplace taking up one wall, long, narrow windows, sliding glass doors, rich carpeting and expensive furnishings.

"What a dream house!"

Tom laughed. "That's exactly the way I think of it. I don't know how I was so lucky to fall into a place like this."

The kitchen was well equipped, sunny and bright. There Tom took a pitcher of iced tea from the refrigerator and got glasses down from the cupboard.

Tom was a big man, taller than Sara had first thought when she'd seen him on the beach, and he had a quiet way of walking, a graceful way of moving. There were touches of gray in his brown hair, and tiny lines around his eyes hinted at sleepless nights.

They carried their tea back to the living room, and on a glassed-in porch, Sara caught sight of Tom's tools of his trade and stepped out for a better look. There were all sorts of cameras and tripods. She also detected a strong smell of chemicals and knew that he must do his own developing. But there was no evidence of the photos he had taken and she was disappointed.

"Do you really use all these cameras?" she asked.

He nodded. "Yes. Different ones for different work."

"I'd like to see what you've done," she said.

"Not yet. It's not ready for viewing," he replied.

"Oh, so you're one of those —"

He laughed with a shrug. "I'll weed out the bad ones first. But when I'm ready for a showing, I'll let you see."

"Good!"

"Now, tell me more about your work in New York. What really interests me is why you chucked it all to come here."

"I worked like a maniac on a layout for a new cleanser called Whiff. It was turned down, and somehow it was the last straw for me."

"I know the feeling," Tom said.

He seemed so relaxed, so friendly, that she liked him more all the time. She wondered what his approach to his work would be, bold and ambitious or careful and studied. She saw a pair of binoculars lay by a window as if in readiness and realized from that particular spot on the porch there was a very good view of the Chadwick place. She wondered if Tom had been peering through the glasses at the turreted house and perhaps had even watched her as she strolled along the beach. The thought made her uneasy. She disliked people watching her unaware. It was a silly quirk of hers. Probing eyes always made her nervous and she especially hated it if anyone leaned over her while she worked on a canvas or a drawing pad.

"Sara —"

"Oh, what? What did you say?"

He laughed. "I just asked you out for dinner sometime soon. I must say you were far away."

"Sorry. Dinner would be lovely."

"Good. I'll give you time to get settled first."

"I'd appreciate that. By the way, I must make a trip to Vincent for supplies. Is there a place I can buy oil paints?"

"Yes. Try Lane's. They should have everything you need."

He lifted his glass with a smile and his eyes were warm. "Here's to a summer to remember, Sara."

She responded with the lifting of her own glass. "I can hardly wait for it to begin."

Tom gave her a long, searching look. "Nor can I, Sara."

5

By the time Sara returned to Windmere from Tom's place, she found that she had been struck with the desire to do absolutely nothing. She didn't even want to drive to Vincent. Perhaps tomorrow. There were things in the cottage she should do. Last night she had barely done anything but unpack the essentials and things were stacked in the closets in boxes, but she had no desire to tackle that either.

Perhaps it was the climate here, the sea air and the warm sun that made her feel so lazy. Or was it just that she was eager to unwind, to put her city life behind her? The pace was so leisurely here, and when in Rome —

No one was on the patio, and Sara decided to sit there in one of the comfortable lounging chairs. She stretched out her legs, put her head back and in an instant was dozing.

She didn't know exactly what it was that awakened her, but she sensed she was not alone and opened her eyes.

"Oh!"

"I didn't mean to startle you, my dear."

The man was gray of hair, small of build and had

the most mischievous twinkle in his eye of anyone she had ever met.

"Let me introduce myself. I'm Wallace Chadwick, Eldridge's brother. You have to be Lee's sister."

"Yes. Sara Denning."

"I live here most of the time," Wallace explained. "Thanks to my brother's generosity. And before you ask, I'm not in stocks and bonds, or oil, or steel, or anything like that. I'm in nothing."

She smiled at the tone of his voice. He announced it almost proudly.

"I'm what is known as the black sheep of the family. But I'm good at parties. People find me entertaining; I have no idea why. And occasionally I run a business errand for Eldridge. My only claim to Dame Fortune is an extraordinary run of good luck I had as a young man investing my trust fund in a silver mine, which, I'm sad to say, has now run out its string."

"Too bad!"

He shook his head at that. "Frankly, my dear, it was nothing but a bother. I've no head for business and never will have. If there's one thing I try to do, it's face reality."

She laughed at that. "I see."

He was surely a delightful, funny, lighthearted man and she liked him instantly.

"I must say, Sara, you're a great improvement to this place. The last people who occupied the cottage were dour and self-centered and as stale as yesterday's mashed potatoes."

"And you think I'm not?"

"Lee seems to be a fine person and I shall expect as much from you. He tells me you paint."

"Yes."

"Portraits?"

"I've never tried one, but the idea interests me. Would you sit for me?"

"All you need to do is ask. My time is your time. Actually, sometimes I find the days very long here at Windmere. Do you suppose that means I'm getting old?"

"I have a feeling, Wallace Chadwick, that you'll never be old."

"Good!" he said, slapping the palms of his hands to his knees. "You've just made my day. And by the way, Sara, everyone calls me Wally. I'd be pleased if you did too."

"What *do* you do all day long?"

"Little as possible. Sometimes, I stroll down to the lighthouse and visit Herb Travis. He's my one friend here. Herb's down-to-earth and we go fishing sometimes, kill a pint of Scotch between us and tell each other lies. What else is left to two old men?"

"It sounds like fun. I've heard about the lighthouse. I must see it sometime."

"I'll take you anytime you want. Herb will like you, Sara. He always had an eye for a shapely leg, the old devil."

Sara was amused. Wally had twinkly eyes but they were also curious and alert. He had taken her in from the tip of her toes to the top of her head, missing nothing in between.

"Lee didn't tell me about you. Just about your car."

"I live in the same house with Eldridge, but most of the time we might as well be a continent apart. I suppose he just has his mind on other things. Business. Buy this, sell that, calculate a risk here — that's not for me. I know people like Eldridge are the ones that make the world go around and he's been more than decent to me, but still — sometimes I'd like to put a dent in him just to make him yell so I know he's really alive and human."

"You surely exaggerate, Wally."

"Probably. I'm so used to telling lies to Herb that I'm telling them all the time," he said with a grin. A tiny flash of gold showed in his teeth. He got to his feet. "Tide's out. I think I'll go down and look for some new shells. That's one thing I do, Sara. I've found some rare ones in my day. I'll show you my collection sometime, all right?"

"Yes, that would be nice."

Then he was gone with a wave of his hand, disappearing down the steps toward the beach. In a few moments she caught sight of him walking at the water's edge, stopping now and then to bend down and retrieve the offerings of the sea.

Sara went back inside the cottage, and with renewed vigor attacked the boxes she had hauled down from New York. This occupied her for the rest of the morning. Then, after fixing a bite of lunch, she decided she would go to Vincent after all. Tomorrow she would begin work in earnest and she would need paints and a few other supplies.

In Vincent, she mailed a note to Diane, ordered a phone installed and found the store Tom had told her about. There she purchased every conceivable thing she would need. Before leaving town, she saw she ought to fill the car with gas. Remembering Lee's instructions, she sought out Mark Williams's station.

Mark came hustling out, gave her a quick look and recognized her at once.

"Hello. You're Sara. Lee told me you would be coming back soon. How was your trip down?"

"Hello, Mark. Lots of traffic. Would you fill it up, please?"

"Sure thing."

Mark whistled while he worked. He seemed eager to please and talked a great deal in a pleasant sort of way, and she saw why Lee liked him. Neither of them was used to this kind of friendliness. Vincent was quite different from New York City and Mark Williams was different as well.

"How are things at Windmere?" he asked.

"Very nice," she said.

"I was only there once. I made a service call when one of their cars wouldn't start. It's impressive all right, but it gave me the creeps when they shut the gate behind me. I'm not much for closed-in places."

"You said the other chauffeur didn't stay long. Do you know why?"

"There was some trouble out there," Mark said. "I think he just decided he didn't want any part of it and left."

Sara frowned, brushing back a lock of dark hair. "What kind of trouble?"

As he polished her windshield carefully, Mark explained. "Well, it seems a girl went over the cliff there — killed her — and the Chadwicks tried to hush it up, but of course it got out. Too bad. She was a pretty thing. She used to stop here for gas. Tania Francis. She was sweet on Ryan and I guess Ryan was really gone on her. He sort of went out of his skull after it happened. I haven't seen him around lately. God knows what he's doing or where he is now."

"What a tragedy!"

"There's some crazy talk about it — rumors that — well, never mind. I wouldn't want to pass them on. You know how people are, they enlarge things, make more out of them than there really is. I just know Eldridge turns purple if anyone mentions it to him."

All of this was very interesting to Sara. She wondered exactly what had happened to Tania. But accidents happen, she thought, no matter how careful people are. Still, it gave her a chill when she thought about it. Windmere was so beautiful, so perfect, that she disliked the thought of a blot of any kind on it, and the death of a girl must have left unpleasant memories there.

Sara started back to Windmere, leaving Vincent behind. She drove slowly, enjoying the day, trying to learn to pace herself to a slower step. This was what she had wanted for so long — to have time to breathe, to enjoy, to look, to savor — and even an ugly thing like an accident wasn't going to spoil that. She was determined.

There was very little traffic on the road and when she made the turn to the left, it was almost like leaving civilization behind. She was surprised to see someone walking down the road a short distance ahead of her. She had always made it a rule never to pick up strangers on the road but wherever this one was going, he surely had a long walk ahead of him, as there were no houses for at least five miles.

Suddenly she became aware of a car coming up fast behind her. It was a small blue sedan and with a blast of the horn, it sped around her. Sara couldn't see who was driving and the license plate was so dusty she couldn't tell if it was a local car or out-of-state.

Then with a tightening of her throat, she saw the car bearing down on the man ahead of her. She screamed.

"Look out!"

The car seemed to pick up speed and swerved deliberately toward the man, or perhaps the driver had only been as startled as she had been to find someone walking there and momentarily lost control. It all happened so fast that Sara was not sure what had taken place, but as the car sped on, going faster and faster, Sara saw the man had either jumped out of the way and fallen or had been struck. He lay at the side of the road.

Sara brought her car to a screeching stop, leaped out from behind the wheel and ran back to him.

"Mister, are you all right? Mister —"

He lay very still. She saw that he was casually dressed, perhaps even sloppily, his face was bearded and his hair was shaggy and curled around his neck. Even like this, there was something familiar about him and in an instant she was certain this was the man she had caught a glimpse of at the railing at Windmere, staring so mournfully out to the sea.

She shook him gently. "Oh, please, open your eyes! Tell me you're all right —"

She was rewarded with a groan. She saw the man's face had been scratched from the gravel in the road and was bleeding slightly. But otherwise, he didn't appear too badly hurt, only stunned and shaken.

"Speak to me, please —"

The man stared at her and tried to sit up. She helped him, but he was groggy.

"What happened?" she asked. "Did the car hit you?"

"Help me up," he muttered.

He leaned on her heavily as he got to his feet. "I'm okay. Go away. Leave me alone. I'm okay."

But he was far from being all right. He began to weave on his feet and she grasped him tightly around the waist. He didn't protest when she insisted he get in the car. She helped him inside and closed the door. By the time she walked around and got under the wheel, she was alarmed to see that he had fainted. A doctor! She must find a doctor. She made a quick decision to take him to Windmere.

She drove swiftly now. The blue car that had sped

around her had long since disappeared from sight and
she wondered where it had gone. The road forked just
a half a mile ahead and branched off to the other
houses in the area. So, it was impossible to even guess.

Sara wasted no time in driving to Windmere and
when she reached the gate, she was annoyed at the
delay of getting out to press the button and waiting
for someone at the house to release the electric gate.

"Elsa, hurry, please," she said when the maid's voice
came over the speaker. "I have a man with me. He's
been hurt on the highway."

"Oh, but Miss Denning, I don't think you should
bring him here!"

"Please, open the gate! He may be badly hurt and
we're wasting time."

The gate swung open and Sara raced the car
through it. The winding road to the house seemed
very long. The man beside her had not stirred and his
eyes were still closed. Beneath the whiskers and the
facial scratches, she was certain he was an attractive
man, perhaps even handsome. His lashes curled long
and dark against his cheeks and there was a boyish
softness about his mouth that was somehow appealing. If this was the man she'd seen at the railing —
and she was certain it was — what had he been doing
there?

When she reached the house, Elsa came running out
and the cook, Mrs. Goddard, was right behind her.
They were not pleased with this but what else was she
to do? Were they all so high and mighty here that

they couldn't give assistance to an injured stranger?

"You can't bring him here," Mrs. Goddard was saying crisply.

Sara had caught a glimpse of the cook-housekeeper that morning but had not formally met her. She was a buxom, efficient-appearing woman with her hair done tightly in a knot on top of her head. She wore a simple housedress, in contrast to Elsa's uniform, and had the air of authority about her.

"What else was I to do? He needs a doctor — can't you see that?"

Elsa went to peer inside the car. She screeched so shrilly that Sara jumped.

"My God! It's Ryan," Elsa said. "Mrs. Goddard, it's Ryan!"

Sara stepped back with surprise. Ryan? Eldridge Chadwick's son? The man who had lost his girl over the cliff? Sara's head whirled trying to take in the whole of it.

Everything happened swiftly then. Ryan was taken to the house and Mrs. Goddard said she would phone the doctor. Elsa was very upset, wringing her hands, shaking her head back and forth.

"Oh, dear, dear, dear!" she said.

"Where has Ryan been?" Sara asked. "Why was he like that —"

"He wanders these days. Aimlessly," Elsa said. "Ever since poor Tania —" Then as if she had said too much, perhaps revealed a family secret, Elsa clamped her lips shut and said no more.

Sara went back to her cottage, unable to take her

mind off all that had happened. Strange that of all people she should pick up Ryan Chadwick on the road. What quirk of fate had taken her to that exact spot at that exact moment? Destiny wove its way in strange manners, she decided.

She remembered Ryan's burning eyes and boyish, vulnerable mouth. Such an unhappy man. She felt compassion well up in her heart.

6

THE REST OF THE AFTERNOON Sara found herself wondering about Ryan Chadwick and she glanced now and then at the road, but she saw no one come. Apparently it had been decided that a doctor wasn't needed. It was really none of her business, she supposed, but it was hard to put the incident out of her mind.

By the time Lee came home that night, it was after eleven o'clock, but Sara was waiting up for him.

"You must be tired," she said.

"A little. It's been a long day. Chadwick had a dinner meeting that lasted forever. How did it go for you?"

"A lot of interesting things have happened to me."

She told him first about meeting Marcia and then her visit with Wallace Chadwick. She saved Ryan until last and as she related the story, Lee's eyebrows went up with alarm.

"Ryan was nearly run down? Sis, you're not hinting that it could have been deliberate?"

Sara sighed. "Oh, not really. But it did seem strange. The car whizzed around me so fast, maybe the driver just didn't see Ryan."

"Did you say it was a small blue car? Did you see who was driving? Was it a man or a woman?"

"Couldn't tell."

"Were there mirrors mounted on the fenders?"

"I couldn't say as to that either. It all happened so quickly, Lee."

"I've noticed a car like that hanging around the station when I take Chadwick to the train. Coincidence, I suppose. A good many people take that same train."

"Ryan must not have been badly hurt, because I never saw a doctor come."

"Or they just decided they didn't want any more talk."

"Because of Tania?"

Lee looked surprised. "How did you hear about that?"

"Mark Williams."

"I see. He told me, too. The Chadwicks seem to be very touchy on the subject."

They contemplated that for a moment and for the first time, Sara feared there might be a serpent in their paradise. The Chadwicks, after all, were an unknown quantity.

Lee seemed eager to dismiss the subject. "I'm going straight to bed. Thank God tomorrow's Friday and Chadwick never goes to New York on Saturday. I'll be glad for Sunday — my day off."

The next morning, Lee had taken Chadwick to the train and returned before Sara was ready for the day. After they had a late breakfast together, Sara made a firm resolution to go out scouting for the first scene she would paint.

Before leaving for a walk along the beach, she went out to the garage to find Lee. He was busy washing the Cadillac with care, his sleeves rolled up and a bucket of soapy water at his feet.

"You treat that car like a woman," Sara teased. "Such a tender touch!"

"It's a great car," Lee replied.

"It must be easier to drive than the delivery truck —"

Lee smiled. "Considerably."

While they were talking, Marcia Chadwick appeared in the doorway.

"You have a customer," Sara said.

"Probably not," Lee said with a frown.

Marcia spied them and came toward them.

"Hi, Sara," she said.

"Good morning, Marcia. It's another lovely day. I missed you on the beach yesterday."

"Something came up," she said with a shrug.

She didn't seem interested in what Sara was saying. She was more intent on watching Lee, and then she deliberately ran a finger over the fender of her convertible, leaving a mark in the film of dust there.

"Will you do my car too, Lee?"

Lee nodded. "Yes, of course, Miss Chadwick."

Marcia tilted her head in a provocative way. "You're a lot more handsome than the last chauffeur Daddy hired."

Lee blushed and was trying hard not to look at her.

But Marcia was easy on the eyes with her golden hair caught back from her face with a bright ribbon, giving her an even younger and more innocent look. She wore a shade of blue that reflected the touch of violet in her eyes, and her beach clothes showed off to every possible advantage the slim and shapely contours of her body.

"You don't talk much, do you, Lee?" Marcia asked.

Lee shook his head. "Just busy, Miss Chadwick."

She laughed at that but made no move to go. Just then, Wally Chadwick happened in. He came to put his arm around his niece's shoulder.

"So, you're in here bothering Lee again," Wally said. "You know you're neglecting your old uncle, don't you? I'm going for a walk. Will you two pretties come along?"

Marcia quickly declined. "I'm for a dip in the pool. Besides, you'll just go down to the old lighthouse and sit around with that funny old Herb. No thanks, Uncle Wally. I'll stay here."

"Well, it's up to you. Sara, you'll come, won't you?" Wally asked.

"Yes. I'd love to."

They left Marcia and Lee in the garage. Sara doubted Marcia would go for a swim. If she didn't miss her guess, Marcia would be hanging around the garage all morning long.

Wally had read her thoughts.

"Marcia's lonely here at Windmere and I suppose I can't blame her. It's not the most jumping place in the world and she's young and full of life. Lee's new and interesting and she just broke up with her last boy-friend."

They had gone only a short distance down the beach when Wally paused. "Sara, I want to thank you for what you did yesterday for Ryan. I don't suppose anyone in the family has had the presence of mind to tell you that."

"I've been wanting to ask. How is he?"

"Bruised and moody but not truly hurt physically. I would say he was lucky. But then Ryan has a charmed life. He's like a cat with nine lives. I can't begin to remember all the narrow escapes he's had. That sort of trouble seems to follow him. Once he nearly drowned out there in the Atlantic when an undertow caught him. He's smashed up a couple of automobiles, endured a plane crash, and was accidentally shot on an African safari on a wild-game hunt."

"I see. Well, I'm glad that he's all right."

"Ryan's a troubled young man these days, but he's my nephew and I just wish I could see him happy again, and Marcia too."

"You're very fond of them both, aren't you?"

Wally nodded. "My weak spot, you might say. Eldridge's kids sort of became my kids because I don't have any of my own."

"And no wife either?"

"Once, long ago. Esther died a young woman and there was never anyone else for me. Now, enough about the Chadwicks. Tell me about yourself."

"There's not much to tell."

But as they walked along the beach, turning right

from the Chadwick place, Sara found he managed to draw considerable information from her. She found him very easy to talk to.

They had pulled up even with another house, where a family named Hanson lived.

"They usually come for weekends and sometimes a month-long visit during the summer. It's a shame to have a place like that and not use it, but the Hansons are not the usual summer-type people."

As they walked nearer, they saw some activity about the place, and Wally lifted his brows with surprise.

"By Jove, I believe they've come! They must not have been here very long or we would have seen Midge Pearson by now."

"Midge?"

Wally laughed. "The Hansons' foster child. You'll meet her, never worry. She knows everyone and roams the beach by the hour. I feel sorry for the tike. I'm not sure she's happy with the Hansons."

They walked on and Wally gave Sara a hand. "The beach gets a little tricky here, but it's possible to get around those rocks and on down to the lighthouse. Or if you're not game, we could cut through the Hanson property —"

"Let's be adventuresome," she said. "I can manage —"

Wally told her exactly where to step and how to do it. They rounded the point easily enough. A few steps more and they were doubling back again, so that soon Tom Barclay's house, which had been visible all along, was suddenly shut out of sight. Just ahead, the old lighthouse rose upward, white and towering to the blue sky, from its place on a rocky cliff.

"Oh, it's lovely! Wally, I'll have to paint it. Will your friend mind if I set up my easel here?"

"Herb would be delighted. He'd feel quite the celebrity. A few years back, before they put those modern buoys and markers out in the cove, they used the lighthouse. Herb worked there and when it was closed, he asked permission to stay on and they've let him."

"What fun it must be to live in a lighthouse!"

"Well, the community likes to keep it here. It's a landmark and why tear down everything that belonged to yesterday? It's time we start preserving a little of it before it's too late."

They climbed a steep flight of steps from the beach and approached the lighthouse.

"Hey, Herb, look what I have!" Wally shouted.

All the way to the lighthouse, Sara had envisioned what Herb Travis would be like, and she was not disappointed. He was not a big man, but had a shock of white hair, wind-tumbled, sea blue eyes, a sun-bronzed skin weathered by wind and years, slightly stooped shoulders and a pair of hands that were large and calloused, surely more at ease with the oars of a boat or a piece of rope than a necktie or a teacup.

"Where did you find her?" Herb asked.

With a laugh, Wally made introductions and Herb gave her a brisk nod.

"Nice to know you, Sara. Welcome to the lighthouse. Want me to show you around?"

"I'd love it, Herb."

The place was obviously the old man's pride and joy. The three of them climbed up the winding stairs to the very top and then stepped out and leaned on the railing to stare out at the sea. From here the roof-tops of the Chadwick place were in view among the trees and all of Tom Barclay's house could be seen. Sara had a bird's-eye view of the outline of the coast and she could see for miles out to sea.

"Oh, I love your lighthouse, Herb!"

"Glad you do. You come anytime you want," Herb said. "Only leave Wally at home next time."

He winked at her and she laughed. Beside them, Wally pretended not to hear.

"Old fool," Wally muttered.

Herb grinned and led the way back down the steps. There was a considerable contrast between the two men. Herb wore heavy shoes, faded blue jeans and a work shirt that was patched at the elbows. Wally was nothing but natty with tailored slacks and a mono-grammed shirt with a silk scarf at his throat. But there was a rapport between the two that was a joy to watch and as she studied and listened to them, the time slipped pleasantly by.

Herb talked about his days at the lighthouse, of a ship that had gone down in a storm and then he told about yesterday's fishing and the storm that would probably hit them later that summer.

"Big bag of wind," Wally scoffed. "You always were bragging about the old days."

"Proud of them," Herb shot back. "Now before we start arguing, how about something to drink?"

"Is there any of that Scotch left?"

"You know blamed well we finished that yesterday."

"I'll bring some more next time I come," Wally said.

"I got soda pop," Herb said. "I'll get some."

So they sat in the old lighthouse at a scarred kitchen table, drinking chilled root beer, and Sara couldn't remember another single day in her entire life that had been any happier. She knew she was beginning to soak up the atmosphere, that it was starting to stir around restlessly inside her head and that before she reached Windmere, she would be itching to put what she had just seen, felt and experienced down in bold colors on canvas.

It was nearly noon when Wally declined an invitation from Herb to stay to lunch and they started back.

"Come again, pretty lady," Herb said.

"Possibly as soon as tomorrow," Sara said. "Or next week for certain."

They walked away, waving to him one last time.

"You liked him," Wally said.

"Very much. But you two are so different."

"That's why we hit it off, I suppose. Besides, I like people, Sara. All kinds. That's what the world's all about — people."

"Yes," she said quietly.

For no reason she could put her finger on, she thought about Jerry, sweltering in New York, slaving away at his desk in the Waterman Advertising Agency, and she felt sorry for him. Perhaps she should invite him down very soon. Still, that might not be such a good idea. Jerry would put the wrong emphasis on the invitation. But she felt a twinge of loneliness just now, even with Wally chatting away beside her. She thought of Tom Barclay with his strong good looks, and she wished he'd come by and take her out to dinner as he had promised he would. But this feeling of loneliness often went with the need to paint. Perhaps that was why her work came out with a kind of haunting quality that made people come back for a second look. Jerry had said she had something special and she wanted to believe it. This summer would prove it to her one way or the other.

Lee was in the cottage devouring a sandwich when Sara returned.

"What was all that with Marcia this morning?" Sara asked.

Lee coughed uncomfortably. "What do you mean?"

"I think she likes you," Sara teased.

"Oh, come off it, Sara. I'm just the chauffeur, you know, and Marcia's the boss's daughter. We're just about as far apart as the moon and the earth."

"Be nice to her, Lee. I think she needs a friend."

"I don't intend to be nasty," Lee protested. "But I have to remember who she is."

Sara made herself a sandwich too and joined him at the table. She told him about her walk with Wally and about meeting Herb Travis.

"This afternoon I'm going to paint. If I don't, I'm going to burst."

Lee reached around to the counter, grabbed her

paintbox and thrust it toward her. "Then here — go, girl, go!"

They laughed at that, but an hour later, Sara was set up on the beach. She had decided to do a sketch of Windmere first and then work up to a full painting of it and later, she would tackle the more complicated motion of the sea.

It was hot and since she was working directly in the sun, she put on a wide-brimmed hat for protection from the heat. The water rushed across the sand, glinting with dozens of tiny mirrors. She was hypnotized with the sights and sounds all around her. She picked up a pencil and started roughing in a sketch.

Her concentration was very good and she must have worked for more than an hour before she realized that someone was watching her. She spun about, startled.

"Oh!" she said.

A young girl, nine, possibly ten, sat on the sand, knees hunched up, her arms wrapped around her skinny legs. She had brown pigtails, large, round glasses and a little face with features that somehow didn't match. She was easily one of the homeliest kids Sara had ever seen. Then she smiled and everything changed. There were dimples at the corners of her mouth, her teeth were surprisingly straight, and her eyes echoed the smile.

"Hi," she said.

"Well, hello. Where did you come from?"

She lifted her scrawny shoulders in a shrug. "From up the beach. I live in that big house there."

"The Hanson place? Oh, so you're Midge."

She grinned. "You know about me?"

"In a way."

"You paint real good."

"Thank you."

Midge pushed up her glasses by the nosepiece and changed her position to that of an Indian pose, legs folded in front of her.

"Did you know that a hundred thousand years from now the Big Dipper will look different? The end of the handle will be bent straight down."

Sara smiled. "No, I didn't know that."

"Did you know the fattest man in the world weighed more than a thousand pounds and they buried him in a piano case?"

Sara blinked and shook her head.

"There's a centipede with a hundred and seventy-seven pairs of legs."

"Really?"

"I know lots of things like that."

"That's very interesting. How on earth —"

"Oh, I read a lot," Midge said with another shrug. "What's your name?"

"Sara."

"Are you going to be here all summer?"

"I hope so. How about you?"

Her face clouded for a moment. "I don't know. Mother's here but Dad probably won't come. How do you do that? I can't even draw a straight line. Fact is, I can't do anything," Midge sighed.

"Give yourself time. I couldn't draw when I was only ten."

"I'm eleven."

"Sorry. Well, I couldn't at eleven, either."

"Could you show me how to paint?"

"Perhaps."

"I'll have to ask Mother if it's okay. She says I'm always being a nuisance."

"I could find time to teach you a little something, I'm sure."

Midge rewarded her with another bright smile.

"That would be great! Well, I have to be going now."

Midge got up, brushed the sand from her shorts and gave Sara's canvas one last lingering look. Then with a wave of her hand, she was gone. Sara watched her for a moment, swinging along, bursting now and then into a short run and then hunkering down to prod a shell from the sand. Sara remembered being that age. Looking back to it now, she thought there had never been a time when she'd felt so free and been so happy. But Midge was not like that and for no reason Sara could truly pinpoint, she felt sorry for the girl.

With effort, Sara turned back to the canvas. It took a few moments to get back into the mood of what she was doing.

It was only when she discovered how low the sun was getting in the sky that Sara realized how much time had passed. But she was happy and content, pleased with what she had accomplished.

She returned to the cottage and found that Lee had gone to Vincent to meet Chadwick's train. She showered and changed, then stepped out to the patio, drawn by the cooling air and the spectacle of the sunset.

"You're the girl," a voice said.

She spun about and found a tall man swinging himself up out of a lounge chair. He was better dressed now and he'd shaved off the beard. His hair looked neat and clean, had possibly just been cut that day. It was hard to recognize him as the man she had picked up on the road yesterday, but his eyes were a dead giveaway. She would have known them anywhere.

"How are you feeling?" she asked.

He came to stand beside her, leaning on the railing. She saw that the scratches on his face had already begun to heal.

"I'm going to live," he said. "Unfortunately."

"What a terrible thing to say!"

"I sometimes wish that car had killed me."

"How can you stand there and say that in the face of such a beautiful sunset? On a day like this how could you want to be anything but alive?"

He didn't reply to that. There was a lost and lonely look on his face.

"I saw you here one other time, didn't I?"

"Yes. But I didn't know who you were then —"

"I can't seem to stay away from here. Usually I come at this time of the day. I don't often come to the house — they fuss at me so much — but at dusk, I like to come."

"You don't live here?"

He lifted his shoulders in a shrug. "Part of the time. Whatever my mood is."

"Why do you come here at dusk?"

He turned his burning gaze to her and she saw the anguish in his face. "Because that's when it happened. One moment Tania was here and the next —"

His voice broke. He gripped the railing tightly and then after a moment, he made an effort to get hold of himself.

"Sorry, I shouldn't talk about it. I don't even like to *think* about it."

She was strangely moved, so much so that she reached out to him. She covered his hand as he gripped the railing and he jumped at her touch. He stared at her for a moment with surprise. She felt foolish and uncertain. He was only a stranger. Why did she feel so much compassion for him?

She turned away, leaving him there alone in the fading sunset, not knowing whether he was staring after her or out to the sea.

7

THE BLUE TIDE INN overlooked the Atlantic and the dining room was arranged so that the windows faced the sea and gave the diners the best view. Sara felt easy and relaxed from long days spent in the sun. She'd been at Windmere nearly two weeks and had painted for hours on end. Best of all, she liked what she had done. No one bothered her when they saw her working; even Wally walked a wide circle around her, trying to be as thoughtful as possible. She loved him for his consideration.

Midge had been her most constant companion on the beach, but she, too, had learned not to interrupt when she was deeply involved with her canvas. But Sara usually made it a point to take a break whenever Midge appeared. Listening to Midge's odd bits of information was always a delight.

Tom had made it a habit to come just as she was about to stop work for the day and they spent pleasant moments together before she said goodbye and went back to her cottage.

Now they were out to dinner, their first time, and Sara was enjoying every minute of it.

"I was afraid you wouldn't come," Tom said.

"You've been so absorbed in your work. I'm surprised you have any energy left when night comes."

"But I do and the change of pace is nice. Thank you for bringing me here, Tom. It's a delightful place."

"One of many around and we'll find them all," he promised. "If you like —"

Tom gave her a warm smile and she knew she'd want to discover them with him. Tom was pleasant and easy to be with.

"Do you know as I came to pick you up this evening, it's the first time I've ever been to the Chadwick house? The iron gate seems a little unfriendly, doesn't it?"

"I've grown used to it, I suppose."

"Do you like it there?"

"Very much."

"What are they like, the Chadwicks? As you know, I'm rather new to the community and they haven't exactly beaten down my doors to make my acquaintance."

"I know Wally and Marcia, but I've not much more than met Eldridge. So, I'm not an authority, I'm afraid."

Tom fingered the frosted cocktail glass before him. "And Ryan? What about him?"

Sara hesitated just a moment. She hadn't seen Ryan again except for a glimpse or two since the night they had met at the railing and stood together for a little while.

"I don't know him either, Tom. Why all the interest in the Chadwicks?"

"Just a normal curiosity," he said. "There are few people around, so those that are here come under a closer scrutiny. And maybe I'm a little jealous —"

"Jealous? Of their wealth?"

"They have it all, haven't they?" Tom asked, and a hard note came to his voice. "Why is it some people have so much and others have so little —"

She was startled by the anger in his voice, and then with a laugh, he shook his head. "Sorry. I didn't really mean it that way at all. It's just that I saw my father work all his life at a mean, hard job and what did it get him? A small pension, a gold watch and obscurity. No one remembers now that he gave his life to the company. No one seems to care. Worse luck, he was in an auto accident a couple of years ago and he was left in a wheelchair — the insurance he'd kept with the company was canceled. Canceled! A man gives his life to them and then they cancel him —"

"What did he do?"

"He was a machinist. One of the best. What he didn't know about the parts of a turbine engine you could put in a thimble. But he didn't have the benefit of a college degree or of knowing all the right people. Oh. I'm sorry, I didn't mean to sound off. It's just that the injustices in the world get me down."

"Are you like your father?"

Tom's face softened. "I couldn't shine his shoes. He's really something, Sara, and I'd like for you to meet him sometime. I phone him about once a week and I try to write often. I've sent him stacks of photos of the beach and he enjoys them."

"Feeling as you do and with his condition, I'm surprised you came here, Tom."

Tom took a deep breath. "It was Dad's idea, Sara. He insisted I come and I'm glad I did. I needed to come for several reasons. Meeting you is a bonus. I was afraid it was going to be a very empty summer."

Sara sipped her drink, not knowing what to say in reply.

"Is there any reason why we can't enjoy each other's company this summer? Otherwise, I think it will be lonely for both of us," Tom said.

She smiled. "I suppose you're right."

"Let's just roll along with the tide and take what comes, and what's washed out to sea — well, it will just be gone. What do you say?"

"It sounds like a good idea. We'll have fun together and when the summer is over —"

He lifted his head and a smile came to her from his tanned, handsome face. "When the summer is over, perhaps everything will be different. Who knows?"

"You must have left someone back in Cleveland."

"A couple of girls that somehow failed to excite me very much. I'm almost afraid to ask about you."

She thought about Jerry. He had been on her mind so much that she had been tempted to phone him, but she'd held back. They'd had some good times together and she knew he loved her. She was fond of him and if it could be more, how simple everything would be.

"There is someone, Tom."

Tom leaned back in his chair, his eyes masked. "I see."

"But he's in New York and I'm here and I don't know if we'll ever be together again. I think that's something I'll have to decide for certain very soon. Maybe that's one of the reasons I wanted Lee to take the job with the Chadwicks. It isn't everyone who gets a chance at a stolen summer, away from it all."

"No," Tom said thoughtfully. "I wish things were —" He paused as if about to say something very significant and then changed his mind. "What can I do to make your stay here a happy one?"

"I don't know what more I could want. I have the sea, the sand, the lovely weather, all the paints I need, new canvas to cover —"

"Is your life really that simple and basic?"

"I hope to find out if I'm truly an artist or if I'm better suited to selling commercial work to promote some new product. I need to know that."

"From what I've seen of your paintings, you're good, Sara. Very good."

"But I seem so amateurish at times. I get out of patience with myself."

"Nothing worthwhile comes easily," Tom said and a frown touched his face. Sara had the oddest feeling that he was not talking about her work at all, but some dark, secretive thing.

He stirred and smiled at her. "Would you like another drink?"

"No. But if you do —"

Tom shook his head. "What I really had in mind was a drive along the coast. If you take the highway south of the lighthouse, there's a really beautiful stretch of ocean and there's still enough moon to make it spellbinding."

They left the inn and with Tom at the wheel, they drove through Vincent and down a road to the shore-line. There was a light burning at the lighthouse, a soft glow in the darkness.

"Herb took me fishing the other day. I thought the weather might stop us, but it turned fair. We caught the sum total of nothing. Herb said it was a bad sign," Tom said.

"A bad sign of what?"

Tom laughed. "He didn't say. A bad sign for every-thing, I guess."

"He is the sweetest old man."

The drive was all Tom had promised it would be. The air was cool as the breeze came in off the ocean and the sea had taken on a nighttime quality, a mid-night blue body of water that showed its smile with the rippling white caps and nibbled at the beach like a caress.

Tom stopped the car. "Let's walk down there."

Hand in hand, they stepped down to the sand and they strolled silently, the night brushing their shoul-ders like black velvet and the rush of water a sym-phony.

A buoy winked its light on and off, a warning to stray ships that the water ran shallow, and as they paused to look at it, Tom put his arm around her shoulder.

"It's like a heartbeat," he said. "Thump, thump, thump, blink, blink, blink."

He turned her gently toward him. His large hand lifted her chin. "My beautiful little Sara," he murmured.

Leaning down, he kissed her for a long moment and it seemed perfectly right and sweet as they stood on the sand in the dwindling moonlight, the surf at their feet. There was no other world but the one they were experiencing this very moment.

"I've wanted to do that all evening," he said. "In fact, I've wanted to do it long before this."

She heard the thunder of his heart beneath her ear and found she could say nothing in reply.

"Shall we walk farther down the shore?" he asked.

"It must be getting late. We'd better go back to Windmere."

The drive back was one of tumbled emotions for Sara. Tom stirred something fresh and exciting inside her. He was so different from Jerry. The night was beautiful, the air fresh and clean, the stars like softened flakes of gold.

When they reached the gate at Windmere, Tom shook his head with despair. "I forgot about this. Does this mean we'll have to get someone up?"

"Elsa has a button in her room so when people come in late —"

Tom got out to ring the bell and in a moment, the gate swung open and they drove through. At the house, Tom walked with her to the cottage door.

"I'll see you on the beach tomorrow?"

"Yes."

"This has been a great evening, Sara."

"For me, too. Goodnight, Tom."

He bent to kiss her once again and then, saying goodnight, was gone. She listened for the sound of his car going up the road to the gate before she went inside the cottage.

Lee's bedroom door was closed, but he'd left a light burning in the kitchen. Sara was not sleepy and she didn't want to go to bed. She decided to step outside once more and went to lean against the cool iron railing and listen to the night.

She thought of the girl who had fallen over here and it made her uneasy. How could it have happened? It was better not to think about it. She wanted no unpleasant things marring the summer. She smiled as she remembered what Tom had said. They would roll with the tide and she wondered what it would bring them eventually.

Drugged at last by fresh air, she went back inside, suddenly tired and sleepy. Never before had she slept as she slept here, asleep when her head hit the pillow, not waking up until she heard Lee stirring in the next room.

They were having breakfast when the house phone rang. Lee arched his brows. If Chadwick was calling this early in the day, it probably meant there had been a change in plans.

He went to answer it.

"Hello . . . Yes, Mr. Chadwick, my sister is here."

Sara looked up with surprise. Why would Chadwick be asking about her? There was a startled look on Lee's face. "Yes, sir, I'll tell her. Yes, sir, in half an hour."

He hung up and shook his head. "I don't get it. He wants to see *you*, Sara, in the den, in half an hour."

"Me? Oh, Lee, do you suppose he's going to ask me to leave? Have I done something wrong? I've tried hard to stay out of his way and I'm sure he can't find fault with anything I've done."

"You'll just have to go and find out," Lee said with a worried frown. "Chadwick's not going to New York this morning. They have a house guest. There was a woman with him last night when I met the train; I assume she's some kind of business associate."

Sara was curious and a little uneasy. The summer held so much promise and if she had to leave here — after breakfast she brushed her hair carefully and put on a little makeup, something she'd scarcely done since coming here.

Later she went to the house and Elsa took her to the den. Once again she saw the huge desk, the rows of books on the shelves, the plush carpeting and the comfortable furniture. She spied the woman at once. Her hair was done in a French twist, she wore a tailored dress with a string of pearls as her only jewelry and her eyes were cool and blue behind horn-rimmed glasses. Sara knew that she was being sized up minutely.

"Miss Denning," Chadwick said, rising from his chair behind the desk. "I'd like you to meet a close business associate of mine. Miss Lorna Cellman."

Sara returned the woman's nod and wondered again why she had been summoned here like this.

"Please sit down, Miss Denning," Chadwick said.

She felt as if she were waiting for some very important verdict as she clenched her hands together in her lap. This was nearly as bad as it had been waiting to hear what reaction Garrison would have to her work on Whiff.

"I'll come right to the point, Miss Denning," Chadwick said. "This is highly irregular and something I don't like to do, but I'm in a bit of a bind. It concerns a business transaction and frankly, it means I have to move fast or all is lost. I can't get away from Windmere today nor can Miss Cellman, as we're waiting for some important phone calls from Europe. The thing of it is, we need a courier to fly to Denver, meet our associate there, turn over some signed papers to him, get a receipt and return. Time is of the greatest importance and there isn't anyone free in New York who can handle this on such short notice. Now, Miss Denning —"

Sara blinked, guessing what he wanted.

"I realize this is an imposition," he said.

"I don't like it, Eldridge," Miss Cellman cut in. "I don't think we should follow through with this transaction at all."

"I've already decided, Lorna," he replied smoothly.

"You're jumping the gun too fast. You should wait another few days —"

But Chadwick was ignoring her and doing it in a manner that told Sara he was a determined man.

Lorna Cellman was getting angrier by the minute. She rose and paced about the room, nervously fidgeted with her glasses and finally turned her back to the room to stare out the window.

"Would you mind helping us out, Miss Denning?" Chadwick asked. "I know it would take your day and part of the evening, but I could have Lee drive you to Atlantic City. From there you can take a mid-morning flight to Philadelphia and make your connection to Denver, nonstop. You would be helping me out of an awkward situation and I know you're a trustworthy person —" He gave her a brief smile. "In checking Lee's background, we also learned a great deal about you, Sara."

"Well, if there is no one else —"

"You're the only person available," Chadwick replied. "Marcia has no head for anything like this, Wally has other fish to fry today and I've no idea where Ryan has gone. I'll gladly reimburse you for your time."

"You've been so kind to let me come here with Lee that it's the least I can do. If you'll give me full instructions —"

Chadwick was already reaching for the phone. While she listened, Sara heard him make the plane reservations to and from Denver and while he did so, he wrote a few instructions on a pad of paper.

"Mr. Madlock will meet you at the Denver airport. You'll have plenty of time before you catch your flight back."

"This Mr. Madlock —"

"You can't miss him." Chadwick smiled. "He'll introduce himself, but when you see a tall man with a flowing mustache and a large diamond ring on his little finger, you've found him. He speaks with a very definite German accent. I'll phone him and tell him you'll be coming."

Sara went back to the cottage, explained the situation to Lee, and changed into appropriate clothes. Then with the papers locked in a briefcase, the key in her purse, she climbed into the Cadillac and smiled at Lee.

"Drive on, James!"

Lee made a face at her. "Easy there, girl. I must say this is quite a turn of events."

"I'm glad to help out and besides, a trip to Denver, even a very quick one, might be fun."

"But doesn't it seem a little strange? Why you?"

"It's because I have such an honest face. Don't make such a big thing out of it, Lee. He wanted a favor, so he's getting it. Don't be late meeting me when I get back."

"I'll be there. Just don't miss your connections."

"Who is Lorna Cellman, Lee? She didn't want me to go to Denver. I thought she and Chadwick were going to have a real quarrel over it."

"She's Chadwick's good right hand, the way I understand it. There are some that say she's more, that she has romantic ideas about the boss too."

"I don't think I like her."

Lee laughed at that as he cleared the gate and

drove on toward Vincent and the highway to Atlantic City.

"You don't even know her, Sara."

"But sometimes I get feelings, you know? Down deep where it counts, I don't get good vibrations from her."

Then Sara put Lorna Cellman out of her mind. The briefcase rested on her lap and she began to worry about it. What if she lost it, what if she missed the man in Denver, what if — there were dozens of ifs and it would be best not to think of any of them. Sara leaned back and tried to enjoy being driven to the airport in a limousine.

Things went smoothly at Atlantic City. She gave Lee a quick wave and rushed through the gate, paused for the customary security checks and then was soon boarding her plane.

A dark-haired man, small of build, sat across the aisle from her reading a paper. But after a time she became certain he wasn't reading a word of it. Now and then he glanced covertly at her and she began to get an uneasy feeling. He was watching her and it wasn't the usual flirtatious kind of look every woman recognized. This was sly, almost devious.

She snuggled the briefcase closer on her lap and began to wish the trip to Denver was over, that the papers had been safely handed over to Madlock and that she was home again, on the beach, talking back to the gulls.

8

SARA WAS SERVED LUNCH on the flight, and shortly after that, they were nearing Denver. She peered out the window and saw the majestic rise of the Rocky Mountains, the higher peaks smudged with snow. There was an unbelievable beauty about them and she wished there was time to rent a car and drive up the winding roads, follow a rushing stream and go as high as she could among the pines and aspens.

She clutched the briefcase on her lap and knew that while she was glad to do Chadwick a favor, she didn't truly like the role of a courier, especially when important papers were involved.

The plane began nosing nearer the earth and she saw Stapleton International Airport ahead. In a moment the wheels screeched down the runways and they thundered along, slowing down. The big bird had reached its destination safely and Sara with it.

She joined the other passengers filing into the terminal, cleared the gate and stepped out into the waiting area, looking around, wondering if finding Madlock was going to be as easy as Chadwick had led her to believe. At the same time, she was trying to watch the man who had been across the aisle from her, hoping that he would simply walk on very quickly and never give her another glance. With a sigh of relief, she saw him melt into the crowd and she put him out of her mind as a very well dressed man with a flower in his lapel and the biggest mustache she had ever seen stopped her.

"Miss Denning?"

"Yes."

"I'm Madlock. Chadwick said to look for the prettiest girl on the plane, and I think I've found her. Do you have the papers?"

"Yes, right in here," she said, patting the briefcase.

"Let's step over there and we'll make our transaction. I won't keep you any longer than necessary."

He seemed hurried and she was relieved to have been contacted so quickly. They sat down in the chairs in the waiting area and as Sara unlocked the briefcase, she gave him an uncertain smile.

"Would you mind very much showing me some identification?"

He laughed and shook his head. "Not at all, my dear. Very sensible of you."

He showed her a driver's license in his wallet along with a few credit cards bearing the name Kurt Madlock. He also produced a receipt and signed it with a flourish.

"An even trade," he said.

Sara took the large brown envelope from inside the briefcase and handed it to Madlock. He took it with a nod.

"It was pleasant meeting you, Miss Denning. I wish

there was time to buy you a drink, but unfortunately I'm expected at my office with these papers."

"Goodbye, Mr. Madlock."

Then he was gone, walking away swiftly, the brown envelope tucked out of sight in his own briefcase. Sara decided she might as well browse about and perhaps pick up a funny little gift for Lee. It was then she caught the barest glimpse of the man who had been in the seat across from her on the plane. Thank God, he no longer seemed interested in her. Had he just spoken briefly to a tall, red-haired woman wearing a blue linen dress? Then she saw him again, and with a start she saw he was following Madlock out of the terminal. Coincidence? Or was he purposely keeping a few steps behind Madlock?

Sara tried to laugh at the notion. She'd done her part of the job and she should forget it now. She saw a small shop and decided to go inside and look around. She was browsing about when she suddenly became aware of the red-haired woman in blue beside her. The woman seemed intent on buying some magazines, but finding her so near made Sara uneasy.

Sara quickly made her purchase and stepped back out to the busy waiting room and double-checked her flight time back to Philadelphia. The woman in blue no longer seemed to be around and Sara laughed at herself. Her imagination was getting away from her, that was all.

She had more than two hours to wait for her return flight and spent most of it reading a book. Then it was time to board the plane.

Once again, Sara feasted her eyes on the mountains as they climbed upward, and when they had disappeared from view, she settled back for the trip home. The next thing she knew, the pilot was announcing that they were over Ohio, and that made her think of Tom Barclay and his father. Tom was nice, different, and he gave the summer an added dimension.

It was a short time later that Sara saw a woman coming down the aisle — and she was the very same red-haired woman in blue! Sara's throat went dry. It surely didn't mean anything. Or was it that the duty of watching her had simply been turned over to someone else? At Philadelphia, Sara was certain she would see no more of the woman, but when she boarded the same flight to Atlantic City, Sara could no longer put it down to coincidence. She was all the more anxious to reach home safely and prayed that Lee would be waiting to meet her.

After Lee had driven Sara to Atlantic City and seen her safely off, he returned to Windmere and advised Chadwick that she was on her way.

"I'll not be needing you today, Lee. Miss Cellman and I will be working here. But when you bring Sara home, please have her stop by the den."

"Yes, sir. I will."

Lee knew there was nothing for him to do in the garage. All the cars were in good running order and if he polished them any more, he'd rub off the paint. So, unexpectedly, he had a free day.

He changed out of his uniform, put on a pair of

swimming trunks and decided to go down to the beach. He had found a little spot up in the rocks near the water where a protruding ledge offered shade and made a roof for a shallow, cavelike room. He had discovered it several days ago and hadn't even told Sara about it. He felt private there. Even as a child, he'd liked to slip away and be alone. The view was stupendous and he could go for a brief swim or stretch out in the sun or simply sit back in the shade and read one of the books he had stashed away there. He was anticipating a lazy day as he climbed the rocks and made his way to his secret place.

As he reached the spot, he was startled to see someone else was there.

"Marcia!"

She lifted her sunglasses and smiled at him. "Oh, it's you!"

"What are you doing here?" he asked.

"Enjoying the day; what are you?"

He flushed. He realized how it must have sounded. The beach belonged to the Chadwicks, not him.

"I'm sorry, I didn't mean to intrude," he said.

He started away but she called after him. "Oh, you don't need to go. I know you've been coming here. I found this place a long time ago when I was a kid. It's very special, isn't it?"

Lee nodded. "Yes, it is."

The sun was making her blond hair even more silvery, almost platinum, and she was probably the prettiest girl Lee had ever seen. But he frankly didn't know what to make of her. The last few days, she'd been in and out of the garage several times, never really wanting anything, but seemingly eager to talk. He had come to look forward to her visits, to listen for her steps.

"Why don't you join me," she said. "The sun is perfect today. It's not too hot and the breeze is just right. It's a gorgeous time of the year."

Lee hesitated. Then with a laugh, Marcia jumped up and came to grasp his hand and tug him up the last step and onto the ledge. Her fingers around his seemed cool and smooth.

"I can't stay long," he said uneasily.

"Don't be silly. You can spend the day. I know Dad doesn't need you. When Lorna comes, he doesn't go to New York. What do you think of her?"

He shook his head, not certain how to answer that. He'd barely seen Miss Cellman and he wasn't one to make snap judgments. Besides, he wasn't going to gossip with Marcia. He knew his place.

"I hate her!" Marcia said with surprising heat to her voice. "She turns Dad into a silly oaf. She has him wrapped around her little finger. Do you think they're having an affair?"

Lee felt his face grow red. Marcia's bluntness caught him off guard, but he knew she was waiting for an answer. "I'm sure I don't know and besides, it's none of my business."

"You're very proper, aren't you? I bug you, don't I?"

"Miss Chadwick —"

"Marcia. You called me Marcia a few minutes ago.

Don't worry, Lee, no one is going to see you here with me and what's the difference if they do?"

He sat down cautiously on the ledge, wondering how quickly he could go without offending her. But she was right about one thing, it *was* an almost perfect day. Sara would have good flying weather. His sister quickly fled from Lee's thoughts as Marcia put her cool hand on his arm.

"Lee, tell me about yourself."

"There's nothing to tell."

"Well, there has to be something!" she said with a touch of exasperation in her voice. "What were you like as a little boy?"

He smiled at that. "I'd rather hear about you. Have you always lived at Windmere?"

"Yes. Other people close their houses and go somewhere for the winter, but Dad always stays. We just weather it out. But then, most of the time, I'm away to school."

"Will you leave in the fall?"

Marcia shook her head. "College's a drag and I don't want to go back. I suppose it's going to mean another row with Dad. Did you go to college, Lee?"

"No, I couldn't afford it. So you see, Marcia, we're very different."

"That's why I like you, Lee. You're for real."

"Am I?"

She laughed at that and then stretched out on a beach towel, sun glasses in place, smiling. For a little while, Lee sat on the ledge watching her and a dozen crazy thoughts went chasing through his head. This was not happening; he was only dreaming and he would wake up to find that Marcia was gone. After a while, he stretched out beside her, closed his eyes for a little while and let the sun caress his face. When he dared look at Marcia again, he found her watching him.

She smiled and the shape of her lips seemed perfect, soft, warm and inviting. He wanted to kiss her. He shook the thought away and wished the knot would leave his throat.

"Lee, what do you think about when you come up here by yourself?"

"Lots of things."

"Do you ever think of me?"

He grinned. "Sure. I think what a pest you are, always hanging around the garage, in the way —"

"Oh!"

She grabbed a handful of tiny pebbles and tossed them at him. They struck his chest playfully and fell onto the ledge.

"Do you always pester your father's chauffeur like that?"

She flung off her sunglasses and he saw her blue eyes raging with anger. "No! Never! It's the first time there was ever anyone like you, Lee."

His heart had begun sounding like a motor with the timing set too high, the pinging of it rattling in his ears, a warning.

"Am I so different?"

She nodded slowly and her voice was barely audible above the rush of the surf. "Yes," she said. "Oh, yes!"

He wanted to reach out for her, pull her close, but he knew that to do so was to open a door to a room that meant trouble. Forbidden fruit always tasted the sweetest, he'd been told. But this was the first time it had been dangled before his eyes and he was sorely tempted.

"Marcia," he murmured.

She reached out and touched his face with her fingers and he held them for a moment tight against his lips. They stared at each other and suddenly he realized she was as frightened as he. With a little cry, she jumped to her feet and she began scrambling down the rocks to the surf.

"Wait," he called. "Wait —"

"Catch me if you can!" she shouted with a laugh.

Then entering into the spirit of the game, he chased after her and they ran into the surf. Since coming here, he had kept his swimming time brief. He knew he felt much better these days, but he had been cautioned to go slow. Swimming took a great deal of effort, and more air than his lungs could supply. But now he dashed caution to the winds and ran into the water after her.

She was a good swimmer and he saw that it would not be easy to catch her. After a few minutes of wild thrashing of his arms and legs to shorten the distance between them, he saw that she was going out so far that he didn't dare try to follow.

"Marcia, come back. Marcia —"

But she gave him a devilish smile and went on. He

saw her go farther and farther and as he treaded water, he began to worry. There were strong undercurrents out there and even good swimmers could drown. Then before his despairing eyes, he saw her thrash an arm wildly as if she were in trouble. She disappeared for a moment, resurfaced and then went down again.

He started after her. There was nothing else to do, and he called forth all his lagging energy. It seemed a very long way to the spot where he had last seen her. He had only one thought in mind and that was to find her, to help her back to the shore, to save her from the blue water that had now suddenly become so treacherous.

When he reached her at last and lunged for her, he managed to get an arm around her and support her.

"Don't fight me, Marcia. Just let me do it. Easy now, you're all right."

The shore seemed a hundred miles away. His lungs were aching miserably and it seemed less and less air was reaching them, even though he tried to breathe deeply and evenly, keeping his face out of the water.

After only a short distance with Marcia in tow, he knew he was laboring to a point of exhaustion and certain peril.

"Can't make it," he muttered. "God, give me strength —"

He didn't know exactly when it was that Marcia came to life, when it was she that was supporting him, when it was she that was saving his life and pulling him to shore.

He felt the sand under his feet, her arms around him, helping him and then he remembered collapsing, chest heaving and his lungs on fire.

He had no idea how long it had been when he opened his eyes and found himself stretched out on the clean sand of the beach, his head in Marcia's lap, her blond hair drying in the sun, her eyes shadowed with worry.

"Oh, Lee, are you all right? You gave me such a scare."

"Some hero I turned out to be. I'm sorry —"

"But what happened out there?"

"I —I'm not supposed to exert myself. An old illness when I was a kid left my lungs weak — but that's beside the point. I went in the water to save you, Marcia. You were drowning —"

Her eyes clouded with tears. "Oh, Lee! What a terrible thing to do to you. I didn't know!"

"I don't understand."

"I wasn't drowning. It was a gag, a joke — I wanted you to chase after me. Brazen, stupid me — oh, Lee —"

He felt her shudder, saw the true compassion in her eyes and they looked deep into each other. He lifted a hand and put his palm against her sun-warmed cheek.

"It's all right, Marcia. Don't cry —"

He wiped away the tear that trickled down her face. Then as he lifted his head, she bent toward him and their lips met and clung for one fierce, desperate moment. When they broke away, they stared at each other.

"You do care," she said softly. "You *do* care —"

The tide swished a wave toward them, but they didn't move, even when it nibbled at Marcia's feet, and there, in the sunshine, with the sky watching, Lee kissed her again and knew for a certainty that he had just taken his first step into the forbidden room.

9

WHEN THE PLANE LANDED at Atlantic City, Sara was
one of the first ones off and she hurried through the
gate, searching anxiously for Lee. She spied him and
rushed toward him.

"Oh, Lee —"

Then she saw that Marcia Chadwick was with him,
and all the worried things she wanted to tell him died
on her lips.

"I thought I'd tag along," Marcia said. "It beats
staying at home and being bored."

Lee was standing apart from Marcia and he looked
tired but somehow elated. Sara glanced from one to
the other and sensed that there was something between the two. But she couldn't think about that now.
She glanced over her shoulder and saw the woman in
blue. As if there was nothing wrong at all, she walked
by them, scarcely glancing in their direction. But it
was a very practiced maneuver, Sara was sure of that.

"Do you happen to know that woman, Marcia?"
Sara asked.

Marcia shrugged her shoulders. "Never saw her before in my life. Why?"

"No reason. Let's go, Lee. It's been a long day."

She was anxious to leave the airport, get in the car and drive back to the peacefulness of Windmere. She wondered if she should tell Chadwick about the man on the plane and the woman in blue and then decided against it. She was not certain about any of it and it would sound more than a little ridiculous.

All the way back, Marcia chattered to Lee and Sara heard his answers, polite and proper, but now and then a little laugh would creep in and a warmth came to his voice.

The road out of Vincent was quiet and empty as usual. Sara began to relax. When they drove through the gate, Lee told her she was to report to Chadwick.

"Yes, of course," she said.

It took but a few minutes and Chadwick seemed pleased that everything had gone smoothly. Lorna Cellman did not say a word but her cool, blue gaze never left Sara's face.

When Sara returned to the cottage, she saw that Lee had not yet come in from the garage. Was Marcia still with him? She decided to make a cup of coffee and by the time it was ready, Lee had come into the room and tossed his chauffeur's cap to a chair. They exchanged a glance and Lee flushed.

"I know what you're going to say."

"Do you?"

"I shouldn't be seeing Marcia — I shouldn't let her hang around."

"She's a nice girl."

"But not for me."

"If you're worried about Chadwick, I doubt he sees or notices anything unless it has a dollar sign attached to it. It's business, business, business with him."

"Maybe. But Marcia is his daughter and who am I? I can't forget how different we are."

"Sometimes these things work themselves out."

Sara had fully intended to talk to Lee about the trip to Denver and her uneasiness over the notion that she had been followed, but he seemed tired and his mind was obviously with Marcia. Besides, here in the cottage, with the sound of the surf crashing on the beach below the rocks, it all seemed idiotic. Perhaps tomorrow she would tell Lee her suspicions.

But the next morning brought a surprise visitor to her door. Sara had slept late, Lee had gone to drive Chadwick and Lorna Cellman to the station, so when she heard someone knock at the door, her first thought was that it was Elsa or Marcia.

"Jerry!"

Jerry Lydell stood there looking at her for a long moment, a slight flush on his cheeks. There was an awkward second or two as they stared at each other, remembering how they had parted. Then Jerry stepped into the room, dropped his briefcase into a chair and pulled her quickly into his arms. His lips came down warm and sweet on hers and for a long time he held her close, laughing softly at her surprise.

"Where on earth did you come from? Why are you here?" she asked.

"One question at a time," he said. "So this is the place —" He looked around for a moment, caught a glimpse of the view and pursed his lips. "I can see why you're so crazy about it."

"I still can't believe you're here, Jerry!"

"I've come down on Bob Waterman's orders. Listen, Sara, I have something in my briefcase that will interest you. At any rate, I have to have an answer from you before I go back on the two o'clock train."

He picked up the briefcase and took out some papers. Then he spread them out on the kitchen table, and for the next twenty minutes, he talked without stopping. It was a small struggle for her to keep up. She'd forgotten that she used to work this way every day. The pace was so fast in New York, so leisurely here.

"The thing boils down to this, Sara. We need a layout for the World Tour Travel Agency, and the trips and package deals they're going to offer have temporarily been named Cloud Nine, and what you're to do is make everyone want to be a part of it. You'll be working on their first tour."

"I'm to make a hard sell in a pretty package."

Jerry laughed. "Sure, you know the bit. Do a bang-up job on this, Sara. It's important and it might lead to better things. But we'll need the work within two weeks. Can you bring it to New York a week from Thursday?"

Her head was spinning. "I'm not sure —"

The whole thing seemed to drift away when she tried to pin it down. It would be a battle to get back into her old routine, to think commercially again. Jerry saw her hesitation. "Darling, it would be a good idea to keep your finger in the pie. I especially want you to do this. You're right for it."

"You convinced Bob of that, didn't you?"

Jerry smiled. "Guilty. It was a way to get to see you and keep you working for the agency too. So, kill me."

She could tell that this meant a great deal to him and she wanted things to be right between them once again. She had missed his friendship more than she had imagined she would, and there were moments when she almost wanted to love him. He was still unhappy with the way things were. If she went along with him on this, it would surely ease the situation. She looked at the papers scattered on the table and drew a deep breath.

"What if I try and it's not good enough — what if I fall on my face as I did with the Whiff account?"

"You won't. We're not dealing with Garrison this time, for one thing."

Jerry began talking again, persuading her, tossing out some ideas of his own, and the first thing she knew, she was getting back in it, asking questions, making notes and offering a few thoughts of her own. Jerry began to smile.

"Does this mean you'll do it?"

"I'll try."

Jerry was elated. With a happy gesture he scooped the papers up to a pile and left them on the table. Then he checked his watch.

"Plenty of time for a walk on the beach and for you to tell me what you've been doing since you came here."

"I'd rather show you."

"Okay."

She got out all the work she'd done — the sketches, the watercolors and the oils — and while it wasn't a great deal yet, it was an impressive lot at that. Jerry examined each piece of work with critical eyes and she was conscious of holding her breath.

"Beautiful, Sara. Just beautiful! I didn't realize you could do this — but I should have known, shouldn't I?"

"The summer's young. I'll do a great deal more, I hope. Oh, Jerry, you don't know what satisfaction there is in doing this, in trying for a certain mood, a particular feeling, a very special color — so different from advertising."

"You almost make me envious," he said, a touch of wistfulness in his voice. "But I'm not sure I could be happy off in a never-never land like this."

"Windmere isn't *that* far removed from civilization," she laughed.

"By the way, how is the great man? I've been hearing things about him. Very interesting things."

"Like what?"

"Let's walk down to the beach and I'll tell you."

They left the cottage, went down the steps and walked hand in hand along the water's edge. Jerry had left his jacket at the cottage, shed his shoes and socks, rolled his trouser legs, and loosened his tie. The change it made in him was startling.

"I like you like this, Jerry."

He shrugged. "Well, I don't have a chance to be casual very often."

"That's what's wrong with the city," Sara sighed. "Here, you step to a different music and usually the tune is of your own choosing. But what were you going to tell me about Chadwick?"

Jerry paused for a moment to bend down and pick up a seashell. He examined it minutely, found a flaw in it and tossed it aside.

"Well, it seems the man is involved in something really big. I hear he's stuck his neck out so far he has practically everything tied up in it."

"What sort of thing?"

Jerry lifted his shoulders in a shrug. "Who knows? It's all very hush-hush. I've heard talk that it has something to do with the government. But whatever it is, you can bet that Chadwick plans to make a small fortune from it."

"I never did understand high finance or big, complicated deals — I guess that means I'll never be a millionaire."

She was wondering if her trip to Denver had something to do with all of this. Perhaps so and then again, that seemed unlikely. If it had been so important, why would he have risked his papers with a comparative stranger?

They strolled along the beach and Sara thought of taking Jerry to the lighthouse. But she quickly decided against it. She wasn't sure he would appreciate its stark beauty or that he would take to Herb Travis. Jerry sometimes made light of the simple things, of simple people. She hated that flaw in him and she didn't want to risk having him put any kind of blot on the paradise she'd found here.

Later, they shared an early lunch at the cottage. Lee had not come back after taking Chadwick and Lorna Cellman to the train, and Sara remembered that he planned to stay in Vincent, pick up some supplies from Mark Williams and stay to eat with him at noon. It was probably just as well that Lee and Jerry did not meet. There was not much love lost between the two.

Jerry nibbled halfheartedly at the sandwich she had made him.

"Sara, I miss you. I wish you'd come back to New York with me, right this minute. Why do you want to waste a talent like yours down here in this fairyland? Can't you do your serious work on weekends or something?"

"A weekend just isn't long enough."

"Don't you miss what we had together?"

She was touched by the wistfulness in his voice. "At times I even miss the office and the crazy things that happened there — but in the next moment, I know how happy I am here. Just give me the summer, Jerry. Is that so much to ask?"

"We always were at odds about something, weren't we?"

They grew silent again and neither ate very much. It was soon time for Jerry to go. He pulled her close and it seemed comfortable and familiar in his arms.

"I'll see you in a couple of weeks," he said.

"I'll take an early train and see you Thursday morning. Goodbye, Jerry."

When he had gone, Sara thumbed through the papers Jerry had left for her. They spelled out the specifics for her. Now all she had to do was get the right idea to put them across to the public. Cloud Nine. A nice name. But what did she use for a fresh approach, for the right angle?

She took a sketch pad down to the beach and sat on one of the rocks there. She made several false starts and wadded them up angrily. She was rushing it, of course. There had to be some time to think about it, to mull it over, pick and choose from the best possible ideas she could find.

Why had she agreed to do it in the first place? Why hadn't she simply told Jerry no? Of course the money would help; she couldn't forever keep drawing from her savings and she would never take from Lee. The work was probably a blessing in disguise. Strange, while Jerry had been here talking about it, she had really wanted to do it — but now that he was gone, the desire had gone too.

"Hi, Sara!"

She saw Midge trudging along the beach toward her. When Midge reached her, she studied the sketch pad for a moment.

"That's different," Midge said.

"This is the kind of work I do when I live in New York. I'm supposed to make this so attractive you'll want to rush out and buy a ticket for the tour."

"I asked Mother if I could take some lessons from

you. She said I shouldn't bother you. I'm always just a bother —" Midge sighed.

She sounded so woebegone that Sara reached out and took her suntanned face in both hands. "Ah, Midge, you're no bother to me. You remind me of myself when I was your age. It's too bad you don't have a brother like I had."

Midge pulled her face into a frown. "I don't even have a real mother and father," she said. "I'm a foster kid, Sara. Didn't you know that?"

"To me, you're just Midge," Sara said.

"Lee's kind of my brother," Midge said. "He's nice."

"I think so too."

"He lets me watch him work on the Chadwick cars. He can fix anything."

"I wish he could fix this!" Sara sighed.

She turned back to the sketch she'd made and sometime later, Midge slipped away, leaving her alone. She made a few more attempts and was about to give up when Ryan Chadwick appeared as he usually did, suddenly, without warning, slipping into view like a quiet shadow.

"Where have you been?" she asked. "I haven't seen you for several days."

"Around," he replied. "I think I know every mile of this beach for ten miles in every direction."

She heard the deep loneliness in his voice and saw the way his lips tightened. She felt a wave of pity for him.

"Your father is always involved in business things. Don't you —"

"No," he said with a shake of his head. "I'm a good deal like Uncle Wally. I do nothing. There was a trust fund set up for Marcia and me when we were kids. It's very generous and thanks to Dad's foresight, it has made me independent financially."

"I see."

"You don't approve, do you? You think every man should have a cause in his life, an ambition, a thing to do —"

"Most men do."

"I'm different," he said. "All my ambitions and causes and reasons to live went over that railing up there. Tania was with me one day, gone the next —"

"I think I would like to have known her."

Ryan gave her a half smile. "You're very much like her, you know."

"I am!"

"She was small and dark too, perhaps a bit taller, and she laughed from the toes up. She was a little flighty — or at least pretended to be, mostly for my benefit I think, but there was always a little corner of her that I never knew, that she held back from me."

"We all do that, Ryan."

"I wish I had known what was in that corner," he said with a frown. Then he ripped off his sunglasses and rubbed his dark-rimmed eyes tiredly.

"Ryan, there's only one thing for you to do now. That's go on the best you can. It always comes down to that."

He stared at her for a moment and seemed about to say something. But he changed his mind and then turned to look up at the rocks where Tania had fallen. He stiffened and came to quick attention.

"What the hell —"

"What is it?"

"Hey!" Ryan shouted up toward the rocks. "Hey, what are you doing?"

Sara looked over her shoulder to see what he was shouting about and was surprised to find Tom Barclay in the rocks above.

Ryan was very tense and angry beside her. "Who does he think he is? What's he doing up there."

"What's it matter?" she asked.

"That's where they found Tania. I don't like anybody tramping around there. It's — well — sort of sacred."

"I'll tell Tom to go away if you like."

"Do it," Ryan said quickly.

She left him to go up the steps. When she drew even with Tom, she called to him.

"Tom, could I speak with you?"

"Sure."

He came climbing over the rocks toward her and in a few seconds was standing beside her on the steps.

"What were you doing?" she asked.

"I'm a rock hound, among other things, and I thought I might find some interesting specimens there, why?"

"Ryan doesn't like it."

Tom glanced down to the beach where Ryan stood tense and angry, watching them.

"I know I'm trespassing," Tom said. "But what's a few rocks?"

"It's where Tania fell. Ryan's a little sensitive about it."

Tom set his jaw and for a moment or two, Sara thought he was going down to the beach to confront Ryan. Then he shrugged his wide shoulders.

"So, okay, I'll knock it off," he said. "Tell Ryan to relax. I'll go rock hunting somewhere else. Why don't you come along, Sara?"

"I couldn't. I have some work to do for my agency. So, for the next week or so, I'll be slaving away."

"I hope that doesn't mean day *and* night," he said with his nice smile. "I think we're due for another night out, don't you?"

"Sounds nice, but I'll have to see."

"I'll phone. And look, I'm sorry if I disturbed any of the mighty Chadwicks."

He started down the steps with her, and when they reached the beach, she saw that Ryan had disappeared. Tom wandered on down toward Widow's Point and Sara picked up her pencil again. She looked once more at the rocks where Tom had been searching. A rock hound? A photographer? What else was Tom Barclay?

When she decided to give up work for the day and went back to her cottage, she found Ryan waiting for her on the patio.

"Thanks for getting Tom to leave," he said. "I know it must seem a crazy thing to you, a small thing —"

"I understand, Ryan."

His dark eyes glinted. "Yes, I think you do, Sara. You know, I hope we can be friends. I can talk to you like I can talk to no one else."

She was flattered and touched. Ryan was a complex man and she sensed he didn't often ask anyone into his private world. She gave him a smile. "You always know where to find me, Ryan."

10

Herb travis had received word from his only granddaughter, Jan Travis, that she would come to spend the summer with him. Jan taught school in Pennsylvania and would be free to come in a few days. Herb had been hoping she would come, and for the last week had put the spit and polish to everything in sight. He whistled while he worked, making things hum, and the place began to look more as it had in the old days when the lighthouse was still in use. He often wished for that time to come back.

"You're dreaming, Herb," Wally always said. "You know darned well that won't happen. The place is like us, time to be put out to pasture."

To that Herb always answered, "Maybe you're ready for that, but I'm not!"

Wally would grin then and Herb would know that he had deliberately goaded him.

When he had been the lighthouse keeper, Herb's life had been rich and full. For one thing, his wife, Martha, had been living and little Johnny had been running around in short pants, into everything, as inquisitive as a rabbit in a garden of lettuce. Now, Johnny had moved away, married and settled down and was middle-aged. Impossible how the time flew by! But the one wonderful thing left to him was his granddaughter, Jan. Thinking of her, Herb smiled. It would be so good to have a young woman in the house again, and because she was coming, the summer suddenly took on new meaning.

After so much cleaning and preparation, Herb discovered his old bones were tired. He was glad when the day ended and he could sit out on the porch and watch the evening come.

"Ho!"

He looked up at the greeting and saw Wally Chadwick swinging along as if he had all day. One thing about Wally, he didn't know how to hurry and *wouldn't* hurry no matter what.

"This place is so shining clean and bright, it hurts my eyes," Wally said.

"Sit down," Herb answered. "This old sea horse is winded."

"When do you expect Jan?"

"Any day now. She wasn't sure just when she would get here. I can hardly wait."

"I remember her as a sweet girl."

"And a good cook. A man was never meant to work in a kitchen; I don't care what anybody says."

"You're going to invite me to supper, aren't you, while she's here?"

Herb fished in his pocket for his pipe and pondered that for a moment. "I suppose we could tolerate it."

Then they laughed together and Wally went inside to get the checkerboard. Last week they had been on a binge of gin rummy. This week it was checkers, next week it might be chess or backgammon. Funny thing about Wally Chadwick, thought Herb. He could go where he pleased, do what he wanted, and yet he chose to come down here to the seaside and play checkers with him. But Herb was glad for his company and if it hadn't been for Wally's friendship over the years, it would have been mighty lonely.

For the next hour they played with hardly a word exchanged between them and they were even up on games when Wally pushed the board back.

"Enough for now. Let's quit while we're even."

"You're just afraid of playing the rub game to decide which of us is the best — you know darned well I'd beat you."

"Want to put your money where your mouth is?"

"Can't afford to gamble, you know that, but you've been eyeing that fishing rod of mine, if you want to wager fifty bucks against that."

"Fifty dollars! That rod and reel isn't worth it and you know it, you old skinflint."

"That's the deal; take it or leave it."

"Then I leave it!" Wally said.

They cleared the board and put the checkers away. Wally was not really angry. It was all part of the game he played, but tonight he seemed restless and kept staring out to the cove.

"Herb, have you noticed the yacht anchored out there?"

The cove was a favorite spot for many sea-minded people and there were usually all sorts of craft there, but he knew immediately which boat Wally was referring to. It had dropped anchor with all indications of making a long stay of it.

"Sure, I saw it," Herb said. "I noticed it one day when I was up on top. It doesn't seem to have plans of moving on."

"Seems a little odd, doesn't it?"

Herb shrugged. "Probably just somebody down from Boston or New York anxious to find a quiet place to spend the summer."

"I suppose. We have more all the time it seems. It used to be the cove was sort of private —"

"Times are changing."

"Sure, I suppose so. Still the yacht has been quiet. Too quiet."

"You're sure interested in it."

"Curious, that's all. Do you want to play some cards?"

"You always cheat."

"Look who's talking! Well, never mind, it's time for me to get back to Windmere anyway. I'll see you tomorrow, Herb."

Then Wally said a quick goodnight and went with a wave of his hand. Herb relighted his pipe, thinking about his friend. Something was eating Wally and it wasn't like him to keep it to himself.

Herb finished his pipe and decided to go to bed. Jan wouldn't be coming this late. It would be tomorrow now.

Wally strolled back to Windmere, the evening sun slipping down to the sea very swiftly now. He scrambled over the rocks at the point, walked by the Hanson house and looked to see if Carl Hanson was about. His wife, Dorothy, had been there for two or three weeks now. Midge had been on the beach every day, but her foster mother seldom ventured out. But then the Hansons were a strange lot, not a bit friendly, and it was no wonder the child went around looking lost and lonely.

Wally thought again about the yacht in the cove. Using binoculars, he had been able to make out her name. It was called *Marybelle* and he knew it was a rental from up the coast. It still struck him as strange that after it had dropped anchor, he had not once seen a line put out for fishing or anyone driving overboard for a swim. Most of the boats that came in and out of the cove held vacationers who played hard before moving on.

At Windmere Wally went in the back way and found Mrs. Goddard in the kitchen. They always had a late dinner because Eldridge did not reach the house until after eight o'clock, but tonight he saw it was nearly ready.

"Why so early?" he asked.

"Mr. Chadwick is not coming tonight. He's staying in town."

"That's not like him," Wally said, snatching a raw carrot from the relish tray and nibbling it.

"It's Lorna, of course; what else would have kept him?"

Wally hid a smile. Mrs. Goddard was usually as quiet as a tomb and would rather take a whipping than talk lightly about any member of the family, but they were friends and she said things to him she would keep from the others.

"They're working on some big deal, I think. Lorna's important to Eldridge these days. She's become a close business associate," Wally said.

Mrs. Goddard's only reply to that was a lifting of her nose in a haughty air.

Wally knew that something was in the wind, although Eldridge had never bothered to tell him so. For one thing, his brother's nerves were showing, and Lorna Cellman seemed as jumpy as a cat these days.

Later, when dinner was served, Ryan was missing from the table, which was not unusual, but Marcia was there, fresh from a swim in the pool. She looked even more radiant than ever. He gave her a long, searching gaze.

"Are you getting serious about Lee?"

She flushed and he laughed.

"I suppose you thought I didn't know. Really, Marcia, you haven't been exactly discreet."

"What business is it of yours?"

Wally lifted his brows. "None, I suppose. But I just don't like to see you get into something you can't handle."

"I *can* handle it!" she said angrily.

"You're only nineteen and you don't know half what you think you do. Lee must be near thirty. He has a head on his shoulders and, I suspect, his own way of thinking. Better tread gently or you'll get your pretty little toes stepped on."

She made a face at him. "Uncle Wally, you're the one that doesn't know half what you think you do."

He laughed at that. Youth! It was a mad, wonderful sort of time and he wished he could turn back the clock.

"Well, we'll see, Marcia," he said quietly, gently.

Ryan didn't appear until later that evening, and when he came to join Wally on the patio under the stars, the evening breeze bringing the smell of salt, Wally sensed his nephew's restlessness.

"How're things going, Ryan?"

"They're not."

"How long has it been since Tania —"

"Two months, three days."

"That can be a long time."

"It's been an eternity for me," he replied.

He sat with his elbows resting on his thighs, hands swinging between his knees, shoulders hunched, and in the dim light from the house, Wally could see that there was still agony in his face.

"It's strange, Uncle Wally. I didn't really know very much about Tania. I didn't even know who to call when she died. The landlady told me Tania had told her a Brad Jennings was a relative in New York and I phoned him. He took charge and Tania's body was shipped to the Middle West. To a town called Vincennes, Indiana. I couldn't bring myself to go and I never heard anything from her family, if she had one — and she must have —"

"Stunned with grief," Wally said. "Give them time —"

Ryan drew a deep breath. "I keep telling myself that, but it's not easy. They probably blame me for letting it happen —"

"She was a secretary, wasn't she?"

"In an engineering office. She seemed vague about it, said it wasn't a very interesting job. I sent them a wire when Tania died and I never heard a thing from them either —"

"There have been a lot of girls in your life, Ryan. I remember some of them —"

"None like Tania," he said quickly. "It all happened so fast between us when we met. You know, she used to wear a locket. It was the one thing she seemed to truly care about, but I don't know who gave it to her and I never saw inside it. I think she was wearing it that day —"

Ryan's voice broke. Wally waited patiently, knowing that it was good for Ryan to talk like this. It was the most Ryan had ever said to him about Tania, and the sooner he said it all, the better he would feel, the quicker he could face the bitter truth of the situation.

"Tania's gone," Ryan said sadly. "A moth on the summer night, here one minute, gone the next —"

Wally heard the melancholy in his nephew's voice and was touched by it. He was mourning himself half sick.

"Let her go, Ryan. I know you loved her even if it was a very brief love, and given time, it might not have worked out at all as you think. Oh, don't look so shocked. Who can tell what the wheel of fortune is going to spin out for us? But she's gone. Bury her once and for all and lift up your chin and go on with your life. There are other women, and you're young. Bury her, Ryan. Let her go."

11

Tom barclay had spent over an hour in his darkroom, a place he had rigged up in the basement. His film had been developed, and when the pictures had dried enough to be handled, he took them down from their clips and carried them upstairs to the bright light of the porch. Only a few pleased him and most of them did not. He tossed the photos aside in anger. It was lack of concentration, of course, and the cost of film these days wasn't to be taken lightly. All he was doing was wasting much of his time and a good deal of his money.

The sky had a hazy quality this morning that would call for special techniques if he went out today to do any filming. He picked up his binoculars on the porch and peered through them, studying the Chadwick house. All seemed quiet, with just the usual activity. He changed the view and looked up and down the beach, again finding nothing of interest.

With an impatient look, he turned the glasses out to the cove and trained them sharply on the yacht, *Marybelle*, which was still anchored there. He scanned the boat carefully, but there was no sign of anyone stirring. He knew for a fact that there was a man and a woman aboard, but so far this morning they had not come up on the top deck. Could it be they weren't even there? A small boat could have come along and taken them off sometime earlier.

With a sigh, he lowered the glasses, put them aside and went to check the coffeepot but found that he had already drunk it dry.

It was time to be getting some kind of order to his book, and he worked for awhile at it, fighting for concentration but not succeeding. Somehow, the morning slipped away and he decided to drive into Vincent for lunch. The town seemed unusually busy and he could spot the tourists, wearing shorts and sneakers, sunglasses shielding their eyes and cameras slung over their shoulders.

At Lane's, the one decent store in Vincent, he restocked his film supply, purchased a few more developing chemicals and put them in his car. Then he made his way to Chaney's, the best place in Vincent to eat.

He was halfway through his meal when someone paused at his table, and with surprise he saw it was Marcia Chadwick. Marcia just missed being truly beautiful. The only thing that marred her loveliness for him was the flinty independence that shone out of her eyes and the hard little jaw that probably meant she could be stubborn if she put her mind to it. In the weeks he had been at Widow's Point, this was the first time Marcia had ever deliberately sought him out.

"Hello, Tom Barclay."

"Hello, Marcia," he said, getting to his feet. "Will you join me? Could I order you something?"

"I've had lunch. I just thought I'd say hello."

But she sat down when he held the chair and he kept wondering why she had suddenly become so friendly. Perhaps she was bored and had idle time on her hands. He kept the conversation light — was the weather always so warm this time of year, did they ever get bad blows and how was the deep-sea fishing in the area? They were all safe topics, and then he dared to mention the trouble they'd had.

"What do you mean, trouble?" Marcia asked, a flash of fire in her eyes.

"The girl died there. Fell off the cliff, someone said. How on earth could that have happened? It was from your patio and I've seen it — it's all enclosed with a railing, a fairly high railing, and yet she fell. Was she ill?"

"Tania was never sick a day in her life that I knew of," Marcia replied.

"Then perhaps she just felt faint or it could have been that she drank too much —"

"Tania didn't drink at all!"

"Strange," Tom said quietly.

He met Marcia's stormy blue eyes. "I don't want to talk about it. I'm sick to death of *thinking* about it. Why are you bringing it up again, Tom? What business is it of yours?"

"Sorry if I upset you," he said. "Let me order you something to drink. Something cool. You name it and —"

She got abruptly to her feet. "I have to be going."

"Look, I'm sorry if I said anything I shouldn't have.

You know how it is, just idle curiosity — something like that doesn't happen every day around the cove, does it?"

Then she was gone without another word and Tom sat back down to finish his lunch.

When he went home to Widow's Point, he took a quick look up and down the beach. It all seemed quiet and peaceful and he could not spy Sara anywhere. She must be down at the lighthouse or working indoors today. Perhaps the heat was keeping her inside. Hardly anyone was stirring and there weren't many boats in the cove. But that damn yacht, the *Marybelle*, was still there. He trained his glasses on it and saw that the people aboard were on the rear deck, and from here he could not get a good look at them.

Tom changed into shorts, rummaged in the closet until he found his fishing gear and then carried it all down to the dock. It was only about the second or third time that he had used the boat. He stowed the things inside, not bothering to uncover the life jackets and other supplies that were kept on board under heavy canvas.

With a couple of pulls of the rope, the motor roared to life and he eased away from the dock and out to the cove. The boat was an old one and it rumbled over the water, vibrating. He did not make a beeline for the yacht but maneuvered away from it as if going to a favorite fishing spot. The engine began to miss, and after a moment of coughing and sputtering, it died altogether.

Tom pulled the rope several times, but the motor

would not fire. He grabbed up the pair of oars kept for such emergencies, fitted them into place and began pulling, heading straight for the *Marybelle*.

When he was within shouting distance, he cupped his hands around his mouth and began to yell. Eventually, the small, dark man he had seen through his glasses appeared at the railing, scowling at him.

"I have engine trouble and no tools. Could you help me out?" Tom asked.

The man stared at him, but Tom ignored him and went back to rowing toward the yacht. Soon the woman had appeared, too, and Tom saw them hold a whispered conversation.

"We've a toolbox somewhere. What do you need?" the man asked.

"Several things. Look, why don't I just come aboard and I'll pick out what I'll have to have; okay?"

By now, Tom had eased his boat up to the yacht. The man lowered a ladder over the side, and Tom swung out, grabbed the ladder and hauled himself up quickly, wasting no time, giving the strangers no chance to stop him.

They were not pleased at having him there, but Tom ignored their angry looks and gave them a smile.

"Awfully nice of you people. I have to get that old motor fixed; that's all there is to it. If I can get it going again, I think I'll forget all about fishing and go home while I can."

"I could radio to shore for help."

"Oh, no," Tom said with a shake of his head. "That's not necessary, as I'm sure it's just a minor adjustment, but I need tools. Let me try to fix it first. Now, where are the tools? In the engine room, I imagine —"

Then before they could stop him, he disappeared below decks. He managed to catch a glimpse inside the main cabin and what he saw tightened his lips. There was some very sophisticated radio equipment aboard. Not the usual stuff, he was sure.

"The toolbox is in here!" the man said, jerking open the door to the engine room. "I'll get it."

"Sorry to bother you," Tom said apologetically, pretending he had not seen anything unusual.

The man was anxious to be rid of him and a small metal toolbox was hurriedly shoved into his hands.

"Thanks. I'll just have a look inside and get what I need," Tom said, fingering the latch on the box.

"Just take the box," the man said quickly. "When you've finished, put it on the deck."

"Oh, sure. I'll do that. Can't thank you enough, Mr. —"

The man licked his lips and gave Tom a quick look. "Thornton. We're Mr. and Mrs. Thornton."

"Very good of you, Mr. Thornton. Have you had any luck fishing? There's a nice spot on the far side of the cove —"

"We're not here for fishing," Thornton said with annoyance. "We're just on vacation, trying to get some peace and quiet. Is there a law against that?"

"Of course not. I mean, I'm sorry — well, I'll be going."

They were glad to see him leave at last and he went back up to the deck and climbed down to his boat.

The Thorntons didn't come above decks. Tom wished he could have had more time to look around.

He tinkered with the motor, adjusting the carburetor and making some minor repairs. Another two or three pulls of the rope and the motor started. It was running rough, but it would get him home. He quickly climbed the ladder again and put the toolbox on the deck.

"Thanks, folks!" he called.

There was no reply and he didn't see either the man or the woman. Back in his own boat, he restarted the motor and began easing away from the yacht. Now and then the motor missed, backfired, and nearly died. He went limping to the dock and as he was tying up, he heard a distinct giggling.

He straightened with surprise and then went to jerk back the canvas at the far end of the boat. Midge leaped out at him, shouting. "Surprise!"

"Midge, you imp! What are you doing here?"

"I'm a stowaway like in that story *Kidnapped*."

Tom looked at her and then out at the yacht. Midge had been aboard the whole time!

"I should turn you over my knee and spank you!"

She giggled again. "I caught you, Tom. You weren't having engine trouble at all, were you? You were just pretending. How come?"

Tom eyed the young girl and reached out with a wide hand to give her a playful swat. "You and your imagination!"

"Well, you put on a pretty good act," Midge said.

"Midge —"

"Oh, it's okay. I won't tell anybody. If you wanted to get aboard the *Marybelle*, who cares?" she asked with a shrug of her shoulders.

Midge gave him another impish grin, and he decided to let her play her little game.

"You must have smothered under that canvas," he said. "Want to come up to the house? I fix a pretty good ice cream soda."

"Okay."

She helped him carry his fishing gear back up the steps to the house, and in the kitchen, she perched on the stool and watched him take the ice cream from the freezer and the soda pop from the refrigerator.

"I used to work behind a drugstore counter when I was a kid," he told her.

"I wish I had a job."

Tom smiled. "You have the world on a string and don't know it. What more could you want? A beach like that down there — most kids would give their eyeteeth to spend a summer here."

"They're fighting."

"Who's fighting?"

"My mother and father. Before we came here, I heard them talking about a divorce."

"Oh."

"That's why Mother's here — she's thinking things over — that's what they called it."

Tom finished with the soda and put it on the table in front of her. He could see how upset she was and he reached out to tug playfully at a pigtail.

"Don't look so solemn. I bet everything works out."

"I've been in foster homes before. I never get to stay. They always send me back —"

She wasn't eating and Tom did his best to get her mind off her parents and eventually she seemed to put it behind her with a long, deep sigh. Then she lifted her chin, squared her shoulders and dug into the soda as if determined to make things work out.

"Herb's granddaughter's going to come here. Did you know that?"

"No."

"She teaches school. Literature. She's not married but she had a sweetheart once."

"Midge, how do you do it?" Tom asked with a laugh. "How can you possibly know *everything* that goes on around here —"

"I'm a snoop."

"I'm afraid I have to agree," Tom said, remembering how she had stowed away in the boat earlier.

"Where did you live before you came here?" she asked.

"Cleveland. But if I could have my choice, I think I'd like to live in the wide open spaces of Wyoming or Montana."

"And be a cowboy?"

"Well, it's a thought."

"Maybe I'll come with you," she said. "I'll just run away and they'd never miss me! What do they care anyway?"

Tom wished he knew what to say. Situations like this caught him off guard and he felt hopelessly inadequate.

Midge finished her soda in record time, looked at the clock and said she had to go.

"Mother said not to be late. If I am —"

A worried look crossed her face and then she was off, running swiftly, disappearing out of his sight as she went down the steps and then reappearing down on the beach. She paused long enough to wave. He watched her until she was out of sight, then he looked back out to the cove. The *Marybelle* was still there, rocking gently in the afternoon sunlight. His visit aboard apparently had made no ripples. So much radio equipment wasn't usually found on a boat of that kind and size, was it?

It was just dusk when Tom took a look at the Chadwick place through the binoculars. He focused on the patio and he saw Ryan Chadwick leaning at the railing, peering down to the rocks. He was not alone. Sara was with him.

Tom stood rooted, watching, wishing he had learned to read lips. What were they saying to each other? He saw the look on Sara's face. She felt sorry for the guy! Then he saw them turn away and leave together, and an unexpected jealousy rippled through Tom's heart. Where were they going together?

"Damn!"

He lowered the glasses, for they were out of view now. But in a moment, he could pick up a whiff of dust on the lane and he guessed they had gone in Ryan's car.

There was a breeze kicking up. Clouds were beginning to move in on the horizon. He closed the shutters on the porch and made sure his camera equipment was safely out of any rain that might blow in.

Then from the closet, where he had put them out of sight of any curious eyes, he took out the enlargements he had made. They were blowups of shots made of the cliff and the railing at the Chadwick patio, the spot where Tania had gone over. He had studied them until his sight was blurred and his head fuzzy. But he got out the magnifying glass and once more he went painstakingly over them, inch by inch.

Nothing, absolutely nothing! Perhaps if he could get another angle, in a different light, from above rather than below —

12

Sara had been surprised by Ryan's invitation to go for a drive, but she took it as a good sign, and after putting in a miserable day at her sketch pad, she was rather glad to put Windmere behind for a little while. Sometimes a fresh atmosphere would create new ideas, and right now she had *no* ideas at all!

Ryan seemed almost impersonal as they got into his sports car and then with a roar of the engine went tearing down the lane to the gate, spewing the gravel under the wheels. All the way to the main road, Ryan said nothing, but gripped the wheel tightly.

"Ryan —"

He shot her a quick glance and visibly relaxed. "Sorry. I go off like that sometimes — down some deep dark tunnel. I have no right to impose it on you, though. You've been working, very hard."

"Yes. I'm desperate for the right idea."

"You like what you do, don't you?"

"If I didn't have some goal or challenge it would be as if I couldn't breathe. That's the way it is with me."

"You're consumed with passion for your work. Must be nice. I'm only consumed with passion for —"

Sara could hear Tania's name trembling on the air,

but Ryan did not voice it. She tried to think of something cheerful to say and wished there was more she could do to break his mood.

They drove into Vincent and stopped at Mark Williams's gas station and had the tank filled. Mark eyed Sara for a moment and then looked at Ryan but said nothing. Then when Mark had finished, Ryan paid him and drove on. Ryan seemed to have no particular destination in mind, and Sara saw parts of the country she had never seen before as they chased down narrow sandy lanes, flicked across country roads and zoomed for awhile along the interstate highway. Then Ryan pulled the car off under the shade trees of a state park, and from their vantage point, they saw the Atlantic sprawling beneath them, magnificent in the growing darkness.

"It's lovely here," she said. "As lovely as Windmere."

"I used to think so, but I don't know. I almost hate the sight and sound of the sea these days."

"It would be foolish to let that happen, Ryan. The old saying that life is for the living is true. I'm sure what you had with Tania was very dear and precious, but now —"

"You sound like Uncle Wally. He tells me it's time to get my life moving again, to forget Tania. That's not easy to do."

"Especially if you don't try," she said.

He turned to face her. She sensed a struggle in him and when he reached out to her, his hands were trembling. Then in a desperate motion, he pulled her close and his lips came down on hers. They clung coldly for a moment, and then as abruptly, he let her go.

"My God, I can't even kiss a girl anymore and mean it! And the strange thing is, I *want* to mean it, Sara. You're a lovely woman. I think in another time, in another place, I could have cared a great deal for you. Now —"

"It's a start, Ryan."

He nodded. "Yes. And you're kind and patient with me. I'm sorry if I was out of line. I just wanted to see if there was any spark left in me, if I was alive at all —"

"I think Tania was lucky, Ryan, to have been loved by you. It must have been an exciting time —"

"Will it ever happen for me again, Sara?"

"Yes. I think so."

"I wonder —"

A few minutes later, they drove on and Ryan turned the car in the direction of Windmere, once again lost in deep thought, into his own dark world.

At Windmere, they said goodnight at the garage and Sara went to the cottage, thinking of Ryan and touched by his unhappiness, wishing there was something she could do to help. His loneliness was like a visible black cloud that swallowed him from the rest of the world.

But she could not dwell too much on Ryan. There was the nagging problem of the work for Cloud Nine. For the next few days, she thrust everything but the project out of her mind. She must have walked ten miles up and down the beach, pausing now and then to stare out to the sea, not really seeing it, but searching somewhere deep inside her for a new idea.

Then, when there were only a few days until the deadline, she awakened in the middle of the night and the idea was there, full-blown, fresh, new and interesting. She lay there awhile smiling into the darkness. Then she went back to sleep, knowing she'd need all the energy she could summon for the hard, demanding work ahead.

When Lee had gone in the morning, Sara spread her materials on the kitchen table. Later, she might move to the beach, but right now she wanted to make some quick sketches, jot down a few quick ideas and see if it would all jell.

She was still hard at it at noon when Lee came back to the house.

"Should I eat in the kitchen at the house?"

"No," she said, shaking her head and tossing her pencil aside. "I need a break."

Lee bent over her shoulder for a quick look. "I never can make head or tail out of what you're doing, and then all of a sudden you finish and it makes sense. Are you happy with it?"

"So far. I don't have time not to be. You know, I never realized it until now, but I've missed this."

Lee went to get some cold cuts out of the refrigerator and made them both a sandwich. "Does that mean you'll be wanting to go back to New York?"

"I don't know what it means and that's the crazy part. I thought I was through with all of this, that I really wanted to wash my hands of it. But you know, this is art, too, a different art, a very commercial art, but still a part of the American way of life, and it's nice to have something to do with that."

"I sometimes wonder if either one of us belongs here, Sara," he said, a frown clouding his face.

Sara knew he was thinking about Marcia Chadwick, and she wanted to draw out his thoughts about her, but she could see he wasn't really ready to talk about Chadwick's daughter just yet. When he was, he would bring up the subject himself. If there was one thing she had learned about her brother over the years, it was that he possessed a very wide streak of independence. He didn't like to be pushed into anything; call it manly pride or stubbornness or just knowing what was right for himself, but that was the way it was.

"What are you doing today?" she asked.

"The speedboat down at the dock hasn't been tuned up in ages. When I've finished with it, I'll probably take it out for a trial run. Want to come along?"

She shook her head. "Couldn't spare the time."

"You can't sit here all day without moving," he pointed out.

"No," she laughed. "I'll take a walk later or move out to the patio if none of the Chadwicks are around. I do try to stay out of their way."

"That's not always easily done," Lee said. "It seems I have a steady stream of visitors in the garage. If it's not Marcia, it's Wally, and even Ryan pops in now and then. I wonder where he goes all the time."

"What do you mean?"

"He comes to the garage with his car all covered with white dust."

"Who knows where Ryan goes or what he does? He's a lost soul."

"You like him, don't you?"

"Yes. And I pity him, too."

As soon as she had eaten her sandwich, she went back to work and wasn't even aware when Lee left the cottage. It was about three when she knew that it was time to take a break. With a sigh, she pushed back from the table and stepped outside to the bright sunlight.

Wally Chadwick was lounging in one of the chairs and when he saw her, he gave her a twinkly-eyed smile and patted the chair beside him.

"Come and sit down. I could use some companionship and I haven't seen much of you lately."

"Busy."

"Cloud Nine?"

She laughed with a nod. She had told him about the project during one of their talks.

"How's it coming?" he asked.

"Slowly. You look fit as a fiddle, Wally. What have you and Herb been up to today?"

"Herb's got a visitor. His granddaughter, Jan, has come to spend the summer. She's a schoolteacher and the light of Herb's eye."

"I didn't know about that."

"Then you haven't seen Midge lately."

Sara laughed. "No, as a matter of fact, I haven't."

"Jan's a sweet girl."

"I'll be anxious to meet her."

"Want to walk down now?"

"I'd love to, but I can't. I have to get back to work in a few minutes. Thursday, I go to New York and that's only two days away —"

"You'll make it," Wally said with a grin. "You have it all together, as the kids say."

She smiled at that. "Wally, you've kissed the Blarney stone one time too many."

Sara made her deadline with an afternoon to spare. Once she reached a certain point, everything seemed to fall in place.

Thursday morning, she rode beside Lee in the front seat of the limousine as he drove Eldridge to the train.

"Wish me luck, Lee," she said.

"I have no worries about you," Lee replied. "See you this evening."

Once aboard the train, she did not see Chadwick and was rather glad of it. Chadwick was nice enough, but she knew making small talk with him would not be easy. They were miles apart. Besides, she wanted to save all her energy for her meeting with Bob Waterman.

At Penn Station, Sara rushed to get a cab, fighting her way through the morning crowd. Ah, New York! She laughed to herself, comparing this busy place with sleepy, wind-touched, sea-swept Windmere. It was almost inconceivable there could be two places so totally different with only a short train ride between them.

She arrived at the office early and had to wait fifteen minutes for Bob Waterman to appear. Then in his office, she showed him her work and he peered at it critically, making a few murmuring sounds to himself.

"Honestly, Bob, you drive me crazy! Do you like it or not?"

Then Bob gave her a smile and she knew all was well. "It's great. How would you like to present it yourself this afternoon? I have a meeting with the World Tour people all set up and —"

She shook her head quickly. For one thing, she had not come prepared for anything like this and Jerry had not warned her.

"Jerry didn't tell me that would be part of the deal. Besides, Bob, you're the best salesman I know, and if anyone can get the job done, it's you —"

Bob nodded. "Okay. Good work, Sara. This is just what we need to launch Cloud Nine."

About then she heard Jerry's voice in the outer office and said goodbye to Bob.

"I'll be in touch, Sara, very soon, I hope," Bob said.

Jerry smiled when he saw her and drew her into his office, closing the door behind him.

"How did it go?"

"Bob likes it."

"That's half the battle! I knew you could do it, Sara. You belong here, you know."

She heard the innuendo in his voice and brushed it aside.

"What kind of a day do you have lined up?" she asked.

"Busy, unfortunately. I tried to save the afternoon for you, but you know Bob. But I did hang on to a couple of hours for lunch. I have a new place to take you, Sara. I know you'll like it."

"Sounds nice."

"The minute I saw it, I thought of you."

Jerry had made it a hobby to search for new, interesting places to take her.

"What are your plans?" Jerry asked.

"Since you're busy, I think I'll go and drop by Diane's office and see her for a few minutes. Could I meet you somewhere later?"

"Sure."

He named a favorite corner, a meeting place they had often used, and thinking of it now brought back a flood of memories. He gave her a smile, guessing her thoughts. He was stacking the cards again.

"See you later," she said.

She blew him a kiss and hurried away. She walked to Diane's office building, and her old friend managed a long coffee break. There was so much to tell each other, but when half an hour had passed, Diane looked at her watch.

"Oh, darn! Where does the time go? We've barely scratched the surface."

"You still haven't visited Windmere and you promised —"

"I know. I'll try. But the family has been putting pressure on me to come home for my vacation. Maybe

I can work out a compromise. You look so terrific, Sara. So suntanned and relaxed —"

Later, after having spent an hour or so in some of the shops, Sara went to meet Jerry. He took her to a French café located in a cellar that was unique, off the beaten path and somewhat private. They talked shop for awhile. Jerry had seen the work she'd brought in and had nothing but praise for it.

"It's some of your best, Sara, and we rushed you at that."

"But remember, I haven't done anything like that for awhile, so, I was fresh, or maybe it was Windmere. It has its own special magic, you know."

"No, it was you, doing what you do best, Sara. Oh, I know your serious work has something special too, but this — well, you truly have a knack for it."

"I recall a good many failures," she replied. "Whiff, for one."

Jerry reached out and took her hand tightly in his. "Come back, Sara. We need you at the agency, and God knows I need you for myself. Life's not the same without you. I miss you, more than you can know. Will you stay in New York tonight? Tomorrow's Friday; we could have a long weekend together."

"Lee's expecting me on the seven-thirty train."

"There are telephones."

She shook her head. "Not this time, Jerry."

She expected an argument and when Jerry took it so calmly, she felt relieved. But there was also a feeling that Jerry was holding his ace until the last minute. She knew him and she was familiar with the way his head worked. Jerry hadn't given up; he was simply waiting for the right minute to spring something on her.

The waiter was hovering to take their order. Jerry gave it to him and for a while made light conversation, telling her news of people they both knew, mentioned some of the work that had passed through the office and then finally, when the meal was ended and they were having a last cup of coffee, he leaned toward her.

She steeled herself. It was coming now.

"Did Bob tell you anything more about Cloud Nine?" he asked almost casually.

"No. What more is there?"

He smiled at that and she knew she had played right into his hand. "If it all goes well, it will be only the first in a series of advertisements World Travel Tours will do. I suppose I shouldn't be telling you all of this, but I wanted you to know. It's an important assignment and there will probably be eight more such layouts — if the one you just did is accepted. If it is and the series goes ahead — it will be your baby, Sara."

She stared at him, taking in the full scope of what he had just told her. "You mean there would be *eight* more —"

"Eight more." He nodded. "It will mean coming back here to work, though. The time schedule will be tight."

"I see."

He gave her a happy grin. "Bob will tell you about

it, when the time's right. You can pretend to be surprised. Just bear in mind what it means —"

She drew a deep breath and looked him straight in the eye. "You really stacked the cards, didn't you, Jerry. That's why you were so anxious for me to take the first assignment —"

He didn't deny it. "Sure. Why not? It's important work, not just for the agency but for you too. Besides, I'd do almost anything to get you back to New York where you belong, Sara."

13

LEE MET SARA'S TRAIN, but Chadwick was not aboard.

"He's not coming tonight," Lee told her. "He phoned about an hour ago. How did Cloud Nine go?"

"Bob and Jerry like it. I should know before too long how it went over with World Tours. What have you been doing all day?"

"I finished putting the speedboat in good repair and this afternoon I went swimming —"

"Alone?"

Lee flushed. "No."

"How's it going with you and Marcia?"

"I don't know. She can be exasperating at times. A tease. There are days I wonder if she has a serious bone in her body and then other times —"

"You can handle her, Lee."

He laughed shortly. "Maybe. And maybe not."

"Have you been to the lighthouse?"

"No. But I've heard all about Jan from Midge."

By the time they reached the cottage, the sun was slipping down. Already the days were growing shorter. Could the summer be going so fast?

As Sara opened the door, she heard the phone and dashed to answer it.

"Sara —"

"Jerry? Is that you?"

He laughed. "Bob said I could do the phoning and pass the news. World Travel took your work on the spot when Bob showed it to them this afternoon."

She sat down with a thump. "So soon?"

"Bob's elated and so am I."

"I hadn't expected to hear this quick!"

"About the other — that's still hanging fire. We won't know for a while, but I know it's going to work out, Sara."

"I'm glad you phoned, Jerry. It's great news — now I can forget it and get back to my serious work."

There was a pause on the other end of the line and she heard the sigh come to Jerry's voice. "Sure, you can do that. Listen, I'll phone again as soon as I hear about the rest of the series."

They talked awhile longer, then said goodbye and hung up. Lee had caught most of the conversation and gave her a victory sign.

"I knew you'd do it, Sis!"

"It's sort of nice to know I haven't lost my touch, but I'm anxious to get back to the real thing."

Tomorrow she would get out some of her unfinished canvases and get back to work. Or should she start something new?

The next morning was particularly bright and sunny, without a cloud in the sky. She knew it was the right time to start her painting of the lighthouse. Then, too, she was eager to meet Jan Travis, Herb's granddaughter.

After breakfast, Sara gathered her things and struck out. It wasn't easy lugging everything over the rocks, but she made it. Herb spotted her from the top and waved to her.

"Ahoy!"

"Hi!" Sara shouted. "How are you, Herb? Are you coming down?"

"I'm on my way."

Before she had reached the lighthouse, Herb was down the steps and coming out to meet her.

"You have to come inside and meet Jan. She's up to her eyebrows in biscuit dough."

Sara followed Herb into the kitchen and there she met Jan, a slight young woman with black hair that had a surprising touch of gray and a pair of hazel eyes that were warm with a happy light. Her smile was quick and bright.

"You're Sara! Grandpa's been telling me about you. It's nice to meet you at last."

Jan had a smudge of flour on her cheek, and the kitchen showed the signs of her labor.

"I just popped in the last of the biscuits. Will you stay for lunch?"

"That's sweet of you, but I came to paint the lighthouse, and if your grandfather can spare the time, I'd like to have him in the picture."

"You want *me* to pose?" Herb said. "Such nonsense —"

"Oh, Grandpa, don't be that way," Jan said. "I think it's a wonderful idea. Now, run along and do as Sara asks. I have to clear up all this mess and then I'll come and watch, if Sara doesn't object."

Herb Travis was finally coaxed into posing, although Sara had a hunch that he was very pleased with the idea of it all. She asked him to sit in his favorite wicker chair and decided then and there to do a portrait of him first and the lighthouse another time.

"Are you sure you want to paint an ugly old mug like mine?" he asked.

She put a hand against his weathered cheek and smiled into his blue eyes. "Herb, you're just beautiful; did you know that?"

She gave him instructions and set up to do a quick charcoal sketch.

"When you get tired, tell me and we'll rest."

Seagulls soared overhead, watching, the surf crashed against the rocks, making its own sweet music, for it was high tide and the waves came rolling in, breaking with spewing white foam, and the sunshine settled down around them.

"Tell me about the time you sailed on a freighter," Sara said.

Herb liked nothing better than to talk about the old days. As he told her about all the places he'd been and seen, his face lighted up, twinkles came to his eyes and Sara got exactly the expression she was looking for. She felt enthusiasm leaping to her fingers. This might well be the best work she did this summer. How could she miss with such a subject as Herb?

It was noon before she knew it and Jan came out to

announce that lunch was ready; she insisted that Sara stay.

The lunch was ample and tasty, and Herb ate with apparent relish. Jan was likable and talked with enthusiasm about her summer here, the school where she had taught and some of her favorite students.

"Grandpa wants me to apply for a job in Vincent and stay with him."

"Could you do that?"

"Possibly. I don't think I'd have any trouble getting out of my contract at home, but getting one here might be another matter, it's so late now —"

"I still want you to look into it," Herb insisted.

"Maybe, Grandpa. I'll see."

The lunch was pleasant and relaxing. Sara found herself liking Jan more and more. It would be nice to have a friend here, and before she went back for another session of work, Jan promised to phone her soon.

"We'll go to Vincent for lunch someday —"

Jan was surprised that Midge had not appeared all day. It was not like her, and she wondered if there could be anything wrong. But more than likely, Mrs. Hanson was just away for the day and Midge was with her.

Sara didn't work too long that afternoon, as it was hot and Herb was getting restless. So she packed up her things, called goodbye to Jan and started back to Windmere.

As she cleared the rocks and started walking past the Hanson place, she looked for Midge, but didn't see her. Sara had caught only a glimpse or two of Dorothy

Hanson, a tall, well-dressed woman with tight lips and a deep crease between her eyes.

When Sara had reached the steps to Windmere, she saw Tom Barclay. He waved to her as he came jogging down the beach, wearing swimming trunks, his browned body strong and virile.

She had not seen him for the last few days. He knew she was busy with Cloud Nine and had not interrupted her. But seeing him now, she knew she had missed him. His black hair was wet from a dip in the ocean and his smile was warm and quick.

"I've been looking everywhere for you today."

"I've been painting Herb's portrait."

"I see. How did it go in New York?"

"Very well, I had a call last night. Cloud Nine was accepted."

"That's great! All the reason more why we should do something special tonight. Will you have dinner with me?"

"Sounds good. Where are we going?"

"My place. I've a fair way with a steak on a barbecue grill, and there's a good one at the house. If you'll toss the salad, I can handle everything else. Are you game?"

"Why not? I feel like celebrating."

"I should warn you, I have other motives for inviting you to Widow's Point besides feeding you one of my steaks," he said, his eyes twinkling.

"Ah — what kind of motives?"

He laughed. "I've been trying to make the selections for my book. I need a second opinion."

"Do you mean I'm finally going to get to see your work?"

"Yes. It's a hard job to pick out a few photos from so many."

"I'll help, if I can," she said. "Are you so near to finishing your book?"

"I think so, but then again, I may decide to try for still better photos. Well, we'll talk about that tonight. Seven? Shall I drive down for you?"

"I'll walk down the beach."

At the steps, he offered to help her with her things up to the patio and she shook her head. "I can manage, Tom."

"Nonsense, let me give you a hand."

He took her easel and paintbox and led the way up the steps to the Chadwick patio.

"Just set them there on the table, Tom, and thanks."

He looked around him curiously, then moved over to the railing where Tania had fallen, and for a long time looked down at the rocks.

"Why do you find that so fascinating?" she asked.

He started and turned back to her with an apologetic smile. "Sorry. I was thinking about the girl that fell. What a tragedy."

"Yes. It was. That happened before you came here, didn't it?"

Tom nodded. "But it was the talk of Vincent. Even the waitress at Chaney's told me about it. I take it that the Chadwicks are often the object of talk."

"Prominent people often are the targets of gossip, most of it untrue."

"I suppose you're right. Do they ever talk about Tania?"

"No. Not very much."

"Not even Ryan?"

"He took Tania's loss very hard. He's consumed with grief. I fear sometimes that he's on the edge."

"You like him, don't you?"

"Yes, and I feel sorry for him."

"Anything more than that?"

"Why all the questions?" she asked. "Do the Chadwicks interest you so much?"

"Well, they're *not* the ordinary family, you know."

"That's very true."

Tom took one more look at the railing and the rocks below and then stared for a long moment at a particular yacht anchored in the cove. It had been there for more than two weeks and showed no signs of moving on.

"I must be going," he said at last. "I'll see you this evening."

Then with a wave of his hand, he was gone, disappearing down the steps. There was something hidden about Tom, and she couldn't pinpoint what it was. He seemed warm and friendly on the surface, but it was the inner man that interested her the most. What lay deeper in him might be the most intriguing thing of all.

14

ELDRIDGE CHADWICK kept a penthouse apartment in one of the better hotels in New York, and whenever he had an occasion to stay in the city overnight, he used it. This happened more frequently in the wintertime. He loved Windmere so much, he begrudged the few times he had to stay, especially now when the weather was so beautiful on the ocean.

Tonight, his disappointment was softened by Lorna Cellman's promise to have dinner with him.

"I know you don't like to go out, Eldridge, so why don't we dine in your apartment? Room service will do nicely —"

"I'll order something special," he said, pleased at the suggestion. "A fine wine and some of those hors d'oeuvres that you like so well. Will you make an evening of it?"

She smiled, and though she always made it a rule to be businesslike while they were at work in his office, she broke the rule this time and reached out to put a hand on his shoulder. The touch was a caress.

"Yes, dear. I've been wanting to have a long talk with you anyway."

He didn't know what that meant exactly, but at the

moment didn't care. He smiled his way through the rest of the afternoon anticipating the time with Lorna. Away from the office, out of those horn-rimmed glasses, wearing something less businesslike, she was a very lovely woman. It hadn't been until just lately that he had begun to realize how lonely he was. He'd been a widower for many years, more than he liked to remember, and although Lorna Cellman was several years younger than he, there was no reason why —

He never let his thoughts go any further than that. Over the years a great many eligible women had made plays for him. The Chadwick name had a magic connected to it, and he had tried to protect it. Men in his position often made damn fools of themselves, and he had no intentions of letting that happen to him. There had never been a hint of family scandal until that terrible thing with Tania had happened.

Ryan came as somewhat of a disappointment to him. The boy simply had no direction. Marcia was still too young, with school to finish, but there was always a long line of eligible and suitable young men waiting to take her out. He anticipated no real worries with her. Right now, he knew she was seeing Lee Denning on the sly. But it was one of those little affairs all girls went through and nothing would come of it, he was sure. If it showed signs of becoming more than a fling, he would take measures to stop it. Lee Denning was a fine young man but not for his daughter. Marcia would be married well, into a family of prestige and background. He would see to it.

When he left his office that evening and went to his

apartment, he phoned the hotel kitchen and left explicit orders as to the dinner he wanted delivered.

"Eight. Promptly. No later," he said.

"Yes, Mr. Chadwick, we'll take care of it."

He hung up with a smile. Lorna always appreciated the extra little trouble he went to, and he wanted the night to be perfect.

As he showered and shaved and put on more casual clothes, knotting a silk scarf at his throat, he thought he looked almost as debonair as Wally. Sometimes his brother's idleness ground at his nerves. That must be where Ryan got some of his waywardness. But Wally was a pleasant sort and good company. If Wally wasn't around Windmere most of the time, Eldridge knew he would miss his brother very much.

He thought about Lorna and looked at his watch. She was due in a few minutes and he realized how impatient he was. There weren't enough times like this, alone with her, shut away from the public view and atmosphere of the office. Even when she visited Windmere, they never truly relaxed together.

The doorbell rang ten minutes early, and he rushed to answer it. Lorna smiled at him, her lips lifting upward in a way that tingled along his nerves.

"My dear —"

He drew her into the room and in a moment, she had put her arms around him and kissed him.

"This is lovely," she said. "We have so little time alone, Eldridge."

"My fault," he said. "I shouldn't go chasing off to

Windmere every night. I should stay in the city more often."

"But you love it there, and no wonder; it's so relaxing, so beautiful."

"It's not fair to you — and I've been a fool not to realize how much I've been missing."

"We can make up for it," Lorna said.

She linked her arm through his and they walked into the comfortable living room.

"I've ordered dinner for eight o'clock. Plenty of time for a cocktail before that. What would you like?"

"Anything you fix will be fine," Lorna said. "Eldridge, I *do* like this apartment. I'm so unhappy with my own."

"More problems?"

"Yes. I'm looking for a new place."

"If I can help —"

"I'll manage. But would you think it terrible of me to want to be closer to this building? It would be more convenient —"

"I quite agree. A sensible idea."

He opened the louvered doors that concealed a bar. He fixed the cocktails and set them on a small tray and served her.

"You could spoil a woman, Eldridge —"

"You're worth spoiling, Lorna."

He lifted his glass in a salute and he watched her blue eyes as they smiled back at him. He took the drink from her hand.

"Lorna —"

He kissed her with more passion than he supposed was still in his old soul and when she dropped her head to his shoulder, his joy was complete.

"What would our associates think if they were to see us now?"

"Who cares?" Eldridge asked. "Besides, I suspect everyone knows."

"I try so hard to hide it; I know you don't like public display of affection, especially between two people like us —"

"At the moment, I'm ready to toss caution to the winds. What I do is my own business!"

"But you were always such a cautious man, and I can understand that. You have a certain prestige to protect —"

"Sh! Let's not talk any more about it. We have the evening, we have each other. Let's make the most of it."

"You're right, of course. You always are, Eldridge."

"I've been leaning on you lately, but you know that, don't you? You're the first woman I ever met that had brains to match her beauty."

She laughed and moved away from him. From a box on the coffee table, she took a cigarette, and he fumbled in his pocket for a lighter.

"You've also remained a woman of mystery," he said. "I know very little about you —"

"I don't believe that. You checked me out thoroughly before you hired me, just as you do with everyone in your employ."

"Parents of German heritage, an only child, graduated from high school with honors and cum laude from college, no serious involvements with men, no financial troubles, a clear head on good shoulders and brilliant in business matters. I think that spoke well of you, don't you?" he asked.

"Summed up like that, I sound a bit dull, don't I?"

"Not to me."

"That doesn't tell the whole story, Eldridge. It doesn't say that I was very poor as a child, that I worked like a maniac to get through school, that college was acquired by a scholarship, that spending money was always at a premium, that my parents still speak broken English, that —"

He put a finger to her lips. "That's behind you, my dear. I've made it a rule all my life not to look back if I can help it."

"Not everyone can do that, Eldridge."

"I can. You can. *We* can —"

A flicker went through her glance and she reached out to touch his face with cool fingertips. At that moment, the bell rang and Eldridge sighed.

"Dinner," he said.

He went to answer the door, and a waiter rolled in the linen covered table, carefully checked the service there and was soon joined by another waiter with a cart filled with the food and wine.

"Would you like me to stay and serve you, Mr. Chadwick?"

"No, we'll help ourselves. Thank you. Don't bother to pick up the table until morning."

He pressed a bill into each waiter's hand and saw them out.

"Let me," Lorna said. "Sit down, Eldridge. I'll take care of this."

She served the food, exclaiming with delight at what she found. "All my favorites! How sweet, Eldridge."

Eldridge held his lighter to the candles and flipped off the lights in the room. Lorna dished up the food and he was pleased to find that the kitchen had outdone themselves.

Why was it food tasted better in the company of a lovely woman like Lorna? It seemed even the candles flickered in a more becoming way. When they had eaten and had drunk their fill of the wine, they moved away from the table, and Lorna went to look out at the lights of the city.

"It's impressive like this," she said. "But down there on the dirty streets, with all the problems and the injustices in the world —"

"You sound bitter."

"This country is sick, and you know it as well as I, Eldridge."

"Perhaps, but we'll get well again."

"You're a blind optimist."

He joined her to look at the view and put his arm around her shoulder. Then she turned to him and they both forgot for a while about the world affairs and the problems of the country.

"You said you wanted to talk to me seriously tonight, Lorna. What's bothering you?"

"You know perfectly well," she said.

There was an edge in her voice. They had come close to a very real quarrel when he'd sent Sara Denning to Denver without explaining just why he was making the transaction. The matter had never been truly resolved between them.

"My dear, I appreciate your concern and I respect your opinion, as you well know, but I'm aware of what I'm doing and *why* I'm doing it."

"You're converting all your capital into cash for this one thing. You're risking your securities, you're pushing yourself to the very edge. What if it backfires? What if you lose your money —"

Eldridge rubbed a finger over his mustache and shook his head. "But I won't."

"This is something for the government; that's all I know. Why can't you tell me more? Perhaps if I were to understand better —"

"It's top-drawer secret stuff."

She made a face. "You mean cloak-and-dagger —"

"In a way, I suppose. I never think of it like that. It's something important to this country and I'm in on the ground floor. It means money in the till and —"

He broke off. He was talking too much and knew it. Lorna gave him a steady look. "That's what I mean. Just when I think I'm going to be told, you clam up —"

"Darling, I don't *like* keeping it from you."

"Then tell me! Please."

"I can't, Lorna, and that's all there is to it. Not yet. Perhaps soon."

She put her head on his shoulder and ran her fingers over the crisp hair at the nape of his neck. A tingle went along his nerves.

"Very soon," he murmured.

She nipped his ear with her teeth. "How soon?"

"After the fifteenth of August. Things should be well settled by then —" He sighed with dismay. "Now, I've done it. I've broken part of the secret —"

"It's safe with me, Eldridge, and you know it. Darling, it's just that I'm concerned for you and I don't like to worry —"

"It's all right, I tell you!"

"You've put every available dollar into this. You made a bad deal in Denver just to get your hands on some ready cash — I hope it was worth it."

"I know it was."

"And you won't tell me any more?"

"No."

She pulled out of his arms and moved away from him. The room suddenly seemed too hot, as if the air conditioning had been abruptly switched off. Lorna lighted another cigarette and she looked cool and impersonal now, not the warm, vital woman he had held in his arms just moments ago.

"Don't be angry, Lorna. Don't do this to me. It tears me apart."

She spun about to face him with flashing eyes. "And what do you think it's doing to me? This is the first time you've ever kept anything from me, Eldridge. Don't you trust me? Don't you know that I only have your best interests at heart? Don't you understand that I'm very, very concerned —"

Eldridge stepped toward her. Uncertainty welled up inside him. Lorna could be as emotional as she could be cool and reserved. He knew both sides of her. He also knew that she was perfectly capable of walking out of his life without a backward glance. She could do that if provoked. There had to be a hard core inside her, for how else could she have fought herself up to the position she now held?

The thought of life without her was almost more than he could bear. Not that it had come to that yet, but he anticipated that it easily could.

He shakily poured another glass of wine and held it in his trembling hand.

"There's a man named Barstow. He's the inventor of a very sophisticated piece of equipment vital to national defense. I shudder to think what would happen if it fell into enemy hands."

"What sort of equipment?"

"I can't explain the technical end of it, but it has to do with nuclear power."

"Nuclear power is not new."

"But the electronic controls Barstow is making are. They come in three parts, each interlocks with the other —" he broke off. Why had he told her that? The real secret of the whole business was the three parts. To the experienced and even the trained eye, one section of the control appeared to be all that was needed. Barstow's idea had been to conceal the real function of the control this way — just as a security measure, he had said. Now, he had unwittingly blabbed out the secret.

"Three parts?" Lorna prodded gently. "I don't understand."

"Three sections of the unit is what I should have said," he answered. "You'll forgive me if I'm vague about it — I'm not trained in the field. Now, please, let's not talk about it anymore. Isn't this enough?"

She looked at him for a moment and smiled. "Yes. Of course. Thank you, darling. I feel so much better now. I understand how you feel. I should never doubt your judgment in such matters."

He began to relax. "I tried to tell you that before, Lorna. Why wouldn't you believe me? Now I've done what I had promised not to do."

"But only to me. It will go no farther."

He held her for a moment, but he felt as if he was shaking inside.

"This Barstow, who is he?" Lorna asked.

"A brilliant man. He's been working on this project for a very long time."

"But he's not subsidized by the government?"

"No. Due to their own folly and a foul-up of red tape. Now, they know what a good thing it is and they regret that they weren't in on the ground floor."

Lorna's eyes shone. "Which means you are and you'll be in a position to make a contract with the government?"

Eldridge nodded. "Barstow desperately needed money for personal reasons. I got it for him in return

for the device. The final stages are being made ready
now. In a few weeks, I'll meet with Barstow and he'll
turn over the blueprints to me and I in turn will deal
with the U.S. government —"

"Darling, it sounds brilliant! The kind of thing only
you could pull off."

She kissed him then and he forgot about Barstow,
the new device, and the fact that he had broken his
promise. Barstow had warned him what a hot potato
they were handling. But it was done now, and in a few
weeks it would be past history. What happened here
tonight would not matter at all. Barstow would have
his money, Eldridge would have his, and the country
would be safer militarily than it had been the day
before.

15

THE SUN was going down. Sara was getting ready to go to Tom Barclay's. Lee found himself at loose ends. Marcia had gone inside the Chadwick house to have dinner with Wally and Ryan. She had plans for the evening, too, and would not be seeing him.

Sara offered to fix supper for him before she left, but he declined with a shake of his head.

"I can fix something myself. Have a good time."

"You never ask about Tom. Why is that?"

Lee grinned. "What's to ask? He's a nice, handsome sort of guy and you like him. If you like him — that's enough for me."

After Sara had gone, Lee changed to swimming trunks, made a sandwich, grabbed some fruit from the bowl on the table, put it all in a paper sack and left. Somehow he always felt easier and freer when he knew that Chadwick was not around. Chadwick had not come home to Windmere since Tuesday, and the family was not expecting him all weekend.

This was easily Lee's favorite time of day. Usually at sundown, with the exception of his day off, he was driving back from Vincent with Chadwick in the back seat of the limousine. By the time they reached Windmere and Chadwick had dismissed him for the evening, the sun had gone. So tonight, it was a treat to go down the steps to the beach and step into the blaze of color of the sunset. The gulls saw him and came squawking overhead. It was not unusual for him to bring them crusts of bread or packages of crackers.

"Not yet, you crazy birds," he laughed. "I haven't had my own supper. You get what's left."

They followed him, circling and calling to him as he walked along and climbed the rocks to the ledge. There, he munched the sandwich, finding it especially tasty, and watched the ships on the horizon. A small yacht had been anchored in the cove for ages now. It never seemed to move and he wondered about it, but only in a very idle sort of way. He was relaxed and happy. Marcia had been especially sweet today while they swam in the ocean, stealing golden moments together. Thinking about her always brought a little tingle around his nerves. He was playing with fire. He knew it and so did she, yet they did nothing to stop it.

"Live and let live, that's what you said your motto was," Marcia had reminded him just a short time ago.

"Yes, but —"

"No buts, not for us, Lee. Don't be such an old stick!"

"I'm being practical."

"That's boring!" Marcia said. "Who wants to be practical? Sometimes, Lee Denning, I don't know what I see in you."

"Nor do I."

He remembered that now as he tossed his last crust of bread to the most persistent of the circling gulls. When they realized the food was gone, they went soaring away, white wings spreading against the red sky, floating free and easy. He envied them their freedom. That was the one thing he disliked about his new job. He was on constant call. Chadwick could summon him anytime, day or night, and he was expected to jump when he did. If he were his own man, maybe had his own business, he thought, he could close up shop at five and forget it until eight the next morning. Still, if he could have a place like Mark Williams's gas station and garage, he'd be willing to work until all hours. He'd be his own boss, independent, solely on his own.

Lee sighed and stretched back, hands under his head, to watch the clouds changing color.

"Hi!"

He hadn't heard her coming, but Midge was always slipping up on him.

"Hello, Midge."

"What are you doing?"

"The sum total of nothing."

"Can I do it too?"

Lee laughed and patted the rock beside him. "Help yourself."

She came to stretch out beside him, wrinkling her nose as she stared up at the sky. "Am I doing it right?"

"You're supposed to relax, and all you're doing is wiggling."

"I don't like relaxing."

"What do you feel like?"

He saw her homely little face screw up into a frown, and her eyes were too bright. "Dad's home. He came this afternoon."

"Good!"

"Not good," Midge shook her head. "He and Mother have been fighting ever since he got here."

"Oh."

He could see that Midge was very upset by it, and he felt sorry for her.

"Hey, you have to look at the bright side. You can't go around with such a long face. Come on, give me that big smile —"

She shook her head and Lee sat up to bend over her. With two fingers he pushed up the corners of her mouth and then leaned back to study her.

"A hundred percent better."

She managed a giggle. "Lee, you're funny."

"Want to go for a swim?"

"Will you ride me out on your shoulders?"

"Sure."

He gave her a hand down the rocks and then they raced across the sand and plunged into the water. Riding his shoulders out to water so deep it was up to his chin thrilled her. When they got too far, he dumped her off, and she shrieked with delight. She could swim like a porpoise, and after so much splashing and water fighting, they would eventually let the tide drift them back to the shore.

Ever since the first day Midge had come here, she had dogged his footsteps, but he didn't mind. Midge filled a spot he had never realized before had been so empty.

After Midge had her fill of the water, they waded out to the beach.

"Let's go up and see Jan," Midge said. "You don't know her, do you?"

"No, but you've been telling me about her until I feel like I do."

"She's nice. Real nice."

They started toward the lighthouse and Midge walked beside him for awhile, then ran ahead and came back to circle him, kicking sand and offering him the prettiest shells she could find. The closer they came to the point where the Hanson house perched like a beacon, the quieter she became. Lee talked faster, trying to distract her attention from the troubles the house harbored.

At last they had rounded the point and made for the lighthouse. It was not yet quite dark and they saw the young woman before she saw them. She was busy in a flowerbed, working a trowel with studying concentration.

"Hi!" Midge called.

She turned around with surprise. "Oh, you startled me, Midge." Then she saw Lee. "Are you looking for my grandfather?"

"We're out walking, and Midge thought it was time to meet you," Lee said. "I'm Lee Denning."

Jan brushed at her knees and took off her gardening gloves. She gave him her hand and a warm smile.

"Hello. I'm Jan Travis. Grandpa has talked often about you. You're Sara's brother."

Lee could not say that Jan was a beautiful woman when compared to Marcia, but there was a certain warmth that came through, and her smile was one of the nicest he had ever seen. There was a look in her eyes that was clear, honest and beguiling.

"Grandpa's not very good about weeding," Jan said. "I couldn't stand this another second. I think he's out in the garage working on a fishing reel."

"I'll go and say hello," Lee said.

"I'm going to stay and help Jan," Midge decided.

With a smile, Lee left them chatting together, knowing from their quick laughter that they were already good friends.

Herb was surprised to see him and put the reel aside.

"Don't let me stop you, Herb."

"Time to quit anyway," he answered. "Have you met Jan?"

"Just now."

"Quite a girl, Lee. I was darned glad to have her come, and since she's been here, she really made things fly. Everything from the kitchen to the flower-bed."

"Midge says she's here for the summer."

"And longer if I can keep her."

They left the garage to join Midge and Jan. They had finished with the flowerbed and were sitting on the steps of the old lighthouse, enjoying the evening.

Jan wore faded jeans and a shirt open at the throat

and had acquired a tan in the short time she had been here. She looked healthy and wholesome, and there was something very special about her. Perhaps it was the protective way she put an arm around Midge's shoulders and flashed her grandfather a smile of adoration. The old man beamed in reply, and Lee sat down in the twilight, glad that Midge had persuaded him to come.

There was a comradeship among them all, and Lee noticed that Midge had forgotten all about her dark mood. Jan made her laugh with funny stories and suggested things they might do together during the long summer days.

"You'll have to show me the beach, Midge. I'm sure no one knows it like you," Jan said.

"Can Lee come too?"

Jan gave Lee a glance and smiled. "Of course. The more the merrier."

It was dark and the stars were out before Lee stirred himself. They had stayed far too long and the Hansons would be wondering about Midge.

"Your parents will be looking everywhere for you," he said to her. "Time to go."

Midge shrugged. "They don't care. Do we have to leave now?"

"Yes."

"You can come again tomorrow, Midge," Jan said.

"Walk part way with us?" she asked.

"All right."

They walked out into the warm night, the sea breeze against their faces, and Midge placed herself between Lee and Jan, took each of them by hand and swung happily along, talking to them both.

Jan's laughter was pleasant and low, a relaxing sound, and Lee didn't hurry, but walked slowly, the sand still warm under his bare feet.

When they reached the point, Jan stopped.

"This is as far as I go. Goodnight, Midge. Lee, it was nice meeting you — don't be a stranger. Come again — anytime."

"Thanks, I will. Goodnight, Jan."

Lee knew the way through the rocks even in the darkness. They rounded the point, and there Lee paused at the foot of the steps leading to the Hanson house.

"I'll see you up," he said.

They went up the steps together.

"Gee, it was fun tonight, Lee."

"Very nice. Now run along before you get in trouble."

"Lee —"

"Yes?"

"Bend down, please."

He bent down and Midge put her arms around his neck. With a laugh, he stood up and swung her about and then gave her suntanned cheek a quick kiss. She returned the kiss with a happy laugh and then she was off and running, shouting back to him.

"Goodbye, Lee. Goodbye —"

"Goodnight, Midge — sweet dreams."

Sara had gone to keep her dinner date with Tom. She wore a white dress and had done her hair high to the top of her head. The sun was sinking, the gulls were unusually quiet and everything seemed tranquil and serene. It was a little like Eden here or like a corner of the world where time had stopped.

Sara felt relaxed and pleased with herself. She had done good work today, and it had been fun meeting Jan. Tomorrow, she would be eager to resume her painting of Herb.

When Tom met her at the top of his steps, reaching out a hand to her, he looked at her for a long moment, smiling.

"You look very happy and content. It's shining out of your eyes."

"Sometimes I think something very special is here, just out of my reach, but *here*, waiting for me and one day soon, I'll find it. Did you ever feel that way, Tom?"

He nodded slowly and pulled her close. "I feel that way when I see you and when I kiss you —"

He kissed her then and held her for a long moment. Then with a laugh, she pulled free of his arms.

"You promised me food, didn't you? And I was to toss the salad."

He followed her into the house and helped her get all the makings out of the refrigerator. Out on the patio she smelled the smoke of a charcoal fire, and on the counter the steaks were ready for grilling.

"What other talents do you have, Tom, besides photographing and cooking —"

"I'm a terrible baritone, but I sing in the church choir at home. Sometimes when no one is looking I play the guitar."

"Really? Do you have a guitar here? Will you play for me later?"

"If you twist my arm hard enough," Tom laughed. "Now, I'll start the steaks and when you've finished in here, come and join me. I get lonely awfully fast."

It didn't take long with the salad, and she set it back in the refrigerator to keep crisp. Then she went out into the dusk of evening and sat in one of the comfortable lawn chairs watching Tom fuss with the steaks.

Later, while they ate, Tom asked more about her work and she told him of a possible series for Cloud Nine.

"Does that mean you'll go back to New York?" he asked quickly.

She took a moment to reply. "Jerry seems to think so. I'm hoping that World Tours won't decide for awhile. If I didn't have to make a decision until after the summer was over, maybe I'd know which direction I want to go. But right now —"

Tom covered her hand with his. His touch sent ripples over her nerves and she wondered that three different men could affect her in such separate ways. Jerry brought out the rebel in her, Ryan Chadwick touched off sparks of empathy she didn't even know she harbored in her heart and Tom Barclay just plain excited her.

"I hope the summer goes slowly," Tom said wistfully. "I keep wanting to hold it back."

After the food had been eaten and she had praised his steaks and he in turn had complimented her salad, they went inside to look at his photographs. He spread them all around the room and she took her time. He had grouped them into categories, the sea, the beach, the birds, the people, the boats and the sky and she found each of them excellent in its own right.

"Oh, how can you choose?" she asked. "They're all so good, Tom."

"You should see what I threw away," he laughed. "I'm afraid they were all bombs. What about this one?"

She found herself looking into her own eyes, seeing her as Tom had seen her, suntanned, windblown, the surf swirling around her bare feet, the Atlantic to her back.

"Do I look like this?" she asked with surprise.

"It's one of my best efforts," he said. "I think it will have a very honored place in my book — with your permission, of course. You're the woman all men want to meet — free and happy and perhaps — mysterious —"

"The camera doesn't lie, but you seem to make it tell all sorts of stories. I'm not like this, Tom — not really —"

"Why do you say that?"

"The girl in this photograph is — well —"

"Beautiful," Tom said, supplying the word. "Don't be modest. You *are* beautiful and you have a free spirit. There's a touch of the will-o'-the-wisp in this photo, and that's exactly what I wanted to capture."

She stared at the picture again, flattered and pleased that he saw her like this.

"How did you learn so much about angles, shadows and special lighting effects —"

"Trial and error. When I was all of ten years old, Dad gave me a small camera for Christmas — it was the start. I still have it. I remember those first pictures I took — terrible pictures actually — but they excited me and I knew then what I wanted to do."

"All the pictures are good. Whichever ones you choose, Tom, I know they'll be right ones."

"You're not going to help me decide?"

"I couldn't! How does an amateur advise a professional?"

He laughed at that. "Enough of this. Let's go back outside."

The stars were thick in the sky, smudged clusters of silver, pinpoints of landmarks she had known as a child, the Big Dipper, Cassiopeia, and the Pleiades.

Tom had gone to the railing and was peering out to the cove. The lights of the yacht that had been there for so many days were visible, little yellow dots on the water.

"Why are you so taken with that boat?" she asked.

Tom turned about with a start. "Oh, no reason except — well — let's put it this way. It's been there so long that it begins to feel like an intrusion. Maybe I'm getting as snobbish as the Chadwicks."

"Who's aboard?" she asked. "Do you know."

"A man and a woman."

"How do you know that? I've never seen anyone —"

"I had trouble with my boat out in the cove one day and went aboard the *Marybelle* to borrow some tools.

They said their name was Thornton. He's a small, dark man and she has the reddest hair I've ever seen. Have you ever seen them around in Vincent or on the beach?"

"I don't think so. Red hair?" she asked quickly. "Did the woman have an oval-shaped face, was her hair parted in the middle —"

"Yes." Tom nodded. "So, you have seen them! I was beginning to think they never got off that blasted yacht!"

"Perhaps I've seen the woman, but I'm not sure —"

Sara's nerves had tightened up as if being wound on a ball of twine. Tom's description of the Thorntons could well fit the man who had followed her to Denver on the plane and it definitely matched the woman who had followed her back! Oh, that was ridiculous! There must be hundreds of people who looked like that in this crazy old world and she was letting her imagination get away from her. More than anything, she wanted to put it out of her mind. The night was lovely and she didn't intend to spoil it with senseless fears.

"Tom, you promised me a serenade, remember?"

"You're sure you're prepared for it?" Tom laughed.

He went inside and came back with his guitar. He leaned his back against the railing and began to pluck the strings. She sat in the lawn chair, listening, the music drifting on the night, blending with the surf. Tom was nearly as good with the guitar as with a camera.

She let the mood wrap around her, the music

touched a mellow part of her heart, and she would always remember Tom standing there, a shadow in the darkness, the music flowing from his guitar. It was one of those moments she knew would live somewhere in the deepest part of her memory. It was a sweet time, a cherished time, as the wind was a kiss against her cheek and the night a cloak to shelter her. But as Tom put the guitar aside and came to kiss her once again, there was one little part of her mind that was fastened on the *Marybelle* in the cove and the people aboard her, one small atom of her soul that trembled with uneasiness.

16

Sunday morning Sara slept late, the evening spent with Tom a sweet memory that laced itself in and out of her dreams.

The smell of coffee awakened her at last, and she opened her eyes to find Lee standing over her, a cup in his hand.

"Sleepyhead! That must have been some night you had with Tom."

"A very nice time was had by both of us," she said with a yawn.

"Here, drink this. It will wake you up."

"You're in a very good mood this morning."

"Why not? If this job of mine gets any softer —"

"Chadwick's staying away a long time, isn't he?"

"For him." Lee nodded.

"He's not coming today either?"

"No," Lee replied, "so I have another free day."

Sara tasted the coffee. "Hmm, this is good, Lee. What's keeping Chadwick in the city so long? It's not like him."

"Marcia hinted that it surely must be some very big, important deal. Small change to millionaires, I dare say," he said with a wry smile. "If you'll fix the eggs, I'll fry the bacon."

"You have yourself a deal."

Lee went to the kitchen to get started, and Sara reached for a robe. She took a look at the day from her window and the first thing she noticed was that the *Marybelle* was no longer there. It had moved on at last. Thank God, she thought! Somehow, it was the perfect way to start the day. Last night, she had imagined all sorts of things about that boat and the people on it.

As Lee and Sara were enjoying their late breakfast, Marcia appeared, wearing a beach robe over her swimsuit, looking fresh and pretty. Sara could tell that Lee thought so too.

"I came over to invite you to swim in the pool and stay for lunch."

"Lunch!" Lee echoed. "Oh, I don't think —"

"Don't be so prim and proper!" Marcia said. "I'm dying of boredom, and even Uncle Wally has plans to be away today. I'll tell Mrs. Goddard to set a couple of extra plates."

"It's very nice of you, Marcia, and I for one would enjoy it," Sara said.

"Good!" Marcia said, giving Lee a triumphant look. "Then it's settled. See you later."

Sara wondered if Ryan would be around too, or if he had disappeared again. It was hard to tell about him, but she was a little anxious to see if any of her advice had taken root.

"Sis, you think we should go over there?" Lee asked.

"I don't see why not. Marcia wants you."

"Yes, but —"

"Relax. We're every bit as good as any of the Chadwicks, aren't we?"

Lee smiled at that. "If you say so."

Later, Sara found the pool especially refreshing, for the sun was hot and the air close. Perhaps a storm was brewing somewhere out there off the horizon. She took turns racing from one end of the pool to the other with Lee and Marcia. Lee seemed stronger every day, and if nothing else came out of the summer, they would have that much. She didn't know why she thought in terms of just the summer. She could probably arrange to stay here the year around with Lee if she wanted. Lee seemed happy enough with his work here. So why think of only the summer?

She stretched out on a beach towel and closed her eyes, the red spots of the sun floating under her lids, and when a cool hand touched her arm, she jumped.

"Oh, Ryan!"

"Having fun?"

"Yes. The pool's very nice. Why don't you take a dip yourself?"

"Not today," he said.

"Remember you promised me you'd try — go put on your swim trunks — I'll challenge you to a race."

He lifted his lips in a wry smile. "What's the prize if I win?"

"I'll think of something."

He looked out to the water for a moment, watching

Lee and Marcia as they frolicked about, and with a shrug, he got to his feet.

"Okay. I'll be back in a minute."

Sara had to give Ryan credit. He did try, very hard, the rest of the morning. He swam with strong strokes and beat her in every race. He laughed, but the laughter had a false ring to it, and when he brought a stereo out and put on some records, the music he chose was blue and moody.

At lunch time, Mrs. Goddard served them on the patio, and she did so with an air that brought a blush to Lee's cheeks and a touch of anger to Sara. Mrs. Goddard plainly did not approve of this, and Sara could understand her feeling. The employees were not to mix with the family — at least not a family like the Chadwicks. But Marcia seemed to enjoy seeing her resentment and laughed about it. Ryan couldn't have cared less one way or the other.

"Don't mind her," he said. "Her nose gets out of joint very easily. She has a thing about us — sometimes she acts like our mother instead of our cook."

"She's just plain bossy," Marcia said. "You should see how she orders Daddy around, and poor, dumb Daddy, he just takes it and does what she says."

"Well, better her than Lorna Cellman," Ryan said with a frown.

"Lorna's not so bad!" Marcia said defensively. "Anyway, she's smart and she never plays it cute with me. She knows better than to try."

"How long has your father known Lorna?" Sara wondered.

"Several months, but she has a good head on her shoulders and Dad trusts her. She's handled a lot of work for him," Marcia said. "Listen, I have a great idea. Let's all go into Vincent later. There ought to be something fun to do there."

No one made any argument, so it was agreed that they would go. After lunch, they spent a lazy afternoon, playing shuffleboard, taking another long dip in the pool and letting the day slip away, so that it was nearly five o'clock when they finally decided it was time to go.

Lee and Sara went back to the cottage to change out of their swimsuits. Lee was suntanned a golden brown and seemed more relaxed than Sara had ever seen him before.

"You're having fun."

Lee sighed. "Yes. But I let down today. I just pretended there was nothing wrong with anything I was doing, and I shouldn't have done that. It might get to be a habit — if it hasn't already."

"You've never talked to me about Marcia."

Lee fingered the tie in his hand, looking as if he had never seen it before.

"I have to admit that she's quite a girl."

"I see nothing wrong if you're truly interested in her."

"What's with you and Ryan?"

"Nothing, really. I'm just trying to cheer him up."

Lee faced her with a worried face. "Sis, is it possible we're both getting too involved with the Chadwicks?"

"Yes, I suppose it is."

"What do we do about it?"

"Nothing. We'll ride out the tide, Lee. We'll see what happens. Now, we'd better hurry or they'll be waiting for us."

"Ryan said something about going out to dinner," Lee said. "I hope he doesn't go to some fancy place —"

Sara took the tie from Lee's hands, slid it under his collar and carefully knotted it for him.

"You look very handsome. Relax. We're out for a good time, remember?"

There were several places in Vincent to offer them a pleasant dinner, and Ryan knew them all. But they ended up going to the one he felt served the best food. It was a plush affair with a look of elegance, the sort of place that Lee avoided and which impressed Sara despite herself. The two Chadwicks were well known there. Ryan asked for the best table in the house and got it.

Ryan took care of the ordering and Lee seemed uneasier by the moment, even when Marcia reached out and held his hand for all to see.

It was a long evening. Ryan seemed in no hurry to bring the night to an end. He sat moodily at the table, saying very little, lost in some deep memory. He scarcely responded when Sara spoke to him, and she knew he was drinking far too much.

Lee took Marcia out to the dance floor only after she threatened to get angry if he didn't. They attracted attention together, both blond and suntanned, both very nice-looking, both young and obviously interested in each other.

At last, Ryan said they should be going. He asked for the check and Lee insisted he wanted to pay his share. Ryan shook his head and initialed the check.

"My show tonight, old boy."

Lee flushed. "Ryan, I want to pay my half!"

"They'll charge it to my account; no sweat," Ryan said. "Come on, let's get out of here."

Lee knotted his fists and Sara saw the anger flashing in his eyes. Ryan had been condescending and it didn't ride well with Lee.

The drive back to Windmere was quiet. Lee had shrunk into his corner of the back seat and Marcia was angry.

"You're such a silly old clod, Lee!"

"Thanks," he murmured.

For one, Sara would be glad to see the gates of Windmere and to reach the garage. She wished Lee was behind the wheel as Ryan drove erratically, either from drinking too much or from sheer carelessness. But Sara knew if she suggested a change, Ryan would get angry. Then the idea went out of her head as a small, blue car went zooming around them.

"I'll be damned!" Ryan said. "That was the car, the one that nearly ran me down that day —"

With an angry burst of speed, Ryan thrust down the accelerator and the sports car leaped forward. It did not take the driver of the car ahead long to realize he was being pursued and to go even faster.

"Hang on!" Ryan said with gritted teeth.

They took the curves at an alarming speed, and

Sara clutched at her seat belt for safety. In the darkness, the taillights of the car ahead disappeared and then reappeared as they chased it up and down the hills. Then abruptly, the car was gone. Ryan slammed on the brakes.

"Where did he go?"

"You've lost him," Lee said. "Maybe he turned off back there —"

Instantly, Ryan shoved the car into reverse and they went rushing back to a road that led off to the left. Ryan spun the steering wheel, the tires howling, and they went down the narrow, rough road, being jostled roughly from side to side. But there was still no sign of the car, and when Ryan reached a dead end, he slammed on the brakes once more.

"Not here," he said. "Now where do you suppose —"

"Hard to say now," Lee said. "There are a lot of little byroads, lanes — who knows —"

"You might have been mistaken, Ryan. It might not have been the same car," Sara said.

"I'd bet my bottom dollar on it," he said. Then with a bitter laugh, he drove on. "Oh, hell, what's it matter? I just wish —"

He left the sentence unfinished and Sara saw the unhappiness on his face, his melancholy like a harsh mask.

"It was a blue car," Lee was saying. "A small blue car with mirrors mounted on the fenders —"

Sara remembered that Lee had often seen such a car at the station when taking Chadwick to the train.

It must be someone living in the neighborhood. But Ryan didn't know the car, nor did Marcia. With so few houses and so few people, that seemed odd. But the strangest thing of all was the way the driver of the car had sought to escape once he knew he was being chased.

17

THE FOLLOWING WEEK after having spent Sunday with the Chadwicks, Sara was pleased when Jan Travis phoned her.

"I'm going to Vincent today. Would you like to come along? We could have lunch somewhere."

"Sounds like fun. But why don't I pick you up and save you the trouble of getting through the gate?"

"I'd appreciate that," Jan said.

Sara was rather glad to get away from the Chadwick place. Things were uneasy there. That was the best way she could describe it, and she couldn't really put her finger on why. Perhaps it was Lee's involvement with Marcia and her own with Ryan. Or the mood of the house itself. Even Wally seemed quieter these days, as if marking time for some kind of calamity.

Jan was as pleasant as the first time they'd met, and conversation came easily between them. Jan had a light, breezy way that was fun.

"I'm going to see about a teaching job in Vincent, mostly because Grandpa wants it so badly. I talked with the superintendent on the phone and I have an appointment with him. Will you mind waiting? It shouldn't take long."

"No problem," Sara said. "And I'll be rooting for you."

The interview lasted half an hour and when Jan came out of the building, she seemed pleased.

"It looks favorable, but nothing definite yet. I'm not going to tell Grandpa until I know for certain. He gets his hopes up too easily. Where shall we lunch?"

"I have a feeling you know more about the town than me," Sara said. "You choose."

"As I remember from my last visit, there's a place in the next block, not fancy, but they have good food."

They found the place, called Johnnie's, and were lucky enough to find a place to park the car. It was high noon and the café was busy. After a few minutes' wait, they were seated and had placed their order when Mark Williams appeared.

"Hey, two of my favorite ladies!" he said with his friendly smile. "How are you, Jan? I heard you were back."

"Hello, Mark. Have you eaten? Would you like to join us?"

"Sure," he said with a laugh. "Slide over."

Mark Williams wore the blue uniform he always wore when he was working at his gas station. He asked about Lee.

"Haven't seen him for a few days. Is he that busy at the Chadwicks'?"

"Lee's the type that always keeps himself occupied," Sara said.

Mark sighed and shook his head. "I like to be busy too. I don't know, it gets discouraging. Maybe I'm not cut out for the business I'm in. I'm thinking of selling out and going west to join my family there. At least it would be a change of pace."

"Last summer when I was here, you were thinking along those lines even then," Jan teased. "I think you're just talking."

Mark frowned. "Well, maybe it's time to stop talking and do something about it."

While they ate lunch, Mark and Jan discussed mutual acquaintances and the local news. Sara felt more or less on the outside of things, but Jan realized this and soon drew her back into the conversation.

"Midge tells me that you're good friends, Sara," Jan said.

Sara smiled. "Yes. She stops by whenever I'm on the beach."

"Are you talking about the Hanson kid?" Mark asked.

"Yes."

"I'm afraid she's in for a hard row of it," Mark said. "They tell me that the Hansons are going to get a divorce, and as for Midge — she'll be up for grabs and it's possible neither one will want her —"

"I've heard this, too," Jan said. "I was hoping it wasn't true."

"It's real enough," Mark said with sympathy. "Midge almost had it made, rich parents, a nice home, all that money for anything she'd need — a far cry

from what she had before the Hansons came along.
Now, it's possible she'll lose it all."

"They wouldn't do that, would they, Mark?" Jan
worried. "They wouldn't put her through something
like that — they couldn't turn their backs on her —"

"She's not adopted. There wouldn't be any legal
reason why they had to keep her," Mark pointed out.
"And the Hansons aren't my favorite people."

"There ought to be something we could do," Jan
said.

"But what?"

Jan gave them a despairing look. "I've racked my
brains ever since I learned of the situation. Of course,
it's none of my business. Still —"

"Of all the crummy things in this world, this takes
the cake," Mark sighed. "But how can I solve it when
I can't even solve my own headaches?"

The worry over Midge touched them all, but they
didn't come up with any help for her.

When they had finished lunch, Mark said he had to
get back to work and left with a wave of his hand.

"See you around —"

As Jan and Sara drove back to the lighthouse, the
subject of Midge came up again. They tossed out
ideas and crazy plans between them.

"There's nothing we can do, Sara," Jan said. "The
truth of it is, our hands are tied."

"I'm afraid you're right."

"She's such a sweet child," Jan said. "We got on
from the first time she came to the lighthouse and in a

couple of days she had me so completely wrapped around her little finger —"

Sara laughed. "I know what you mean. She seems to affect everyone that way —"

"Everyone but the Hansons, apparently," Jan said sadly.

Sara dropped Jan at the lighthouse, waved goodbye and drove back to Windmere. The problem of Midge was a heavy stone in her heart, and when she reached the cottage, she knew she had no desire to work today. She thought of looking up Lee and talking to him about Midge but decided against that too. Lee hadn't quite been himself since their Sunday outing with the Chadwicks and she knew that he and Marcia had quarreled.

Sara thought of Tom, remembering the night she had gone to his house for supper, and she wanted to see him again. She strolled down the beach toward Widow's Point, anticipating the sight of Tom Barclay. She'd known a lot of men, but there was something special about Tom. How else could just the sight of him stir so much interest inside her heart?

When she knocked at Tom's door and he came to let her in, he was delighted to see her.

"I'm not interrupting anything, am I?" she asked.

"Even if you were, it wouldn't matter. This is the nicest thing that has happened all day."

He reached out a hand and drew her inside. She was keenly aware of him, as she always was, and she couldn't quite explain why she was so drawn to him.

"Are you working?" she asked.

"Not this very moment, but you know, this might be the right time. There's something I've been wanting to do everytime I see you. Sara, would you pose for me?"

"You're not serious!"

"I want to do a series of shots for my own personal collection. Please, Sara —"

"But, Tom —"

"Humor me," he insisted with a smile. She found him hard to resist, and before she knew it, she was agreeing.

Tom began setting up his equipment, taking great pains, and she watched him, realizing how professional he was and pleased to find him so. She respected his integrity and as he teased and prodded and got exactly the right look from her, she knew that Tom probably worked as hard at everything he did.

"I understand now why people freeze up when I do a painting of them. Tom, aren't you about finished? You've had me posing for nearly an hour."

He came to take her face in his hands and study her deeply.

"One more, Sara. Now hold it just like that —"

He clicked the camera enthusiastically and finally under protest agreed to stop.

"I could never get enough pictures of you, but you must be getting tired. I didn't mean to be thoughtless."

He put his camera away and Sara stretched lazily, reaching her arms over her head. "I know now why models earn so much money. How much film did you shoot?"

"I got thirty poses. I'll develop them later."

"Why not now?"

"I'm anxious to see them too, Sara, but photos never take the place of the real thing and why waste time in a darkroom when I have you right here —" He reached out his hands to her. "Sara, let's have the rest of the day together. We'll do whatever you like, go where you want, just as long as I can be with you —"

His hands were warm and tight around hers and his eyes seemed to probe deeply into her heart. "I want to know all about you, Sara. Everything — from the first thing you can remember until now."

"That would take hours and hours to tell."

He smiled. "That's what I had in mind."

"And in turn will you tell me about yourself?"

"Would you be interested in knowing that at the tender age of eight years I climbed up on the roof of our house and couldn't get down?" he laughed.

"What were you doing up there?"

"Rescuing a cat that had fallen from a tree branch to the roof and was in real trouble. All the thanks I got was a few scratches from the pussy and a scolding from my mother. Should we walk down to the beach? We could find a quiet place."

The sand was warm, the sun bright, and the clouds went whispering across the sky in pursuit of secrets. The day wrapped around Sara and she wanted to hold the moment forever still.

For awhile, they walked hand in hand and Tom talked about Cleveland and his father, and she liked the warmth in his voice, sensing that his feelings went deep for family and home.

"Tom, do you know about Midge?"

He paused for a moment. "What's happened to her?"

She told him and Tom listened, shaking his head with despair. "Oh, no!"

"I feel so helpless, Tom. If there was only something we could do."

"The injustices of this world!" he sighed. "Maybe we can think of something."

"There doesn't seem to be any solution. The Hansons are divorcing and that's the beginning of the end for Midge."

"I hate divorce!" he said angrily. "Except in very unusual cases, people should make more effort to stay together. Do you agree?"

"Yes, but many people today would think it a square idea, Tom."

"Not me," he said. "I'm glad you feel the same way. Somehow, I knew you would."

After a while, they grew tired of walking and they moved back from the water under the tall shade of a pine tree and sat down. Tom stretched out and put his head in her lap. She studied the strong planes of his face and put her fingers in his black hair.

"It's strange," he murmured. "How I came here — and so did you — how we're together now. Do you believe in fate?"

"Sometimes."

"What else could this be?"

"The first time we went to dinner, you suggested we

let it be a carefree summer — we'd roll with the tide, I believe was the way you put it."

A flush came over Tom's face. "Sometimes, I say things in haste and have to repent later. I was a fool to have thought this would be a casual summer affair. I should have known the minute I saw you that you were destined to be mine."

"Yours?" she teased. "Sir, you assume too much —"

He sat up and leaned toward her, eyes twinkling. "Oh, *do* I? I've got you right here in my clutches and I won't let you go —"

She scrambled hastily to her feet and began to run. With a shout he entered into the game, chasing her along the wet sand until he caught up with her, and then he pulled her tightly into his arms and smiled down at her.

"Kiss me or I won't let you go."

"Never?"

"Never!"

"That's a long time."

She reached up and kissed him lightly, but it didn't end there and when he let her go at last, the light had deepened in his eyes and there was an excited feeling around her heart.

They grew quiet as they walked on down the beach, strangely aloof with each other now, as if each had withdrawn to reassess what was happening. They began to talk again, and it was as if both of them couldn't wait to tell the other something important, something they felt or thought or had experienced.

They wandered on and the afternoon began to ease

away, and the farther the sun dropped in the sky, the closer they became. They walked back toward Widow's Point at last, and she wondered about his book.

"You've never told me, did you make your final choice?"

"I'd like to show you."

They went back to the house and there Tom got out his photos and showed her the ones he had selected and the order he wanted them in the book. She found them starkly beautiful; even the tiniest detail was made to seem important and gave depth to his work. She knew he was a man with an inner goodness, with an eye for beauty and truth. At the same time there was a hard honesty about him that would not be swayed.

This afternoon, she had grown to know Tom, and now as she watched him proudly showing off his work, waiting anxiously for her approval, she knew that she cared for him, perhaps deeply. Could it happen like this?

"Will some publisher be interested in the book?" he wondered.

"How could they help it?"

"I know something like this isn't easy to sell. But I had to try. Coming here was my one chance in a lifetime and I needed it. But I'm a newcomer to this sort of thing —"

"They'd be blind not to take it."

"You truly think so, Sara?"

"Yes."

He began to put the photos away and he seemed

more relaxed now, more sure of himself. "If you think
so, then I'll stop worrying. But it's still wait and see,
isn't it? It will probably take several weeks or even
more to find out. By then, it will be time to leave
here."

"Back to Cleveland?"

"There's my work there to think about and my responsibility to Dad. He has no one else, Sara, and he
needs me."

"I understand."

"Sara, will you go back to New York, whether it's to
work on Cloud Nine or some other assignment?"

She hesitated. "I don't know."

"I don't want to go back to Cleveland and I don't
want you to go to New York. I want both of us to stay
right here."

"Here? I've heard it called a never-never land, a
fairyland, and maybe that's all it is. A passing
fancy —"

"It started that way, but it's not that way now, is it?
No matter what happens to us or where we go or what
we do, this place, this summer is going to be one of
the most important in our lives. Because we found
each other. Sara, you know how I feel, don't you? You
know I've fallen in love with you."

"Oh, Tom —"

"I want it all, Sara. A home, a family, a wife and
kids with freckled faces — as sweet as little Midge."

The tears burned her eyes. He held her close and
pressed his lips to her hair. "I know you're on edge. I
know you came here looking for yourself and I know

I'm rushing you. I try to be patient, but with you, I can't. I love you so much, Sara."

She didn't know what to say so she clung to him and tried not to think about New York or her work or Jerry or anything before this very minute. But she knew she couldn't do that. The next moment always came and tomorrow rose up with the dawn.

"Don't say any more, Tom. Give me some time —"

"You don't want to be pinned down," he said with a sigh. "You're a summer butterfly and you want to flit your wings and land here and there and taste all the flowers, is that it?"

She laughed. "Maybe."

"I'll give you the summer, as long as you come back to me when it's over. Someday soon, I'd like to take you to Cleveland to meet my father."

"I'd like that."

"Good!"

She stepped away from him, needing to be on safer ground, at arm's length from him. The afternoon had been heady and sweet, but it had also nearly over-whelmed her. Too many emotions were surging through her heart at one time. She needed time to sort them out. Tom sensed how she felt.

"Why don't I fix us something cold to drink?"

"I think it might be a very good idea!"

She could hear him making noises in the kitchen and she went back to flip idly through the photos he had selected for his book. One of them slid to the floor and wedged itself between the carpet and a closet door. Afraid of tearing it, she opened the door to retrieve it. Her shoulder brushed one of the shelves inside and a large brown manila envelope fell to the floor, spilling out more photos. She began scooping them up to return them to their rightful place when suddenly she became aware of the subject of the pictures.

It was the Chadwick place! Dozens of photos of the house, the railing where Tania had fallen and the rocks beneath it! Most of them were enlargements made from photos that had more than likely been taken with a telescopic lens. The close-ups were almost minute in detail. She had a second shock when she found pictures of herself, most of them with Ryan.

Why was Tom spying on the Chadwicks like this? After a stunned moment or two, knowing that Tom would soon be back with the drinks, she hastily returned the pictures to the envelope, put them back on the shelf and closed the closet door. Her head was reeling and she felt a chill chase up and down her back.

Tom came into the room seconds later, the glasses tinkling with ice.

"Here we are," he said.

She took the drink, seeing her hand was trembling. Tom studied her for a moment. "What is it, darling?"

Something was not right here. There had already been strange things happen, and it unnerved her to think that Tom might in some way be a part of it.

"Sara —"

To hide her confusion, she put the drink aside and wound her arms tightly around him, pressing her cheek to his shoulder. With a laugh, he held her and she tried to blot it all out, to let her feeling for him win over the newly born doubts. Above the sound of the surf below, she could hear the thunder of his heart, echoing her own.

18

Ryan spent restless nights prowling the house, smoking too many cigarettes and staring for long stretches of time out to the sea. God knew, he was not responsible these days, and his thoughts twisted in and out of dark places, seeking the light. His emotions were in a tangle over losing Tania. They colored everything so that he found it difficult to think straight, to reason, to listen to anyone. Wally had told him to bury Tania, forget her. Go on with his life. But how? That question welled up in him with its torment, and he knew that the answers were not here at Windmere. There had been something strange about the way Tania had fallen. There *had* been something she was holding back from him. Of that he was certain, even in his muddled mind. There was only one thing to do.

Wednesday morning, he left the house early, tossed a bag into the car and drove away without a word to anyone. At Mark Williams's station, he had the car filled with gas.

"Going on a vacation, Ryan?" Mark asked.

"Not exactly. I'm out to bury some ghosts."

Mark gave him an odd look but said no more and in a few minutes, Ryan was on his way.

The drive to New York was familiar to him. He had done this often when he'd been seeing Tania. He thought about the blue car and his futile chase. For the last two days he had prowled the neighborhood, but it seemed no such car existed. It probably was not significant anyway. Some damned fool had accidentally run him down that day a few weeks ago. Maybe he'd lost his woman too and was out of his skull with grief. Ryan could understand that.

The blue car didn't really matter. First things first. He had to find answers, he had to know some things about Tania. The logical person to seek out was Brad Jennings, the man who had been listed as Tania's next of kin at the apartment house where she had lived. Brad Jennings had been a man in his late forties, a rather short, common-looking person, who had told him Tania was his cousin.

"We have only cousins left now," he said. "But I'll take care of things, Mr. Chadwick. Not a thing for you to worry about."

And like a poor, blind, heartsick sheep, he had followed Jennings's lead, not asking enough questions, not getting enough details. He only knew she was to be buried in a family plot in Vincennes, Indiana. He had been too heartsick to attend the services, but now wished he had.

Jennings had given him his address and a phone number. Once Ryan got to the city, he took a room at a health club where he was a member and used the phone. Jennings's number was no longer in use — he got some crazy recording. A search in the directory and an inquiry to the information operator netted him nothing. There was no Brad Jennings at that number and address. His next move was to get a cab. He gave the driver Jennings's address and after several minutes' ride, the street abruptly came to a dead end and they had run out of houses.

"You must have the wrong address, buddy," the driver said. "There is no such number."

Beads of perspiration began to form on Ryan's face. He knew now that Brad Jennings had lied to him all the way. But why? What was wrong here?

"Okay. Then let's try Johnson Engineering."

He gave the address as Tania had given it to him and he was enormously relieved when the driver found the building. He paid his fare and got out.

The building was not impressive and was just like any of the others in the neighborhood. He wondered why he had expected the building where Tania had worked to be any different. She was just a girl, he reminded himself, a girl who worked at a dull job as a secretary. How many times he had heard her lament about that!

He took the elevator and rode it to the eleventh floor and stepped off. It took him a few minutes to find the right office, and he was stopped by a girl at the receptionist desk.

"May I help you?"

"I'm looking for friends of Tania Francis."

The girl stared at him blankly. "Who?"

"Tania Francis. She worked here until about three months ago."

"I've been here for five years and there was never a Tania Francis or a Tania anybody."

"This is Johnson Engineering, isn't it?"

"Yes."

"I don't understand," Ryan said. "There has to be a mistake. Tania said she was employed here. You must have just forgotten her —"

The girl shook her head. "I know all the girls, all the employees."

"Tania was small, dark, had a lilt to her voice and she always laughed a lot," Ryan said desperately.

The girl shook her head. "Listen, you must have the wrong place. There are lots of girls that fit that description. Have you got a picture of her?"

Ryan shook his head. "No, she never liked to be photographed."

His ears were ringing. The girl plainly thought him a fool. He knew he was in the right place, he *knew* what Tania had told him and yet, she was not known here!

"You've got the wrong girl in the wrong place," the girl behind the desk told him.

He murmured something to her and let himself out in the hall, and he stood there for a full five minutes comprehending what this meant. Why had Tania lied about where she worked? Was she so ashamed of her job that she had made up this one? But God knew, there was nothing very impressive about Johnson

Engineering. In fact, if anything, the office had been rather shabby.

Where did he go from here? In one wildly insane moment, with his head throbbing as if there were a dozen drums pounding inside, he began to wonder if Tania had only been a pleasant dream, if she had ever truly existed.

Vincennes, Indiana. Yes! That was where he must go. There — he would get answers.

An hour later, he was driving out of the city, intent only on driving across the country in search of the truth about Tania.

Tania *had* been real, he told himself. How warm and snug she had been in his arms! A restless little pixie, unable to sit still, full of cute tricks and mischief, bubbling with curiosity.

"Your father's a big, important man, isn't he?" she had asked.

"I suppose so. I don't think of him that way."

"What's he do?"

"He's an investor. He buys companies and things — why?"

"What sort of things?"

"I don't know."

"How can you be so indifferent?" she asked.

He smiled at that and pulled her into his arms. "Why bother? I couldn't care less. I have you. That's all that matters."

He remembered with aching poignancy their times together. Tania was so close in that moment he could almost reach out and touch her. He could imagine her half-skipping, half-walking to keep up with his long strides.

"Don't walk so fast, Ryan," she used to say when they were walking along New York streets.

"Sorry. My long legs just naturally cover the ground in a hurry."

"You're always in such a rush when you're walking with me!"

"Because I can't wait to get you in some dark little supper club or a hallway or somewhere where I can kiss you without half of New York seeing us."

"My sweet Ryan," she had said, and she kissed him right there anyway, drawing amused stares and a few encouraging shouts from cab drivers.

The drive to Vincennes took Ryan longer than he had expected and it was in the evening of the next day when he arrived. He took a motel room and from a telephone directory, made a list of all cemeteries. The next day he methodically visited them all, one after the other, spoke with the caretakers and kept hearing the same thing.

"No record of Tania Francis."

"It would have been just a few weeks ago —"

"Sorry. You must have the wrong place."

He spent the next two days searching the cemeteries himself, certain there had been a mistake in the records. He went to all within a radius of several miles from the city and at last, exhausted, dismayed and groggy with the significance of it, he started driving back home, eyes glued open but seeing little, the stubble on his face growing black and heavy.

It was late the next night when he reached the gates of Windmere and drove through. There was still a light in the den and once he'd left the car, he went straight there. Lorna Cellman was in the room with his father and Ryan wished she would go away. He didn't like the woman and he needed desperately to talk with his father.

"What is it, Ryan? Where have you been? Why are you in this condition?"

"I have to talk with you, Dad."

His father took off a pair of reading glasses and smoothed a hand over his gray hair. Lorna Cellman gave Ryan a lofty look, annoyed with the interruption. Nothing was to interfere with her precious business meetings with Dad, but Ryan could think now only of Tania.

"What is it, Ryan? Can't it wait? I'm in the middle of a very important —"

Something snapped inside Ryan. He went to lean on the desk and looked straight into his father's eyes. "You don't give a damn, do you? You don't care that Tania's dead and it's as if she never existed. I can't even find her grave! My world's gone smash and all you care about is your precious money, your stocks and bonds and silly business deals —"

"It might do you well to take an interest in such things instead of letting yourself go like this!"

Ryan gave him a cold smile. "Oh, sure! Be a good

little boy and follow in your footsteps. What does that matter now? Don't you see, everything's wrong — everything —"

He was startled to hear his voice break, a sob catch in his throat. He was surprised when Lorna Cellman came and took his arm, flashing a look over her shoulder to his father.

"Let me talk to him, Eldridge. Go ahead with the work and I'll be back in a few minutes."

She propelled Ryan gently from the room and outside to the patio where they could be alone and the sound of the sea was oddly soothing.

"You've had a bad time of it, haven't you?" she asked gently.

He was surprised that she seemed so warm and friendly. He had never once thought of her like this, and her voice seemed to open the door and in a moment he found himself telling her everything, desperately needing to tell someone. She listened closely and murmured sympathetic words.

"I'm sure there's a logical explanation for all of this," she said. "There's just been some crazy mix-up. It happens every day, Ryan. There's so much red tape to everything. You know, I met Tania and I liked her."

"Did you? Did you really?" Ryan asked. "I don't think Dad did."

"Your father is reserved and he seldom says what he really thinks. I remember Tania so well that last day. I was working with your father. She was wearing that pretty little blue dress and a locket —"

Ryan lifted his head. "You remember the locket?"

"Yes. It was very unusual. I asked her about it. She gave me some vague answer about it being a gift from someone. Did you give it to her, Ryan?"

"No. She always wore it, always had it with her, but she never wanted to show me what was inside. I thought that strange."

"Perhaps the picture of an old flame," Lorna said. "And probably there was nothing at all. She liked to create a little mystery about herself — I think it was part of her charm. By the way, did you keep the locket or —"

Ryan shook his head. "No. I didn't even think about it until — afterwards. But I don't think it was on her when they found her. She must have lost it when she fell. . . ."

"Ryan, you simply have to go on — you have to pull yourself together. Your father has high hopes for you, even if he doesn't voice them. Someday, he'll want you to take over —"

He let Lorna's words drift over his head. His weary, numbed brain had fastened on the missing locket and suddenly he was obsessed with the need to have it, to hold it in his hand, to open it for the first time and see whose picture Tania had carried close to her heart.

It had to be down there in the rocks where she had fallen. He had never been able to go near the place — but, yes, the locket was surely there!

19

Lᴇᴇ ᴡᴀs ᴅᴏᴢɪɴɢ, stretched out in the shade of his little hideaway. He had been dreaming of Marcia, and he awakened with a start, feeling uneasy. Marcia had been very cool the last few days, barely glancing at him, avoiding the garage, and by her very indifference, she was showing him that she was still angry.

After the Sunday outing with Ryan, they'd had a row, their first, and he had been a little startled to learn how hotheaded and stubborn she could be. But it bothered him; in fact, it worried him. He liked Marcia and he hated it that things were wrong between them. He kept telling himself that he shouldn't have been surprised that this had happened. In the final outing, their differences had to tell.

He came to attention, listening. Did he hear someone coming? Maybe Marcia had finally gotten over her mad. He leaped to his feet and called out her name. Then to his embarrassment, he saw it wasn't Marcia at all but Jan Travis, Midge at her heels.

"Oh!"

"Ah, so we've discovered your hideout," Jan said with a laugh.

He felt himself blush and he knew that Jan had

perfectly well heard the name he'd called out, but she was discreetly ignoring it.

"Lee, will you go swimming with me?" Midge said.

It seemed an easy way out of an awkward situation, and he blessed the child for it.

"Why not? A dip in the ocean would feel good right now. How about you, Jan?"

"I'm not much of a swimmer. I'll watch from the beach."

Lee snatched up his beach towel and with Midge's small hand nestled in his, he led the way down the rocks and out to the ocean.

At the water's edge, they left their beach towels with Jan, and then with a laugh, Midge was off and running. Without her glasses, Midge looked less owlish, but she squinted in the sun and perhaps did not see too well. Lee cut the water with his arms, marveling at the new strength he'd been finding lately, and for nearly half an hour, he played games with Midge in the water, making her laugh.

At last they waded out to the beach where Jan waited for them. Both of them were tired now, and Lee stretched out on the towel, face to the sun. Midge stood over him, dripping water.

"Can I snuggle, Lee?"

"Snuggle?"

"You know — snuggle —"

He laughed as the little girl lay down close to him, and after a moment, he extended his arm and gave it to her for a pillow. She nestled so close that he could smell the sea water in her hair and feel her breath against his face. He looked at Jan and saw a softness come to her eyes. Midge promptly fell asleep and he didn't want to move his arm even after it began to feel numb. Still, it was a nice sensation to have a child curled beside him, one arm wrapped around his neck, as if to keep him there beside her forever.

"She adores you, Lee," Jan said in a quiet voice. "She talks about you all the time."

Lee laughed. "I don't know why."

"She needs a man in her life."

"But doesn't Carl Hanson —"

"From what Midge has told me, he was never an affectionate person, or Mrs. Hanson either, and the child is starved for love."

"What a rotten shame —" Lee said through gritted teeth.

"Do you know the situation at the Hanson house?"

"Yes, Sara told me," Lee said.

He had been appalled and sick at heart. Neither he nor Sara could truly believe the Hansons would desert Midge, but when he'd talked to Mark Williams about it later, Mark had given him a long look and shook his head.

"You don't know people like the Hansons, Lee. You've a wide streak of honesty and decency in you — but I'm not so sure about the Hansons. I hate people like that!"

Lee looked at Midge cradled in his arm and in that moment hated them too.

"I've thought of talking to Mrs. Hanson," Jan was saying. "But what business is it of mine? How can I go knock on her door and say she's not being fair to the child, that she's thinking only of herself?"

"You can't," Lee agreed.

"I should be used to such things, I suppose," Jan said. "Teaching school, I see so many children who get a short stick at home, parents who have no time for them, who simply show no interest, broken homes — all sorts of things."

"Sara told me you were trying to get a teaching job at Vincent."

"Yes. I'm waiting to hear, but no luck yet."

"Herb would love it if you stayed."

"He'd get terribly spoiled," she laughed. "But I'd like to spoil him a little."

Lee shaded his eyes so he could get a better look at Jan. The sun had worked its magic since she'd come here. She had tanned a golden brown and her black hair was glossy. There was a brightness in her eyes, but he wasn't sure which color dominated; were they more green and brown or were they gray and brown? He couldn't tell. But her smile was always so warm, so nice. There was a gentle kindness about her, but more than that, something seemed hidden deep inside. Now and then a little glow of it came through. Was it an unanswered passion, a longing?

"You came looking for me," he said. "Was there something special you wanted?"

"Grandpa told me you're a good mechanic. I hate to ask, but he insisted that you wouldn't mind. It's my car. There's something wrong with it."

"I see. I'd be glad to take a look at it."

"I know it's an imposition. I could take it to Vincent and ask Mark Williams about it."

"Let me have a look first. I don't mind at all. Why don't I come down this evening?"

She seemed pleased. "Good. That's very nice of you, Lee."

Midge began to stir and after a moment, she opened her eyes and sat up quickly, wondering for a moment where she was.

"Oh, hi, Lee," she grinned.

"Hi, princess."

Lee gave her a bear hug and then she was off and running, shouting for him to come in the water again.

"Show me how far you can swim and then I'll come," Lee said.

He was suddenly reluctant to leave Jan. It was pleasant beside her and he watched as she let a handful of sand sift through her fingers. A gull cried overhead and the sky was brilliantly blue. On the horizon a sailboat tipped in the breeze and the moment held, burning itself into his memory. He knew it would stay there a long time and he would remember Jan sitting there in the sun, smiling, her eyes warm and dancing with tiny lights.

Then Midge was back and after another brief swim, Jan said she must be getting home. Midge went with her, leaving him alone, and the day suddenly became empty, the surf lost its magic and the sun slid behind a cloud.

Suddenly, he didn't want to linger on the beach any longer. He gathered his things from the ledge and started back to Windmere. Before going to the cottage, he looked inside the garage. Marcia's car was gone.

"Ho!"

He looked up to see Wally Chadwick.

"Have you seen Marcia, Lee?"

"Not all day, and her car's gone. She must be out."

Wally gave him a meaningful look. "Something wrong?"

Lee gave him a twisted smile. "Why do you ask?"

"I'm not blind, you know. I know you and Marcia have a little thing going. I know that something's happened too. She's been in a real tiff for days."

"Maybe it's just as well," Lee said. "I knew it wasn't going to work. I tried to tell her from the beginning."

Wally smiled. "You're forgetting something, Lee. Marcia has a mind of her own and even though she's angry at you now, it doesn't really mean anything. She can be a handful, I know."

Lee shook his head. He didn't really want to talk about Marcia. Thinking about Jan's car, he began gathering a few tools he might need and putting them into a small box. After a time, Wally strolled away. Lee was just about to go to the cottage and change out of his damp swimming trunks when he heard Marcia's car on the drive. She always drove too fast, especially on the narrow, winding lane, and with a screech of brakes, she came charging into her parking slot in the garage.

She saw him at once, got out with a slam of the door and glowered at him.

"Where were you all day?" she demanded. "I came looking for you and you weren't here."

Lee set his jaw. "I was on the beach most of the time."

"Oh, really?"

"You already knew that, didn't you?"

"I saw you with Jan. I *saw* you! It looked real, real cozy. You're out playing cute with Jan Travis while I'm catching hell from Dad because I've been seeing you every chance I get!"

Lee swallowed hard. Wally had not told him this, but Lee wished he had. He might have been better prepared for it; even though he had known it would happen sooner or later, it caught him off guard now.

"What about your father, Marcia?"

"He told me to cool it with you. I didn't tell him that I'd already decided you were impossible!"

Lee gave her a cool smile. "I see. What else?"

"I told Daddy I'd do as I pleased."

Lee laughed shortly. "Yes, I can imagine you did. You like to have things your own way, don't you?"

At the same time, Lee felt a coldness in the pit of his stomach. He could smell doom. Chadwick had the perfect excuse for firing him now, and it would probably happen, just when everything was so perfect. Why hadn't he used his head, why had he let this happen in the first place?

"I knew it wouldn't work, Marcia," he said with a sigh. "I tried to tell you that —"

"You don't *want* it to work!"

He closed his eyes for a moment, trying to think what to say, how to make her understand.

"Marcia, don't say things like that. So, okay, I locked horns with Ryan. Why shouldn't I? I have a little pride too, you know. All I wanted that Sunday night was to pay for my own girl's dinner — is that so terrible?"

Marcia stared at him for a moment. "I suppose not," she said in a low voice.

"Okay, then."

Her blue eyes were rimmed with tears and in a moment, she had flung herself against him. Gingerly, he held her, bewildered and uneasy. She kissed him anxiously and he laughed.

"I do think you should be more careful about that, Marcia. If your father saw us now, he'd fire me on the spot and we'd never see each other again."

"That's not true. I'd go with you. I'd follow you to the ends of the earth. I'd scrub floors for you and cook and do all those things women are supposed to do for the man they love —"

He smiled at her and let her think he believed it. But Marcia often got carried away. She had no idea what she was really saying.

He sent her on her way at last and listened to the sound of her steps, heard a door open and close and knew she had stepped back into the world of the Chadwicks.

With a sigh, he finished putting his tools in the box. By then, he heard Sara calling to him and he left the garage and went to the cottage.

"Jan was looking for you earlier today. Did she find you?" Sara asked.

"Yes. I'm going down to the lighthouse this evening to work on her car. Want to come along?"

Sara shook her head. "Not this time."

They had supper together and then Lee left for the lighthouse.

Jan was waiting for him. Herb sat on the porch puffing at his pipe and "taking his leisure," as he called it.

Lee wanted to look at the car before darkness fell, and it didn't take him long to pinpoint the trouble.

"You have a bad sparkplug wire, Jan," he said.

She had come to lean against the fender to watch him work, her dark hair lifting in the evening breeze. There was a scent about her he had noticed before. He wasn't good about such things, but he thought it was jasmine.

"Will it cost much?" she asked.

"No. Usually if they replace one wire they replace the whole set. I can get what's needed at Mark's the next time I'm in town, and it won't take long to install."

"I appreciate this, Lee. I'm afraid I don't know much about such things. I fixed a pitcher of lemonade. Why don't we have some?"

They joined Herb on the porch. He was full of stories tonight. He seemed more mellow every day, and Lee knew it was Jan's influence. Lee leaned back and listened to Herb spinning his tales, the insects hammering at the screen door, the surf a soft shushing sound, and now and then, there was the faraway clang of a bell buoy coming on the wind.

He stayed much longer than he had intended. It was getting late and he said he must go.

"I could drive you back," Jan said. "If you think the car will hold up that distance."

"I'll go by the beach; it's quicker that way."

He wanted to ask her to walk with him part way as she had the other night but decided against it. He called goodnight and walked away. He stopped once to look back. They had gone inside the lighthouse, but Jan was silhouetted in the doorway, a slim figure of a girl who was startlingly different from Marcia. He had enjoyed the evening and he felt at home with Jan and her grandfather. With Marcia, he had often felt as if he were walking on eggs. He had never known when she might flare up. In the back of his mind where good sense dwelled, he had always known he did not belong in the Chadwicks' world.

Jan's world was different.

20

THE MARYBELLE was back! Sunday morning, as Tom looked out to the sea, he saw it anchored in the same spot where it had been before. He searched out his glasses and quickly focused on it, but as usual he was rewarded with the sight of very little activity. The Thorntons were certainly taking an extended vacation!

Tom's lips set at the thought. It was more than a vacation, and he'd stake his life on that fact. He put the glasses aside and went to make some coffee. While he waited for the percolator to do its work, he used the binoculars again, scanning the beach and dwelling for a long time on the rocks below the Chadwick house.

"I'll be damned —"

Ryan Chadwick was there, searching methodically, paying particular attention to a certain area where Tom knew Tania had come to rest after her terrible fall. Tom's hands were trembling and it was hard to hold the glasses steady. His eyes burned and his arms ached from holding them in one position so long.

Then as he watched, he saw Ryan straighten and shake his head with despair. A moment later he seemed to abandon his search and disappeared toward the direction of the house.

Tom lowered his glasses, thinking. Then he went to the phone and soon had his father on the long distance line.

"It's been two weeks since you called, Tom," his father said. "I was getting anxious."

"If there had been any news, I would have been in touch," Tom replied.

"Then there's still nothing?"

"No."

His father coughed on the other end of the line.

"Dad, you are all right?" Tom asked anxiously.

"I've been a little under the weather," he admitted.

"What is it?"

"Just a cold, I think. You know how summer colds are, a real nuisance."

"You're taking care of yourself, aren't you? Have you seen the doctor? Maybe you should have Mrs. Darwin make an appointment for you."

"Don't fuss, boy; I'm fine."

They talked a few minutes longer and Tom suggested he come home for a few days.

"Better not. Stay right there and stop worrying about me; I'll get along," his father said.

"I'll call again soon," Tom promised.

They said goodbye and hung up, but there was a new worry inside Tom's head now. His father hadn't sounded natural. He was no longer a strong man since the accident, and even a minor illness could easily develop into something major.

Later that morning, Tom decided to take a walk. With a camera slung over his shoulder, he started out. He had explored most of the beach in the immediate area, but there were still narrow roads he had not walked and patches of trees he had not investigated.

The sun was hazy, not especially ideal for taking pictures, but he had special film and a high-powered lens in his camera bag.

As he tramped away from the house on Widow's Point, he thought of Sara. Her very name rippled along his nerves and he knew how much he had come to love her. He only wished she loved him as much. But he was sure she didn't. She seemed uncertain, confused, unwilling to commit herself. As she had phrased it to him once, "It's a bridge I have to cross, I know. I'm just not ready yet."

Something was holding her back, and he was afraid he knew what it was. Jerry Lydell, without a doubt! She was taken with Ryan Chadwick too, but he did not really concern himself with that. Sara felt compassion for Ryan, not much more. He *hoped* it was nothing more! Ryan Chadwick was poison; everything he touched went sour. Like Tania falling over the cliff — poor, sweet, beautiful Tania.

Despite a hazy sun, the day was warm, and Tom pushed north from Widow's Point, going farther than he ever had before. The houses were scattered here, and there was practically no beach. He focused his camera on the shoreline, using a telephoto lens, and he was surprised to find a dock below.

He decided to investigate. There was brush and a

tangle of dwarfed trees, but if someone had been using the dock, there would be some telltale sign of a path down to the water.

He could see nothing. He was about to give it up as a bad idea when he heard someone coming. Instinctively, he shrank out of sight. He was startled to see Wally Chadwick, and immediately — almost automatically — he began to photograph his actions.

Wally often took long walks — everyone knew that — but this was a good distance from Windmere. Tom was about to call to him when he saw Wally come to a surprised halt. It took Tom a moment to see what it was that Wally had found. Cleverly hidden with branches cut from the nearby trees was a small blue sedan.

Tom quickly surmised it belonged to the Thorntons on the *Marybelle*. Perhaps they came to shore, used the car when they needed supplies and then hid it again when they came back. But why the camouflage? Did they fear thieves or vandals?

Tom saw that Wally was now examining the car carefully and making a note of the license plate number. Then he put the branches back as he had found them, brushed his hands with a silk handkerchief and left, going in the opposite direction. When Tom was certain Wally had gone and would not see him, he came out of hiding. He wanted to look at the car himself, but thunder had been rumbling for the last few minutes and the skies had changed from hazy to dark, angry clouds. A storm was brewing, and it was a long way back to Widow's Point.

He walked as swiftly as he could, but by the time he neared the house, the rain had started. He ran the last several yards, but was drenched by the time he got inside. He changed into dry clothes and went down to the darkroom in the basement.

A few minutes later, he was examining the pictures of Wally and the car. It did not look as if Wally was merely curious. It had a tone of being more than that. Tom went to get the envelope out of the closet, and on the kitchen table he spread the photos, the ones of the Chadwick house, the rocks where Tania had fallen, the people who had appeared at different times at the railing on the Chadwick patio, the *Marybelle* and a blurry and very poor picture of the Thorntons. To all of those he now added the ones he'd just taken of Wally Chadwick.

It was a new and interesting piece in the jigsaw puzzle.

Sara had been putting the finishing touches to Herb's portrait and since the day was rainy and damp, she was working inside. The phone rang, and even before she reached out to answer it, she felt it was going to be Jerry.

"Hello, darling."

"You sound in a cheerful mood," she said.

"Why not?" Jerry asked. "I have great news."

"About Cloud Nine?"

"Yes. World Travel has decided to go ahead with the series — and Sara, they want *you* to do the work!"

Sara gripped the telephone tighter. "I see."

"You'll do a layout for all the countries where they offer tours — Spain, Italy, England, even one to Russia — and you'll do them all! Do you know what this means, Sara?"

Despite herself, Sara was suddenly caught up in a web of excitement.

"It sounds like a challenge," she said. "And hard work."

"You can do it, Sara."

"Jerry, I'm not sure I'm interested."

There was a stunned silence on the end of the line. "I can't believe this! You aren't going to let this slip by, are you?"

"Could I do the work here at Windmere?"

"Absolutely not. The World Travel people want to work closely with you on this, step by step — this is a big project, Sara."

Sara licked her dry lips. If she took on the rest of the Cloud Nine series, she would have to leave here — probably very soon.

"When do they want the project started?"

"In about two months. But we have to have your decision in a couple of weeks. We can't give you any longer than that to make up your mind, Sara. If you don't want to do it, we'll have to find someone else."

"Two weeks —"

"Why don't you come to New York and we'll discuss it. I'll go over all the details with you — you'll see how important it is —"

She knew that New York represented a trap. Once she got in Jerry's office, back in her old surroundings and with Jerry giving her the hard sell, her good sense would begin to fade away. She would find herself caught up in the rat race again — but did she want that?

"If I didn't have to come so soon, I might be interested," she said. "Maybe in September —"

"Not a chance, Sara. I'll expect a call from you *two weeks* from today with your decision — and sooner if possible."

"All right, Jerry."

"And darling, don't be foolish. Don't throw away this one big opportunity. It could mean so much to your career here at the agency. Now promise me you'll give it careful thought. And while you're thinking about it, remember one thing. I love you. I want you back. We're right together, Sara. We belong here —"

Sara hung up thoughtfully. Two weeks to decide what to do! Another bridge to cross. She knew she had not heard the last from Jerry. He would give her a few days to mull it over and then in sly little ways he would begin to pressure her. He could do it in such a charming way. Worst of all, it was hard to deny him. He brought out the fighter in her, the desire to get ahead.

The summer was going fast. It was the first of August, and she had never truly looked beyond September. It was time to start doing that. It was still raining, but she went out and down to the beach anyway. She found a private spot among the rocks and sat down there, arms wrapped around her legs, knees pulled up under her chin. The rain was warm and refreshing against her face. The mist rolled in from the cove and she watched the thunder clouds crashing their heads together and felt the lightning cut through her like a clean flash of fire.

The sea was as stormy as she was inside. Uncertain, unsettled, searching, pounding away at the shore as if in search for peace. Tom loved her and wanted to marry her. She was drawn to him and when she was with him, she felt more complete than she ever had before. But there were nagging doubts in her mind too. The hidden package of photos she'd found had built an uneasiness inside her. Why was he spying on the Chadwicks? Why couldn't she simply ask him about it?

The storm began to ebb and, drenched to the skin, hair streaming from the rain, she went back to the house, changed into dry things and towel-dried her hair. But she felt clean and her head was clear. She looked at Herb's unfinished portrait and reached for a tube of paint.

By the time the day was over and Lee came to the house for supper, she had finished it.

"What do you think, Lee?"

"You have him exactly, down to the twinkle of his eye and the untied shoelaces."

She laughed. "Do you think he'd like to have it?"

"He'd be a fool to turn down a picture like that, and if he doesn't want it, I know Jan will. I'm going down there in a little while. Why don't you come along?"

"Don't you have to meet Chadwick's train?"

Lee shook his head. "He didn't go to New York

today. Have you seen him lately? The man looks sick."

"Is he?"

"I don't know. Maybe he's just worn out. I've seen a light in the den 'way past two o'clock for several nights now. And when Lorna's there, they really dig in. Elsa says they hardly stop to eat."

"Why are you going down to the lighthouse? I thought you were there last night."

"I was. I'm doing some work on Jan's car and I got the parts today."

Jan and Herb were on the porch when they reached the lighthouse and Herb spied the canvas under Sara's arm at once.

"What's that?"

Sara laughed and carefully removed the brown paper she had put around it for protection.

"The paint's hardly set up yet, so be careful of it, Herb. Here you are —"

Jan gasped with pleasure when she saw it and Herb straightened with a blink of his eyes.

"By golly, Sara, that's mighty good!" he said.

"If you want it, it's yours," Sara said.

"But, Sara, you could sell this," Jan protested.

"I'd like you to have it."

"That's very generous and before Grandpa can say a word, *I* accept!" Jan laughed.

"Wait until Wally sees it," Herb crowed. "He's going to be green with envy!"

"Have you seen Wally today?" Sara asked.

"No."

"Eldridge is ill. I just wondered if it was anything serious —"

Herb frowned. "I know Wally's been worried about his brother for some time now. I don't mean to tell tales out of school, but Wally says his brother has stuck his neck out too far this time, whatever that means."

"Maybe it's not so easy being a millionaire after all," Sara sighed.

Herb held a match to his pipe. "You know, things haven't been really right down there since that girl died. It sort of put a blot on things, if you know what I mean."

"Yes," Sara murmured. "Even I get an eerie feeling about it now and then —"

Lee left Sara and Herb talking while he took his tool box to the garage. Jan went with him.

"You can help, Jan. I'll need you to hold the light."

In the garage, Lee raised the hood of Jan's car, reached for a trouble light that Herb kept handy, snapped it on and gave it to Jan.

"How was your day?" she asked.

"I kept busy working on Marcia's car."

"Oh."

Lee lifted his head. "She drives it like the devil and it's a touchy machine. It's hard to keep it running smoothly."

Jan grew quiet for a moment and Lee wished he had not mentioned Marcia's name. Then she asked about Midge.

"Haven't seen her," Lee said with a frown. "Even

though it was rainy most of the day, I thought she'd come by as usual."

"I've an awful feeling that things are coming to a head at the Hanson house. I suspect, for one purpose or another, they only took Midge in the first place to hold together a shaky marriage."

"It makes me boiling mad whenever I think about it. Midge is an innocent child and if they've merely used her —"

"I feel so helpless," Jan said. "And I've grown to love her."

"Me too."

He worked silently for awhile, finding that a wrench in his hand and a motor to fix had a calming effect. When he had finished at last, he put the hood down and cleaned his hands on an old rag.

"I have the new sparkplug wires in, but tomorrow night I'd like to give it a tune-up. It needs it."

"Lee, I feel guilty taking so much of your spare time —"

"Don't be silly. I'm glad to do it."

"I sometimes think that you should be a garage man, not a chauffeur."

"Mark Williams has it made. I wish I had a place like his."

"Did you know he wants to sell out and go west?"

Lee nodded. "Yes. I've heard him talk about it. But it takes capital to buy a place like that. I have a good job at the Chadwicks'. I'd probably be a fool to consider leaving it. Besides, I have no capital."

"It's hard sometimes to make changes."

"What about you? Have you heard anything from the school at Vincent?"

"As a matter of fact, I heard some time ago, but I didn't want to tell Grandpa just yet. There's an opening if I want it. I haven't made up my mind that I *should* stay, but I can't wait much longer to tell them. It's irregular as it is — contracts are usually signed in the spring, before school lets out — but there were some unusual circumstances at Vincent . . ."

"I wish you would stay!"

They looked at each other for a moment and then Lee cleared his throat and began to gather his tools.

"Why did you say that?" Jan asked.

"It's nice having you here, and Herb would be the happiest man in the world —"

"Yes, Grandpa *is* hoping I'll stay on, but the winters here are long and lonely —"

"They wouldn't have to be," Lee said. "I'm just up the beach. We could have some great times together."

"But what about Marcia? I know about the two of you —"

Lee felt the heat come to his face and he reached out to snap off the light so Jan couldn't see the blush that came to his cheeks. She had never mentioned Marcia to him before. They had avoided the subject purposely.

"Are you in love with her, Lee?"

"She's a nice girl, different than you might think —"

"That isn't what I asked."

She seemed very close in the darkness. When he didn't answer, she turned to leave. Her arm brushed his and without thinking, he reached out to stop her.

"Don't go, Jan."

He turned her to him and in a moment, she came into his arms. He kissed her for the first time, a gentle, surprised kind of kiss.

"We'd better get back," she said.

"Jan —"

"Don't say anything. You don't have to."

"But Jan —"

She walked out of the garage, and in a moment he followed her.

Before he and Sara went home, Jan made coffee and they sat around the table talking. Lee found he couldn't keep his eyes off Jan. At first, she seemed to avoid his glance, a flush coming to her cheeks. Then she gave him a smile filled with sunshine, and when it came time to go, he went with a feeling of reluctance.

21

THE NEXT MORNING, Sara and Lee lingered over breakfast. Lee still had not been summoned to take Chadwick to the train and they assumed he was not going. Lee seemed in a thoughtful, quiet mood and Sara suspected it had to do with Jan Travis, but she didn't approach the subject. They were having a final cup of coffee when Tom suddenly appeared outside the door. Sara took one look at his face and knew something was wrong.

"What is it, Tom?"

"It's my father. I talked to him yesterday and he was not feeling well. The woman that looks after him, Mrs. Darwin, just phoned me. To make a long story short, I'm going home for a few days. Sara, I'd like you to come with me."

"What?"

"Cleveland's about five hundred miles from here — it's a long drive, but we could drive it straight through."

"You mean you want to leave *now*?"

"That's what I had in mind," Tom replied. "I know this is sudden and I'm sure you think I'm a little crazy, but I want you to meet Dad and I just don't want to wait another minute before leaving."

"How long will you be gone?"

"That depends on Dad, of course. A couple of days, anyway. If I see I must stay longer, I'll send you home on a plane."

She didn't know what to say, but she was aware of the desperate way Tom stood there waiting for her to make up her mind.

"Please, Sara?"

"All right. But you'll have to give me time to pack a bag."

"I'll come by in about an hour. Will that do?"

"Yes."

Tom disappeared as quickly as he had arrived. Lee went to get her suitcase out of the closet and snapped it open for her.

"Maybe I shouldn't have agreed to go."

Lee laughed. "You never could say no to anybody that needed help, and poor Tom looked like his world had caved in."

"He's devoted to his father."

It was the most hurried packing she'd ever done, but she wouldn't need many things. She was ready when Tom came for her. With a quick hug, she told Lee goodbye.

"Take care. Have a safe journey," he said.

Tom put Sara's things inside his car, waved to Lee, and they were soon leaving Windmere behind.

"What's wrong with your father?" Sara asked.

"Pneumonia. Dad's just not strong anymore and

lately, things have been too much for him. He's lost heart, I'm afraid."

They reached Vincent and pushed on. Soon they were driving on the interstate highway toward Philadelphia, and from there they would push west and a little north to Cleveland.

Tom had little to say as the car hummed along. He seemed lost in another world. Finally, Sara suggested a cup of coffee.

"Or an early lunch," she said. "You look so tired, Tom."

"I didn't sleep much last night. I had this awful hunch about Dad — and this morning when Mrs. Darwin called —"

"I'm sure it's not as serious as you think."

"Maybe driving was a mistake. We should have taken a plane."

"Connections are bad out of Vincent, and in the long run you will probably get there just about as fast this way."

"I suppose you're right."

They stopped for lunch, and after they'd eaten, Sara suggested she take the wheel for awhile. Tom began to talk nervously, seeming to want to tell her about his life in Cleveland, his work there, the kind of father he had.

"You'll like Dad and he'll like you," he said.

"Can you be so sure of that?"

Tom smiled. "As well as I know the sun will come up in the morning."

Gradually, Tom stopped talking and dozed off. Sara

kept her eyes on the highway and drove at a steady pace. What strange roads life took one down! She had never dreamed this morning that she would be doing anything like this before night.

The miles ground away under the wheels, even at the new slower speed limits, and about sunset they stopped for supper. Tom calculated the time they would reach Cleveland.

"Eleven o'clock, I'd say, or possibly even sooner."

He guessed it about right. They reached Cleveland at ten-thirty and Tom drove to the suburbs. When they came to a modest-looking house with green shutters and a ramp built up to the porch to accommodate a wheelchair, he told her they had arrived.

A light was still burning inside, but the door was locked and Tom rang the bell. A small, short woman came to let him in.

"Oh, Tom, you finally got here."

"Hello, Mrs. Darwin. How is he?"

"Your father is still awake. I told him you were coming and he refused to go to sleep. He had an uneasy day, but he's feeling better now. The doctor said he would have to go to the hospital tomorrow if he wasn't any better, so he's putting up a fight."

"That sounds like him," Tom said. "Mrs. Darwin, this is a friend of mine, Sara Denning. I think I'll go see Dad now. Sara, make yourself at home. Mrs. Darwin, you might fix some coffee or something —"

Tom disappeared toward another part of the house, and Sara was left in a comfortable living room while Mrs. Darwin made noises in the kitchen. Sara looked around with interest. It was an average room with furniture a little worn and arranged so a wheelchair could move about easily. A half-finished jigsaw puzzle was spread out on a card table. There were a stack of books beside it and several newspapers, things a confined person would make use of.

Sara spied a framed photograph sitting on a bookshelf, and she had just gone to look at it when Mrs. Darwin called to her. The girl in the picture was young with dark hair and a pretty smile. She looked vaguely familiar. Mrs. Darwin appeared in the doorway.

"The coffee's ready. Would you like to come to the kitchen —"

"Of course."

Sara could hear the murmur of Tom's voice talking with his father. The kitchen was pleasant and clean, and the coffee smelled good. She accepted a cup gratefully. The long trip was beginning to catch up with her.

"I'm glad you've come with Tom," Mrs. Darwin was saying. "It's such a lonely drive all by yourself."

"He's so worried."

"Tom's a good boy," Mrs. Darwin said. "One of the best."

Sara drank her coffee and in a few minutes, Tom appeared. She could see relief in his face and he gave her a smile.

"Dad says he's feeling much better and he even bawled me out for coming," Tom said with a grin.

"If he's getting cranky, it's a sure sign he's better," Mrs. Darwin replied.

"I'll want to talk with the doctor the first thing in the morning," Tom said.

He helped himself to the coffee and joined Sara at the table. Mrs. Darwin scurried away when she heard a bell ringing.

"Dad's signal that he wants something," Tom explained.

"You're not so worried now. I'm glad."

"I think I got a little panicky. Dad's all I have left."

Mrs. Darwin was back in a few minutes and told them that Tom's father wanted to meet Sara the first thing in the morning.

"Actually, he wanted to see you now, but he needs to rest. I have the guest room ready. Your room too, Tom. You both look tired," Mrs. Darwin said.

"It's been a long day," Tom replied.

The next morning after a restful night's sleep, Sara had just finished her breakfast when Mrs. Darwin told her that Barclay was expecting her. Tom took her to see him.

She found the bedroom cheerful, and there were fresh flowers from the garden. The man in bed had fierce dark brows, a heavy face and the same bone structure as Tom. When he smiled, the resemblance was even more noticeable. In his day, he had been a strong man, but he seemed weak and withered now.

"So, you're Sara," he said.

"Hello, Mr. Barclay."

"Tom's been telling me about you, over the phone and in his letters — now he's brought you all the way out here. It must mean something."

Sara's cheeks went warm and she glanced at Tom, who gave her a quick smile. "Dad knows me pretty well," he said.

"I've heard about you too," Sara said.

"Tom, go away and leave us alone. I want to talk to this pretty girl by myself."

Tom lifted his brows, but after a moment left the room. Barclay gave Sara a long, long look.

"I can trust you," he said. "You have an honest face and I know you're a fine person or Tom wouldn't love you so much, Sara. I have to tell you something."

She leaned a little closer and saw the serious light in his eyes.

"I'm not long for this world. Oh, I'm better today, but I know — a man gets to be my age, he senses things. Tom's going to be all alone soon. I'll rest easy if I know he has a woman like you."

She swallowed hard. What on earth had Tom told him? She groped for the right words, but as it was, she didn't need to say anything as Barclay rushed on, talking now in rapid spurts, as if exceedingly eager to have it all said.

"He takes things to heart. If he says he loves you, he means it, Sara, and he'll love you till the day he dies. He's like that. I'm glad he's found you. I worry about him — not right for a man to be alone — especially when I'm at fault. He doesn't want to leave me —

now, isn't that ridiculous? I'm knocking on seventy years old and I've had my taste of life — I want him to have his."

"I'm sure he will."

"With you?"

She met the older man's eyes and even though he was sick, perhaps seriously so, she found she could not lie to him.

"I don't truly know. I'm fond of him, and yesterday, driving here, I felt I knew him more and more every hour. But —"

Barclay closed his eyes. "I see."

"I try not to rush into things. I want to be sure."

"Smart. You're smart. And very pretty and talented too, I hear. No wonder Tom fell for you, hook, line and sinker."

He seemed to be tiring so Sara got up to leave him to his rest. He clutched at her hand.

"Sara, we've had some bad times, Tom and I. But you're like a ray of sunshine. Bless you for coming."

She squeezed his hand, gave him a smile and then slipped out of the room in search of Tom.

He wasn't in the living room, and she was about to go to the kitchen to look for him when she noticed that the picture she had seen last night on the bookshelf was no longer there. Strange!

Had Tom spirited it away? Why? Was it the photo of an old flame, someone he had not told her about? The girl had been pretty, had even looked familiar. It was one more strange thing to add to the others she had stored in her head about Tom, like a closet full of unexplained photos, and the tendency to spy on others on the beach. Now he was hiding a picture of a pretty girl. None of it made sense, but it made her uneasy and, more than that, a little suspicious. Perhaps Tom Barclay was not what he seemed.

22

ELDRIDGE CHADWICK had returned to his New York office after a few days of illness at Windmere. He knew the illness could be attributed directly to nervous tension and fatigue, but he could not afford such luxuries just yet. So he had taken the seven-thirty train in as usual and had come home on the eight o'clock.

Lee met him with the limousine, and Chadwick had barely spoken to him. He was too tired to tend to the usual pleasantries and he frankly didn't care what Lee thought. He was weary to the bone, but within the next few days the nightmare would be over. The deal would be completed. He would meet with the officials in Washington, D.C., and as arranged, he would turn over Barstow's blueprints and specifications. The secrecy he'd been impelled to keep, the feeling that he was carrying a loaded bomb around in his briefcase, would finally be over.

The briefcase rested on his knees. It was never out of his sight these days, for inside it were all the blueprints and plans for Barstow's device, save one, the final plan they called Core Red that would link all the units together to make them workable. While the others were vastly important, Core Red was the key to all of it. Core Red would be delivered to him by Barstow himself, Eldridge would pay the inventor a cool three million dollars and Core Red would be his. Once it was turned over to the government, Eldridge knew that his three million dollars would soon be returned many times over.

He knew it was probably foolish to be carrying around the papers inside his briefcase, but he could not bring himself to leave them anywhere. Lately, his nerves ragged, he had imagined all sort of things. In New York, he thought one day he was being followed. He contemplated locking the papers in a bank vault or hiding them in his office, but of all the many plans he made, he quickly discarded them, one by one. The papers were safe only with him, in his hand, within his sight.

As Lee drove through the gates of Windmere and down the lane, Eldridge thought of Lorna. She would come tomorrow and stay until the transaction with Barstow was safely behind him. He wouldn't go to New York again until it had been done. He no longer felt safe in the city, for he trusted no one. But at Windmere, locked behind the gates, he felt more secure. He might even be able to relax. The long hard road was just about ended and he had pulled it off. He was ready to meet with Barstow — the money was in hand.

Windmere sat in the rosy hue of sunset and he admired it every time he saw it. The gate closed behind them with a satisfying clang and Eldridge found himself anticipating the sight of home, a good dinner, and the peace of the ocean.

Lee stopped at the front door of Windmere, leaping out to assist Chadwick. He found Lee agreeable, prompt and a conscientious worker. If only Marcia — Eldridge sighed. This was one of the things he had been letting get out of hand due to the pressing business of Core Red. But soon he would take steps to correct it.

"Thank you, Lee. I'll not need you any more this evening," he said.

"Yes, sir. Goodnight, sir."

Eldridge went inside the house and Elsa came to meet him, reaching out for the briefcase.

"Good evening, Mr. Chadwick," she said.

"I'll keep the briefcase," he said. "I'll be in my den for a while. How soon is dinner to be served?"

"Ten minutes," she said.

"Good."

He walked down the hall to the den, his office away from New York, and closed the door behind him. The briefcase was too large for the small wall safe he had here, but the desk was sturdy and had a good lock. There was a large bottom drawer that would accommodate the case, and he put it there, carefully locked the desk and put the key on the key ring with the one that opened the briefcase. Then he pocketed them both and did so with an air of relief. The keys would not leave his person until Barstow had come with Core Red.

A few minutes later, he went to have his dinner, and Wally gave him a long, hard look.

"You look as if you could drop in your tracks, Eldridge. You went back to work too soon."

"I'm fine," he insisted.

"Does that mean you've about wound up this big deal of yours?"

Eldridge gave his brother a brief smile. Wally had been curious about the whole affair but Eldridge had told him practically nothing. The only person who really knew what was going on was Lorna. He was glad now that he had confided in her, for it had taken some of the burden from his shoulders.

"Everything is well on its way, Wally. In another week, it will be over."

"Thank God!" Wally said. "Maybe you'll be yourself again."

Ryan came to the table with scarcely a word or a glance in his direction. Marcia arrived late, and he knew from one look at her pretty face that she was angry about something.

After dinner was over, Chadwick heard Ryan leave in his car. Wally was relaxing on the patio and Marcia had gone to her room with a slam of her door.

He went to see his daughter, knocking lightly.

"Marcia —"

"What do you want?"

"I'd like to speak with you for a few minutes."

Marcia opened the door at last and he stepped in. The room was fluffy and feminine, and coming here always gave him an odd feeling of delight. She was such a lovely girl, much as her mother had been at that age, when he had first known and courted her.

"You seemed unhappy at dinner," Eldridge said. "Is anything wrong?"

She gave him a stormy look from her blue eyes and she lifted her chin. "I can handle it."

"Well, I certainly hope so, but if I can be of help —"

She laughed in such a way that he guessed immediately that it had to do with Lee Denning. He had to bite his tongue to keep from saying anything. He could have told her that getting involved with Lee would lead to headaches as well as heartaches, but she was a strong-willed girl and she would not have listened anyway.

"It will soon be time for you to be thinking about going back to college," Eldridge said.

She made a face. "Daddy, that's weeks away!"

"But they have a way of slipping by. I've been thinking, once I have this business of mine all wound up, why don't we go somewhere? The three of us, you, Ryan and me. Maybe a short cruise or a quick trip to Europe. We haven't had a vacation together in years —"

She said nothing, but Eldridge could see that the idea left her cold.

"I think Ryan needs to get away from here. He's still grieving over Tania. A change of scene would be good for all of us," Eldridge said, appealing to her sympathy.

Marcia began to pace around the room, twisting a

hairbrush in her hands, then finally tossing it into a chair and moving to the window that looked out to the sea.

"I might as well tell you now, Dad; I'm not going back to college."

Eldridge stood very still, letting the words sink in, trying to evaluate them. "You *must* get your education, Marcia; you know how I feel about that."

"What do I need it for?"

"That was such a stupid question. I'll not even answer it."

"College is a bore. I don't want to go back and I *won't* go back."

Eldridge's head began to ache in earnest and he suddenly discovered that Mrs. Goddard's excellent meal was beginning to rest uneasily inside his stomach.

"Marcia, you can't mean that! You can't throw away the time you've already invested —"

"Everything's an investment to you, isn't it? Don't you know lots of the kids aren't finishing anymore? They start but they don't finish."

"And just what do you propose to do if you don't go back to school?"

Marcia's cheeks were flushed, and he saw that she was not going to tell him. There was a scheme hatching inside her head, but she intended to keep it there. It was not the first time he had encountered her stubbornness.

"Marcia, dear —"

"I won't tell you," she said. "Because I know you

wouldn't approve, I know what you'll say — and I'm in no mood for a fight tonight!"

"Nor am I," Eldridge said tiredly. "But we'll have to talk about this again."

She didn't reply. Eldridge said goodnight and left her. He went back to the den and stepped inside the darkened room.

"Oh!"

He started. Elsa was in the room.

"What on earth —"

"Sorry, Mr. Eldridge. I remembered the light bulb in this lamp was burned out and I came to put in a new one —"

He flipped on the ceiling light and Elsa stood there, looking frightened.

"You startled me, sir," she said. "I'll — I'll go and get the fresh bulb."

"Don't bother with it tonight, Elsa. I won't need that lamp anyway."

"As you say, sir. Goodnight."

Elsa hurried away, bumping a chair as she went. Eldridge shook his head. Elsa had been with them for several months now and had worked out well enough, but why must she bother in here when he was home? It irritated him, but he realized part of that was due to his own nervousness.

He saw Wally out on the patio and decided to join him. He liked his brother's cheerful company and right now he could do with a little of it.

Wally motioned to him to take a chair beside him and offered him one of the expensive cigars he sometimes smoked. Eldridge accepted it, even though he didn't really want it.

"Wally, you know my children pretty well. I suspect they even confide in you."

"Occasionally," Wally said.

"What's Marcia up to?"

Wally shook his head. "Don't know. I know she and Lee haven't been getting along too well lately. I don't know much more than that."

"She doesn't want to go back to school."

"Not surprised. She has a rebellious streak in her and she never did like college."

"How do I reach her; what do I say to her?"

"Well, my dear brother, that's exactly why I was rather glad that Esther and I never had any children. I would never have been able to guide them properly and I know it. But I've enjoyed yours. I've had the pleasure of them without the responsibility. You know me and responsibility. The two just never mixed."

"You're always degrading yourself, Wally. Why do you do that? It annoys me."

"When the brains were passed out in this family, you got them all, Eldridge. I'm only glad that the trust fund Dad set up for us has managed to keep my head above water — that and your generosity in letting me stay here all these years."

Eldridge rolled the cigar around in his fingers for a moment and scowled out into the darkness.

"Do you think you could teach me to loaf all day as you do?"

"Why do you ask?"

"When this thing is finished, I'm thinking of retiring from the business world. I'll put my affairs in the hands of a reliable broker and sit back and enjoy the rest of my days."

"Does that mean this big deal of yours will fix you up financially for the rest of your life?"

"For all of us," Eldridge replied. "I tell you that in confidence. It's the biggest thing I've ever dared touch. That's why it's so important."

"You've never told me much about it —"

"Couldn't. It's too hot, Wally. Top drawer secret stuff."

"My word, Eldridge, aren't you out of your league?"

Eldridge smiled. "Yes. Lorna certainly thought so, but it was the golden opportunity a man gets only once in his lifetime, if at all, and I couldn't let it pass me by."

Wally's cigar glowed red in the dark. "I hope you know what you're doing."

"I do," Eldridge said. "I'm home now until the deal is set. Lorna will be down tomorrow to help with the final details."

"You going to marry that woman?" Wally asked.

Eldridge was caught off guard by Wally's bluntness.

"She's a business associate, Wally, nothing more," he said, stammering a little.

Wally laughed. "I know better. Who do you think you're kidding?"

"I'm not young any more and Lorna's many years my junior — but I'll think about this later, after the deal is set."

The next day, Lorna arrived before noon, and Eldridge was very pleased to see her. He wanted his children to like her, but neither of them had ever truly warmed up to her. Well, it would take time, of course, he expected that. Perhaps if he could instigate a cruise or the trip to Europe, he could arrange to take Lorna along. Marcia and Ryan would get to know her then, and the trip would be good for them all.

He spent the day working with Lorna; much of the afternoon was used up by phone calls and ironing out time-consuming details.

"We're just about all set," Eldridge said. "I hope you're as glad as I am, Lorna."

She came to put a hand on his shoulder. "Ah, Eldridge, I only want what's right for you. You're such a good, dear man —"

He took her hand and held it to his lips for a moment.

"Thank you, my dear. In a few days, it will be all behind us and Barstow will be in the past. We will be able to forget."

"I wait for the day!"

That evening, Ryan was not at the dinner table, nor was Marcia. Lorna's face went white and she clenched her lips tightly. Wally made light of it.

"They're off on their own pursuits, that's all. Don't be offended, Lorna."

Lorna made no reply. Mrs. Goddard served them with a tight look on her face. She did not like nor approve of Lorna either. Eldridge found the whole business almost more than he could bear. He put his uneasiness down to nerves. The fifteenth of August was creeping up fast — D-Day for him, the day Barstow would come to Windmere with Core Red.

That night, long after he had retired, Eldridge still could not drop off to sleep. Against all good sense, he began to worry about the plans locked in the briefcase in the desk. He had checked earlier to see the case was there, safe and sound, and then had relocked the desk.

Still it nagged at him, and he put on his slippers and robe, picked up the keys from his dresser and went down the hall to the den. He snapped on a light and found the desk tightly locked. Still not satisfied, he pulled the briefcase from the drawer and tested the catches, making certain they were fastened. It was then he noticed the tiny little scratches around the locks. Could he have done that? It was very doubtful. The case was brand new. He had locked it only once, when he had put the papers inside. Then how did the scratches get there?

Frantic now, he fumbled with the key and unlocked the case. Perspiration dotted his forehead. He ripped open the case and was relieved to find the plans inside just as he had put them. Then he noticed that a corner of one of the blueprints had been bent down, as if someone had put them in the case in a big hurry — he knew the crease was new, that it had not been there when he had last handled the papers.

His stomach lurched. The room seemed to squeeze in on him. He relocked the case and carefully put it back in the drawer and locked the desk.

He was surely imagining it. The scratches, the fold

in the paper — everything was a part of his imagination. But if it wasn't — the coldness gripped him again. It would mean someone in his own household had been snooping, perhaps was even guilty of more than that —

Eldridge snapped off the light and put the room in darkness. He went to look out the window to the ocean and pressed his forehead to the cool glass, closing his eyes. What did he do now? Where did he turn? Whom did he trust?

23

SARA AND TOM stayed in Cleveland for three days, and in that time, Barclay made a rapid improvement and hospitalization was not necessary. On their last day, he managed to get up in his wheelchair for a little while and later Tom told Sara he had done it to impress upon them that they were no longer needed.

"Is it true? Is he that much better?" she asked.

"The doctor says so," Tom said. "I'll have to put my trust in him. I'll take you back to Windmere tomorrow. Will that do?"

"Yes, but I've enjoyed my stay here, Tom. It's been a pleasant change."

"I've enjoyed it too. I'll even go as far to say that I loved it — for a number of reasons. Mostly because I've had you to myself, away from the Chadwicks, your painting — everyone and everything. For these few days, you've been mine."

Tom had been sweet and thoughtful, and he had seen to it that she was not bored. His father rested a great deal and while he slept, Tom had shown her the city. He had saved his photographer's shop until last. Then on their final afternoon, he drove her there. Everything had been protected with dust covers and

Tom looked around him thoughtfully. "It's awfully stale in here."

"It's a very nice place."

"I had a good business. I've lost money by closing up, these summer months, but I wouldn't have missed the beach for the world."

"And you have your book ready to send in."

"Yes. That's something I always wanted to do. But the really important thing that happened was finding you, Sara."

He came to put his arms around her, and there among the dust covers and the backdrops he used for his portraits, he kissed her for a long moment. She nestled against him, her heart drawn two ways at one time. She knew she could not go on like this, loving him one moment, doubting him the next. But she could not bring herself to question him, at least not yet.

"You know something, Sara? I don't think I want to come back here."

"You mean you'd leave Cleveland for good?"

"Why couldn't I start a similar shop in Vincent? I admit the town's small, but there would still be graduation pictures, engagement and wedding sittings, those little toothless people who smile for their proud parents and all sorts of things — why couldn't I work there as well as here?"

"What about your father?"

"I'll take him to Vincent. The sea air might just be the ticket for him."

"Would he come?"

"Yes. I think so."

"Well, it sounds interesting, but that will be for you to decide."

Tom shook his head slowly. "No, darling, it will be for *you* to decide. Would you stay there with me? Would you marry me and be my love? You could paint; everyday you could drive down to the sea if you wanted — as long as you always came home to me."

"Tom —"

"We'd have the world in our pocket, Sara! In my spare time, I could take more pictures for another book and you could —"

"Don't, Tom. Please!"

She turned away, and her hands were cold and trembling. He was making it very difficult. How could she bring herself to question him in the face of this? How could she accuse him of being more than he seemed on the surface. Yet, she feared he was. Until she had all the answers about him —

"It's Jerry, isn't it? And your New York job. You're going to take that new assignment, aren't you?" he asked with despair in his voice.

"I don't know. I haven't decided. But I'll have to make up my mind soon."

"What can I say, darling? What more?"

She reached up and kissed him tenderly. "Nothing, Tom. Nothing more. I just need some time."

They left Cleveland the next day, getting an early start.

For the first hundred miles or so, Tom seemed to have little to say. He was lost in some deep thought, and Sara, too, found that now the pleasant interlude was over, she had to face up to a few things. She must decide about New York and the Cloud Nine series and she had to decide how she felt about Tom.

"Are you sorry you came?" Tom asked at last.

"I wouldn't have missed it for anything. I'd like to do a sketch of your father — from memory — and send it to him. Would he like that?"

"I have a feeling anything you gave him he'd treasure," Tom said. "He fell in love with you, just as I did."

They made good time on the trip back and had a late dinner in Vincent. Tom drove her to Windmere and left her at the cottage. Lee was not there.

"I'll see you tomorrow," Tom said. "Goodnight."

Sara had started to unpack when someone knocked at the door, and she was surprised to find Marcia.

"I saw Tom's car just driving away," Marcia said. "So I knew you were back."

"Come in and tell me what's been happening at Windmere since I've been away. Oh, how I've missed this place!"

Marcia came in but didn't sit down. She prowled the cottage restlessly, and Sara recognized all the little signs. Marcia's temper was simmering around the edges.

"What's Lee done now?" Sara asked.

Marcia spun about to face her. "He's been going down to the lighthouse nearly every evening. He says he's fixing Jan's car! Some excuse!"

"He was working on it when I left. I know that to be a fact, Marcia."

"Who does he think he is, Sara? Does he really think he can do this to me? I will not stand for it!"

"I can't speak for Lee, Marcia. You'll have to take it up with him."

"I'll take it up with him all right! I'll scratch his eyes out and Jan's too!"

With that, Marcia flung herself out the door, letting it slam noisily behind her. Sara decided to let the unpacking wait. After the long drive, a stroll on the beach would be relaxing.

She went down the steps to the sand and stepped out to the water. The stars were out, but there was a hint of cold in the air. She decided to run and loosen her muscles, breathing deeply of the sea air. It was good to unwind like this after the long hours in the car. When she was winded at last, she walked back slowly, watching the surf as it rolled in and out.

By the time she returned to the cottage, Lee was home.

"Hi," she called.

He came to meet her at the door and gave her a hug. "I saw your things. I figured you were down on the beach. You look great, Sara. The change was good for you."

"But it's nice to be back."

"How's Tom's father?"

"Much improved. Tom's visit did him a world of good. By the way, Marcia was here looking for you a little while ago."

Lee frowned. "I don't want to see her."

"Oh?"

"She has another mad on and I'm trying to stay clear of her."

"By running off to Jan's?"

He looked up with a start and then grinned rather foolishly. "Well, I'm still tinkering with her car. It needed a tune-up —"

"By now you've had enough time to overhaul the complete engine."

"Okay, okay, enough of that! I'm afraid the big news is Midge."

Sara felt a sense of alarm. One look at Lee's face and she guessed what had happened.

"The Hansons —"

"They're leaving at the end of the week — separately — and Midge is going back to the orphanage," Lee said.

Sara closed her eyes for a moment, her heart bursting with pity for the little girl.

"Oh, no, Lee! I can't believe it!"

"I'd like to personally go and wring Carl Hanson's neck with my own bare hands!" Lee said through clenched teeth. "What kind of monsters are they?"

"Lee, we can't let that happen. Isn't there something we can do?"

"Jan's trying, but so far, she hasn't been very successful. Jan's even entertaining ideas of taking Midge herself. But they frown on single people taking a child — even though God knows it would be better than sending her back to that orphanage —"

Lee was so upset that he was trembling. Sara went to lean her forehead against his shoulder for a moment and then gave him a sisterly pat and tried to cheer him up.

"Well, the Hansons haven't crossed that bridge yet. Maybe something will happen, something will change their mind —"

Lee's face was gloomy. "I never believed in that kind of miracle, Sis. It never happens when it should."

"How's Midge taking it?"

"Like a trooper to everyone but Jan. She lets down with her and bawls her eyes out. I want to do something for that kid, Sara. Give her a party or something. But a going-away party — that sounds terrible. It just reminds us all of what's happening —"

"It could just be a party, couldn't it? Why not a birthday party?"

"Her birthday's in January."

"What's the difference? We'll celebrate early. So what if it is a nutty idea? It's the sort that would appeal to Midge, and we could all spoil her a little — show her that we care. I think in the days ahead she's going to need that."

Lee thought it over for a little while and then began to smile. "You know, it might just be the thing. We'll have games, party favors, ice cream and cake — the works. Sara, you're a genius!"

"Oh, I'm glad someone has finally recognized me for what I am," she said with a teasing laugh.

"I think I could use a cup of coffee," Lee said. "The wind has a nip in it tonight."

"Fix one for me too, will you?"

Sara was once again trying to unpack when the phone rang. Lee answered.

"Sara, that was Elsa. You have company coming down the lane. She just opened the gate for him."

"Company? Who?"

"Jerry," Lee said.

"Oh, dear!"

"What's that supposed to mean?"

She didn't want to explain. It was hard to tell why Jerry was coming here at this time of night. It might have been a spur of the moment thing, or it might have to do with Cloud Nine. Whatever it was, she knew Jerry would probably be difficult.

When she heard his car stop at the cottage, she went out to meet him.

"Sara —"

Jerry came striding toward her, looking tired and rumpled. His tie was loosened and he carried his jacket over his shoulder.

"You look beat," she said.

"It's been a long day. I suppose you're wondering why I've come so unexpectedly."

"Yes."

He stared at her for a moment and then lighted a cigarette. His eyes were stormy in the flicker of his lighter.

"I have to talk to you, Sara. It couldn't wait another minute. So I fought the traffic and drove down after I left the office. I'm not leaving here until it's settled between us."

24

Jᴇʀʀʏ sᴛᴏᴏᴅ with his feet planted solidly in a way that told Sara he meant business.

"Lee's making some coffee. I think you could use a cup," she said. "Come in."

Sara wanted Jerry to relax before they talked. She could tell that he was wound tight, that his mainspring was about to break. But more than anything, she knew the moment of truth between them had finally come. Jerry was going to settle things this time, one way or another, and she was floundering for an easy way to let him down.

Lee gave Jerry a polite nod. "Nice to see you," he said.

Jerry scarcely replied.

"Look, I know you two want to talk. I'll tinker in the garage awhile."

"I'd appreciate it," Sara said.

"You'll spend the night, won't you, Jerry?" Lee asked. "You can use my room. I'll bunk on the couch."

"Decent of you," Jerry said.

Then Lee was gone, with a wave of his hand and a long look at Sara. He, too, had noted the tenor of

Jerry's mood. When Jerry wasn't looking he had held up two crossed fingers for her to see.

Sara gave Jerry a cup of coffee and he drank it quickly.

"Would you like to take a walk on the beach?" she asked. "It's nearly as fascinating at night as it is in the daytime."

"All right. As long as we talk."

They left the cottage and went down the steps. The breeze coming off the water was still cold with a hint of autumn in it. Was summer so nearly gone?

The Chadwick house was dark now except for a light in the den. Lorna Cellman had come that morning and Lee thought she was staying several days. Could she and Eldridge be working so late?

Beside her, Jerry seemed a little less tense. He took her arm as they walked along, and then he broke the silence and voiced the question she knew he had come to ask.

"You haven't made up your mind about Cloud Nine, have you?" Jerry asked.

"Would you believe I don't know what I want to do?"

Jerry paused to face her in the darkness, and in the starlight she could see the firm set to his lips and the hardness of his shoulders.

"This isn't like you, Sara. You were one of the hardest-working people in our office. You were the original eager beaver, and now you're content to roam the beach, dab in your paints, let time drift —"

"Yes, I *am* content to do that for the moment. Not forever. Just for now — I need it, Jerry. Sometimes, we lose our sense of direction and I wasn't sure I was doing what was best with my life — I wish I could explain it better."

"Was it the work or me you were running from?"

"Both," she said honestly. "But losing the account with Whiff was somehow the final straw."

"It happens to everyone," Jerry said. They walked on for a little while, saying nothing. Then Jerry paused again and she knew the moment had come. His fingers tightened around hers.

"I have something to tell you. I think you'll be surprised, in fact, I surprised myself a little for even considering it. Do you know a company called Columbia Advertising in California?"

"Yes. Everyone in the business knows them. They're very good."

"I've had an offer from them, Sara. It's a very good job and there's a chance to move up to one of the top rungs, something that will be a long time happening at Waterman's."

She was more than a little surprised and caught completely off guard.

"You mean you'd *leave* New York? After the way you've been trying to tell me there is no other place on earth like it?"

Jerry laughed shortly. "I guess that's why I feel like such an idiot. But it does bother me, Sara. New York is home and I've been happy there. It's where it's at, or at least I always thought so. Now there's Columbia and they've sure made a tempting offer."

"I'm glad for you, Jerry. You've worked hard and long for Bob Waterman and I never did think you were appreciated there like you should have been."

Jerry drew a deep breath. "Well, I talked myself into going out to California to at least look at the job. I've taken a two-week vacation. Bob doesn't know about the offer — so — "

"I wish you luck, Jerry."

He faced her with a quick motion. "But I want you to come with me. That's why I'm here. I could take the job, we could buy a house on the beach so you could paint, and we could be happy — "

Her throat swelled shut. He had already included her in his plans. Why did Jerry always leap before he looked?

"I don't want to go without you, Sara," Jerry said softly.

"Oh, Jerry — "

He tried to pull her close but she held him off. Despair leaped into his eyes.

"Sara, don't shut me out. Think of all we've had together. Think of what we could have now — "

For a moment, she let her thoughts go back to those happier times together. The swish of water turned back to the buzz of traffic on busy New York streets, and she remembered in a flash their favorite little supper clubs, the concerts they'd gone to, the long, long talks over midnight coffee in her apartment, the lazy Sundays when they had done everything they could think of or nothing at all.

They were fun times, busy times, good times. They had been special and she would remember them along with other nostalgic things in her past.

"Come with me, darling," Jerry urged. "Make me the happiest man in the world. We're alike, you and I. We belong together."

"When are you going to California?"

"When I leave here. I'm due out there next Monday, but I want my answer now."

She looked at him and met his anxious eyes. It would be wrong to give him any kind of false hope.

"Jerry, I don't know how to say this. But I don't want you to think, to plan, to include me in your future."

Jerry stared at her, his jaw hard and set. "You don't love me?"

"Only as a friend. A very dear friend."

"I don't believe that! I won't believe it!"

"Why do you persist? Why are you making this harder? I want you to take the job in California if it's what you want. Make a new life. It might be best —"

He grasped her arms tightly, his eyes burning. "I won't give up. I won't!"

Then after a moment he sighed deeply and let his hands fall to his sides.

"You're tired," Sara said. "You've been keyed up over all of this. Why don't you relax while you're here, enjoy the beach — it would be good for you."

He gave her a wry smile. "At least you try to let a

man down in style. I suppose I could stay overnight. Does Lee's offer of the use of his room still stand?"

"Of course!"

"Then I'll stay. It's better than driving back to Vincent, and with all those crazy roads, I'd probably get lost in the dark."

They talked until Lee came. Sara saw to the comforts of both men and then, calling goodnight, went to her own room. It seemed everything was crowding in on her at once. There were only a few more days before she must give Waterman her decision about Cloud Nine.

The next morning, Jerry got a late start and had barely gone when Lee came in from the garage to talk with her.

"I spoke to Jan last night about a party for Midge. She thinks it's a great idea. She suggested we invite the Hansons — what do you think?"

"I suppose out of courtesy, we should."

"After what they're doing to Midge?" Lee said with a stiff jaw. "I'm not sure I can hold my tongue or my temper —"

"Then don't ask them. We don't want to spoil things for Midge. This is to be her party, her day, and we want everything as perfect as possible."

"How about the day after tomorrow? That would give us time to get everything lined up. I won't be very busy, since Miss Cellman is here. Chadwick never leaves then."

"That would be the fifteenth. Sounds good. Who are we going to invite?"

"Herb, Jan, Tom, Wally — I think that's about it, except for us."

"What about Marcia?"

Lee took a moment to answer. "No, I don't think so. Midge doesn't know her very well, and I'm not sure —"

"How Marcia and Jan would hit it off?" Sara laughed. "I suppose you have a point."

"What's with you and Jerry?"

She told him in detail about what Jerry was doing and what he wanted of her.

"Did you tell him you would go to California?" Lee asked.

"I'm sure California is very nice and I'd probably like it there, but how can you beat this?"

"I don't think you can," Lee said thoughtfully. "You were right to want me to come here, Sis. I never knew how lousy I was feeling back in New York. I think I want to stay around here, maybe not as Chadwick's chauffeur but in this area —"

"Lee, do you have plans you're not telling me about?"

He grinned at that. "Not really. But there's a thing or two stirring around inside my head. I'm glad you said no to Jerry. I think I'll go down to Jan's and start making plans for the party."

With that he went whistling away, and Sara decided to get out her paints. She set up her easel on the patio and was soon joined by Wally.

"I saw you had company last night," Wally said. "Did he stay over?"

"Matter of fact, he did."

"Something going on?"

She laughed. "Jerry's just an old friend from New York, Wally. Now, that's all I'm going to explain to the likes of you!"

Wally grinned at that. "Okay." He lighted one of his fancy cigars and squinted at her through the smoke. "By the way, did you see anything unusual last night — around that yacht out there?"

"No. Why?"

Wally shrugged casually. "Oh, no reason. Maybe I dreamed it. I thought I saw some lights flashing on board — maybe they were having difficulty of some kind."

Then Wally walked away, trailing cigar smoke, and Sara frowned. She stared out at the *Marybelle*. It was strange how it seemed to lurk there like a bad dream, doing nothing. A flashing light could have meant a signal, but to whom? And why?

She looked up to the house. Windmere lay in a direct line from the yacht. It seemed the same, as sprawling and beautiful as ever with its tiled roof and turret rooms, but she wished Wally hadn't mentioned the lights.

25

LEE WAS BUSY in the garage polishing the Cadillac limousine when Marcia appeared. He was surprised to see her. She had tied back her blond hair with a ribbon, and she wore shorts and a boyish shirt knotted at the waist.

She came to lean against the limousine and gave him a sly look. "Aren't you even going to say hello?"

"I wasn't aware that you cared to speak to me."

"Oh, Lee, knock it off, will you?"

He gave her an angry look. "You love calling the shots, don't you? I'm just supposed to roll over and play dead until you tell me to sit up and beg, is that it?"

She flushed at that and shook her head. "No! It's really not like that. If you're going to be mean —"

She looked as if she were about to cry, and Lee weakened.

"Okay. What is it you want?"

"Do you have to do that now? I want to talk."

"You know your father likes his car kept spotless and the lane is dusty these dry days."

"Lorna's here for a few days, so that means he won't

be going out. Can't you take a few minutes to talk with me?"

He finally tossed the polishing cloth aside. "Okay, so what do you want to talk about?"

"Us. Our plans."

Lee could only stare at her. "I've no idea what you're talking about."

"Oh, Lee, I have the most marvelous idea! How would you like to go to Europe?"

"Europe!"

"I'm not going back to college. Dad can't make me go! I want to live, see the world, have fun — darling, think what it would be to go to Europe — together —"

"You're out of your mind!"

She came to put a finger against his lip and then her hand caressed his cheek and the back of his head. He felt a tingle along his nerves. Being so close to her, he felt uneasy, and his throat went dry.

"We'll bike until the weather gets bad. Then we'll settle down in Paris or London or Rome and we'll live in some little flat — I think I'd like Paris best, don't you?"

Lee swallowed hard. "Marcia —"

"I've some money. Not much, but enough. Later, when I'm twenty-one, I'll come into a trust fund. We could manage until then, couldn't we? Lee, think what it would be like!"

"Marcia, you're not thinking straight —"

"All the kids are doing it. I'm sick to death of fashionable girls' schools and silly colleges, and I just want to get away from here!"

"It might not be as much fun as you think. It's not pleasant when there's no money. Marcia, you're pretty naive about things like that."

"But you're not. We'd make it, Lee. I know we would and we'd have a ball. Don't you want to go? Deep down, don't you want to go?"

Lee went back to polishing the car, his head spinning.

"This is just some crazy idea you have in your head," he said.

"Crazy! Oh, Lee, how can you say that? How can you —"

He swallowed hard. How was he going to tell her? He liked her and she was a sweet kid, but there was Jan. Lately, he hadn't been able to get Jan out of his mind. He found himself making excuses to visit the lighthouse, just so he could see her. They had walked together on the beach, kissed in the moonlight, and every time he touched Jan, he knew that Marcia was fading out of his life and soon she would be only a pleasant memory of a summer spent at the sea.

"Marcia, don't get your hopes up," Lee said with a firm voice. "I won't go to Europe with you. I can't."

"Because of Daddy? Don't be silly. He can't stop us —"

"It's not your father, Marcia."

She grew very quiet at that and straightened, the fury coming to her eyes. "It's Jan, isn't it — you and that schoolteacher!"

"She's a very nice woman, Marcia. We're similar. I belong in her world; I don't in yours."

"How can you say that?"

The tears had welled up in Marcia's pretty eyes and Lee felt like a heel. God, give me strength, he thought. How was he going to handle this, make her understand that this summer was only a pleasant interlude? In time, she would feel that way too, possibly as soon as next week.

"I hate you, Lee Denning! I hate you —"

With a sob, she ran out of the garage, and Lee leaned against the limousine, sick at heart. If she went running to her father with this, Chadwick would probably fire him. Maybe it was as well. He had gotten too involved here. He hadn't used good sense.

It was late that afternoon when Chadwick came to the garage and Lee tensed. Was it going to happen now? He tried to read Chadwick's face, sense his mood, but it wasn't easy. Chadwick was not himself these days.

"I want you to meet a Mr. Barstow in Atlantic City tomorrow at the airport," Chadwick said.

Lee breathed a sigh of relief.

"Yes, sir, what time?"

"Nine in the morning, on the Allegheny flight from Philadelphia."

Lee had another reason to feel relieved. They'd set Midge's party for two in the afternoon. He'd have no problems getting back in time for it.

"I've a favor to ask, Lee," Chadwick said.

Lee tensed again.

"I'd rather you didn't use one of our cars to pick up Barstow. Would you mind terribly taking yours?"

"Why no. But I don't understand —"

"The limousine is conspicuous. As a matter of fact, all our cars are. I'd just as soon no one knew Barstow was coming here. It's a business thing. Come home by an indirect route and take note that no one follows you."

"Yes, sir."

"I'm trusting you, Lee. Barstow is an important man and he's carrying important papers. If anyone asks where you're going, please tell them you're on a personal errand —"

With that Chadwick left, leaving Lee puzzled and curious.

Sara stood on Tom's patio, looking out into the night. Behind her, music was playing softly on the stereo. Tom came up behind her and wrapped his arms around her, pulling her back against him.

"Darling, I love you so," he murmured.

"It's been a lovely evening, but it's getting late."

"I don't want you to go yet," Tom said. "And it isn't that late."

"Have you noticed that the lights on the yacht have been out all evening, but now they're on again?"

Tom seemed to stiffen, but then in another moment, he relaxed. "Yes. I've a hunch they came ashore in a small boat, maybe went to town for supplies."

"You don't miss anything, do you?"

Tom laughed. "I'm not sure I know how you mean that, Sara."

She turned in his arms to face him. "You say you love me, Tom, but you're not being honest with me."

Tom brushed the back of his hand against her cheek. "Of course I love you! I thought I had convinced you of that."

"You're evading the issue."

He let his arms drop and he moved away from her, taking a comfortable patio chair. He lighted a cigarette, and for a moment a tiny flame lived and died.

"If something's bothering you, Sara, you haven't told me, so in a way you haven't been honest with me either."

"I discovered a package of photos in your closet the last time I was here — quite by accident — I wasn't snooping. Why are you so fascinated with the Chadwick house? Why did you photograph it like you did, as if you were searching for something?"

Tom was silent for a long time and then stirred restlessly. "Is there anything else?"

"I get the awful feeling that you're spying on everyone around this area, including that innocent yacht out there! And why did you hide a picture of a pretty girl when we went to see your father in Cleveland?"

Tom stiffened at that. "Oh, so you caught that too, did you?"

"She was beautiful, young, sensitive looking — who was she, Tom?"

"Just a girl, Sara."

"She was more than that! Why didn't you tell me

about her? Who was she, an old sweetheart? Someone in your past that you conveniently forgot to tell me about? I've told you all about Jerry. You're not being fair —"

Tom reached out and took her hand and held it tightly for a moment. "Sh! Sh! Don't say that. It's not true."

"Then who was she?"

Tom lifted his head. "My sister. She died not long ago, and it breaks my father's heart to think about her or to talk about her. I was afraid you'd see the picture, ask about it — stir up memories for Dad. That's all."

"Your sister!"

"I'm sorry if you don't believe me, but it happens to be the truth."

She felt foolish now and she didn't know what to say.

"About the photos you found, yes, I've studied the Chadwick place rather thoroughly and with good reason. I've never felt the story they put out about Tania was true. I was certain there was a clue to the real story — perhaps there in the rocks where she fell —"

"How could you hope to find a clue there?"

"There was a locket," Tom said. "Tania wore a locket the day she died and it's missing."

Sara stared at him through the darkness, able to make out the planes of his face in the light coming from the house, but his eyes were shadowed and she could not see the expression in his gaze.

"How do you know that? Did Ryan tell you?"

"I believe it was Wally," Tom said.

"Wally!"

"Now, do you have any other questions? I'm sorry if I seemed ambiguous. It's just that I have a theory about the way Tania died. I don't think it was an accident."

"But why do you suspect a thing like that?"

"Hunch more than anything."

"Why are you so interested in all of this?"

"Maybe because I saw something the other day. I was out walking, looking for things to photograph. Wally Chadwick was nosing around. He discovered a blue car, covered with branches and camouflaged so that it was very cleverly hidden out of sight. He seemed very intrigued by it —"

Sara's hands grew cold. "A small, blue car?"

"Yes."

"That's the kind of car that nearly ran Ryan down!"

"Yes. But it was the way Wally acted — suspiciously — that somehow didn't seem quite right to me, Sara. There's something going on at Windmere. I don't know what, but I'd bet my last dollar Wally Chadwick is mixed up in it."

"Wally? I can't believe it. He's so debonair, so carefree —"

"Maybe," Tom said. "Now, let's not talk about this any more. Let's not waste our time together speculating uselessly about the Chadwicks. Let's think about tomorrow and Midge's party."

26

Sᴀʀᴀ ᴄᴏᴜʟᴅ ɴᴏᴛ ɢᴇᴛ Tom out of her thoughts, and the morning of the fifteenth, with Midge's party planned for the afternoon, she wanted to get back to work, to try and blot out everything. There was a mood in the air — she couldn't pinpoint just what it was — but there was an uncanny feeling in the back of her mind that something was about to happen. Lee had told her in confidence about his arrangements to meet a man called Barstow at Atlantic City, and it wasn't hard to tell that the whole thing worried him.

"Something's not right," he had told Sara at breakfast. "Why am I to *sneak* Barstow to Windmere?"

"A good question."

There were so *many* questions. She wanted to believe the story Tom had told her last night. But why was it she kept thinking that there was more, that she still did not know it all?

The party was to be a surprise for Midge, and Jan had taked with Dorothy Hanson to make sure there would be no hitch in plans. Sara found the morning warmer than the day before as she set her easel up on the beach and made a real effort to concentrate. But she was rather glad when Midge came along and interrupted her.

The child looked even more owlish than usual behind her large, round glasses. Her skin seemed pale beneath her tan, and Sara could see she was near tears.

"What is it, dear?"

With that Midge clouded over in earnest and Sara quickly put down her brush and opened her arms to her. For a little while, Midge sobbed against her shoulder and Sara stroked her hair and kissed her tear-wet cheek.

"Want to tell me what's happened?" Sara asked.

"I kept hoping they'd change their minds, but they haven't," Midge sobbed out. "They're going to get a divorce and I'm not going to live with either of them — I'll never see them again."

Sara held Midge closer and realized rather abruptly how much Midge had come to love her foster parents.

"I've made a habit all of my life to never cross a bridge until I get to it," Sara said.

"It's going to happen; I know it is!" Midge said.

"I wish there was something I could do," Sara said.

She was sorely tempted to tell Midge about the surprise party but decided against it. Lee and Jan had worked so hard on it.

"Tell you what," Sara said. "Would you like to mix some paints for me? I'll tell you exactly how to do it."

This was something Midge had wanted to do several times, and Sara had never permitted it. But now

Midge brightened at the thought, and in a little while the tears had vanished.

About noon, Midge disappeared and Sara went back to the cottage. Lee had just arrived.

"Well, I got Barstow here and you wouldn't believe the route I took coming back from Atlantic City."

"Forget about it," Sara said. "We have a party to give, remember? Let Chadwick worry about his own deals and his visitors."

Lee laughed. "I guess that's pretty good advice. I can't wait to see Midge's face —"

Lee had arranged to have Midge meet him on the beach for a swim about two o'clock. When Midge appeared, they had all gathered, and she stared at them with surprise.

"What's going on?" she asked with her eyes wide.

She had spied the huge birthday cake, the colored balloons and the mound of brightly wrapped packages.

"It's going to be your birthday today," Lee laughed, giving her a hug. "So, Happy Birthday, honey!"

"Oh! But it's not my birthday!"

"We're pretending," Lee said. "We have games planned with prizes and all kinds of ice cream and soda pop — why, we're going to have a day to remember!"

But even before they got the party under way, Sara was aware of the dark clouds rising on the horizon. She feared their well-laid plans would get rained out. Half an hour later, a few drops of rain began to fall.

"What terrible luck!" Jan said. "Maybe we could

make it to the lighthouse before it starts pouring."

"Not a chance," Wally said. "These squalls always move in fast. We'll move it up to my house. We can use the enclosed patio there and be safe and dry and still have plenty of room for games."

Sara was not certain Eldridge would appreciate the intrusion, but Wally was insistent. As the rain began in earnest, no one argued. Midge ran ahead of them all, shouting and laughing.

Their arrival at the Chadwick house was met by Mrs. Goddard with total surprise. But Wally had a way with her, and soon she was helping set up the party again. Eldridge came out to investigate, a frown on his face. Sara went to speak with him.

"I'm sorry, Mr. Chadwick; I'm afraid we're disturbing you."

Chadwick looked about in a harassed way. "I *am* trying to conduct an important business meeting inside. I'd appreciate it if you held down the noise and keep everyone out here — please."

"Yes, of course —"

Lee and Jan were getting the party started again, and they had to modify some of the games in the enclosed quarters. The rain was falling more gently now and the air had turned very cool.

Sometime between pin-the-tail-on-the-donkey and blindman's buff Lorna Cellman appeared on the patio, looking stylishly businesslike, but there was a frown on her face as well, and Sara knew she did not approve of the party.

In a moment of roughhousing, Lee was whirling

Midge around and around and Midge was laughing hysterically. Sara tried to motion to them to be quieter, for Lorna was standing very still now, watching them with cool, studious eyes. What fascinated her so about Midge? Midge was just a suntanned child with pigtails. A gold chain of some kind had come out from beneath the neck of her blouse and was swirling around her neck in mad confusion. Midge squealed with delight as Lee spun her one more time.

"Okay, enough," Lee said. "It's time to eat some of the cake and ice cream. Then — you get to open presents."

Sara went to help with the serving and was surprised when she saw Lorna speaking with Midge. Lorna had never struck her as a warm kind of person, but she seemed intent on talking with Midge now, crouching down to eye level. Then Midge frowned and began to shake her head. What was Lorna saying to her? Midge started away, looking frightened, and Lorna detained her.

Sara was about to go and see what was wrong when Tom went to Midge's rescue. Lorna straightened at Tom's appearance, murmured something in a muffled voice and quickly disappeared. In a moment, Tom brought Midge to the table, a bright smile on his face, talking to Midge and teasing her about the spanking he would give her later.

"What's a birthday without a spanking?" he asked.

"But it's only a pretend birthday," Midge was saying.

Their conversation drifted over Sara's head. Tom

looked all right on the surface. He even sounded natural, but there was something wrong. His eyes betrayed him.

The party was over. Lee and Jan had taken Midge home, the little girl's eyes shining, her arms filled with gifts, declaring it was the best day ever. Tom had quickly disappeared and Sara had found no chance to speak with him.

The rain had stopped by the time Sara helped Mrs. Goddard clear away the last traces of the party. She knew Lee planned to stay at Jan's for the evening.

A time or two Sara considered walking down the beach to Tom's house, but something held her back. Instead she spent a lazy evening catching up on some reading and having a leisurely bath. She did not expect Lee until after midnight.

She had just turned off the light and gone to sleep when something awakened her. Had someone tossed a handful of gravel against the screen at the window and called her name?

"Sara!"

The hoarse whisper brought her up to a sitting position, hand at her throat.

"It's Eldridge Chadwick. I must speak with you. Would you come outside? Don't turn on a light or make a sound —"

Was she dreaming? But the voice was very real and when she peered out the window, she could barely make out the figure of a tall man leaning against one of the pine trees near the cottage.

"Hurry!" he called urgently.

This was crazy! She couldn't believe it was happening. But there was something in the tone of his voice that impelled her to obey.

She did as she was asked, throwing caution to the wind, and her good sense with it. Why would Eldridge Chadwick want to see her under such bizarre circumstances?

She approached the tree poised to run and scream if necessary. Perhaps it was not Chadwick at all but some kind of —

Then Chadwick reached out and tugged her into the shadows beside him.

"Sorry if I've frightened you," he said.

"What is it? What on earth —"

"Sh!" he said. "Keep your voice down, Sara. Now listen and listen carefully. This is very, *very* important."

"Mr. Chadwick —"

He tightened his grip on her arm, and she was caught up in the web of excitement and desperation he weaved around her.

"I trust you, Sara. I *have* to trust you. I no longer know about the others — there's a traitor at Windmere; that much I know."

"A traitor! Mr. Chadwick, what are you talking about?"

He was trying to be patient, but his voice was raw with nerves and urgency.

"In this briefcase are some very important plans. I'll only say they have to do with national defense. I've bought them from Barstow and want to turn them over to the federal government."

Sara's throat went dry. This sounded like extremely hot material and dangerous to handle.

Chadwick shook her arm gently. "Sara, listen to me. You have to help me. Barstow has just brought me the last part of the plans, the key part, Core Red we call it. I'm to deliver all three plans to Washington tomorrow. Now, I'm afraid to go —"

"Can't you phone for help? Can't the government send someone here —"

"I don't think I'd have a ghost of a chance of getting out a message now — I'm sure the phone is tapped, my room is bugged, I'm not at all sure I haven't been seen coming out here —"

Sara's blood ran cold. Suddenly, she was in as deep as Chadwick!

"I'm changing the plan. It's my only chance. I will leave for Washington as scheduled tomorrow morning. But I want *you* to take the real plans to Penn Station. You'll be contacted there by a man —"

"But how — if you've been watched and bugged and —"

Chadwick's voice was tired in the darkness. "I had presence of mind to set up a backup plan some time ago, just in case something went wrong, and I thank my lucky stars I had the foresight to do it. My man will be there and he'll be looking for you."

"You mean, you planned to implicate *me* all along?"

"Only if necessary. You handled the matter in Denver so well — yes — you were the right choice."

This was all coming too fast for Sara. She couldn't really believe this was happening, even when Chadwick pressed the briefcase into her hand.

"I can't impress upon you the importance of this, Sara. If the plan goes awry, it can mean complete financial ruin for my family — but more important than that, the safety and security of this country could well be put in jeopardy. Do you understand?"

Sara's lips were dry and her heart was thudding so loudly in her ears she wasn't certain she heard half what he said. But she nodded dumbly.

"Listen carefully. This is how you will be contacted. A man in a raincoat will approach you at the information counter and ask you how to find a cab —"

Sara geared her brain to absorb all he said. It was like something out of a James Bond movie.

He went over the instructions a second time, but it wouldn't have been necessary. She knew them by heart. Then Chadwick gripped her shoulder with a trembling hand.

"Sara, you do this for me and I'll amply reward you —"

"For the first time all summer, I wish I had never come to Windmere!" she said, swallowing a lump in her throat.

He left her then and she waited a few minutes before going back to the cottage, making certain no one had seen them. The surf sounded thunderous in her ears. Even the singing of insects seemed magnified and her pulse pounded so hard it made her entire body ache.

At last, Sara ventured out from the shadows of the tree. Had she heard something, a furtive step? Unable now to go inside without knowing, she stepped out toward the patio.

"Oh!" Sara gasped.

"Who is it?"

"Elsa, is that you?" Sara asked anxiously.

"Sara? Oh, I'm sorry I startled you. I was restless, so I came out for a walk."

"Uh — me too," Sara said.

She wanted to run to the safety of her cottage, but she made herself say a few more words to Elsa and then walk away very slowly. If Elsa had been able to see the briefcase in her hand through the darkness, she must have wondered about it. Strange, Elsa being out there — never before had she seen the maid on a nightly walk!

Sara wanted to laugh at her fears, but Chadwick had frightened her so, had honed her nerves to a fine edge. She reached the safety of the cottage at last and bolted the door behind her, breathing fast, perspiration on her face. She went straight to her bedroom. She couldn't believe how frightened she was or how she had permitted herself to be lured into any of this. What kind of fool am I? she asked herself. How could I have let this happen — oh, dear God, see me through!

27

Sara had scarcely slept a wink all night. She had tried hiding the briefcase in a dozen different places, but none of them seemed safe. The briefcase was much like a briefcase she owned herself, except that the locks seemed better. First she hid it in the closet, then under things in the chest, and finally put it in bed beside her, feeling foolish, but too frightened to find any amusement in it.

Lee came at midnight and was surprised to find the door locked. She got up to let him in.

"Something wrong?" he asked.

She shook her head. "No. Just a silly feeling — I thought I saw someone prowling around out there earlier. You didn't see anyone, did you?"

Lee frowned. "No. Sara, what's this all about?"

"Just nerves, I guess. You were so upset about Barstow and the way you brought him here —"

"Did seem strange," Lee said. "But I assure you, things seem very quiet and peaceful out there."

She wanted to believe him; she *needed* to believe him. She had a terrible feeling that before it was all over, she would wish she had never heard of Barstow and Core Red.

Sara relocked the door and went back to her room and tried to put it all out of her mind. But nagging questions and new fears leaped out of the shadows, drifting before her eyes in a series of images. She tried to convince herself that Elsa's presence on the patio had been sheer coincidence.

And there was the next day to face, the enormous responsibility of delivering the briefcase to a man in Penn Station. Core Red. It sounded like something out of an apple and she giggled nervously at the thought, wondering if she were bordering on hysteria.

The next morning, hoping her voice didn't give her away, Sara told Lee she was going to New York to see Bob Waterman.

"You've decided about Cloud Nine?" he asked with surprise.

"I want to discuss some of the details with him before I make up my mind."

"Where does this leave Jerry?"

She shook her head. "Poor Jerry. I'm afraid —"

Lee smiled. "I'm glad. He's not right for you, Sara."

"Funny, you never told me that before!"

Lee shrugged. "I didn't want to interfere. But if it had gotten down to the wire, I might have. What train are you taking?"

"The seven-thirty."

"Then I can't drive you. Chadwick is taking the eight-forty to Washington and he'll not want to leave that early."

"I'll just take our car and leave it at the station. Okay?"

"Sure. Have a good trip."

"I think I'll go prepared to stay over. Diane can put me up."

"Might be a good idea. You were so jumpy last night — a change of scene will do you good."

In that moment she very nearly told Lee what she was about but managed to hold it in. Chadwick had stressed that *no one* was to know and that meant Lee too.

"Have a good trip and I'll see you when you get back," Lee said.

When Sara left the cottage, she was carrying her overnight bag and a briefcase. She put them casually inside her car, feeling as if a dozen pairs of eyes were watching her. Chadwick said there was a traitor at Windmere — Elsa? Or was it the gardener, Sam, whom she had scarcely seen since the dry weather had set in, or Mrs. Goddard, Ryan, Marcia? Wally? It was inconceivable to her that any of them could be guilty.

The drive to Vincent was uneventful, but she gripped the wheel tightly and tensed up whenever she met a car or saw one behind her. At the station, she bought her ticket and sat down to wait, the briefcase and overnight bag very close beside her, but she took pains not to be overpossessive of them.

The train was late! With every passing second her nerves grew more jagged and she wished she was a thousand miles away. It was an effort to keep her eyes from the briefcase and when she heard the train at last, she leaped to her feet nervously.

"Sara —"

She spun about in time to see Ryan racing toward her. There was no time to talk to him. She must board —

"Sara, I have to talk to you," Ryan said.

"I'm taking the train, Ryan. I'll see you when I get back in a couple of days."

"It can't wait!" he said.

He kept trying to detain her, and there was a strained, desperate look on his face. What was she going to do? She didn't want to attract attention to herself. The whole thing was to be as low-key as possible and now Ryan was getting insistent and a little loud.

"I have to go to New York, Ryan," she lied. "I have an important appointment."

He followed her all the way out of the station and as far as the train. Then she pulled free from his grip and stepped aboard. The incident had shaken her. She couldn't imagine what Ryan wanted, but she was free of him now.

Sara took a seat by the window, glad the train didn't seem too crowded. She put her things in the seat beside her, hoping to discourage anyone from sitting down beside her. She knew she could never make any kind of sensible small talk with anyone today.

"Sara —"

Her heart plunged. Ryan was in the aisle, cheeks flushed, his eyes glittery. With a quick motion, he scooped up her things and stowed them on the rack above their head. She started to cry out in protest, but clamped her lips shut. Moving her things out of the seat was a perfectly normal thing to do.

Ryan sat down beside her.

"I'll buy my ticket from the conductor," he said. "It's a good thing the train was late or I would have missed you. I stopped by the cottage and Lee told me you were going to New York."

Sara's throat was dry. "So, you chased me down — why?"

Ryan put his head back for a moment and closed his eyes. Sara could see that he looked tired, that lines were deep in his forehead and there were dark shadows beneath his lashes.

"I don't know where to begin, Sara."

"What's happened?"

"So many crazy things. All of them having to do with Tania. She made a fool of me, Sara."

She didn't know what he was talking about and it was difficult for her to concentrate on it. Her mind was rushing ahead with the train, speeding toward New York and her rendezvous in Penn Station.

"It's a funny thing about love," Ryan was saying.

Then to her surprise, he reached out and took her hand.

"You're cold. Is something wrong?"

She laughed nervously. "No. Maybe I am a little edgy about meeting my old boss. I've an important assignment coming up — if I decide to take it —"

She was rambling, not certain she was making any sense but Ryan didn't seem to notice. He was caught up in his own world, his own problems.

"Sara, from the beginning, I've been able to talk to you. You're a very special sort of person to me. Last night, it came to me what a fool I was being, crying after Tania when she didn't love me at all. She lied to me, tricked me, deceived me — that can't be called love anyway you look at it."

Sara was struggling to follow his train of thought, but it was difficult. Then he leaned toward her, his dark eyes blazing.

"Sara, it would be different with you. I know that now. I guess this sounds crazy, but I couldn't let another minute pass. Sara, I want to live again, I want to reach out, be a man again. With you, I can make it."

She blinked, his last words penetrating at last.

"Sara, what I'm trying to tell you is that I want to see you, be with you — and in time —"

"Ryan, what are you saying —"

"That I think I'm falling in love with you. I never thought it would happen, but it has."

She couldn't believe any of this. Her head began to ache. Ryan was almost obsessed with the idea, and the more he talked, the more apparent it became that he intended to make her an important part of his life.

"Do you doubt me?" he asked anxiously. "Don't you know that I'm sincere?"

She saw the look in his dark eyes and she felt the old stirring of the compassion she had always felt for him. When he leaned toward her to kiss her, she didn't pull away.

"You — you overwhelm me, Ryan!"

"I intend to," he said. Then he smiled and he was

like a different man. Even in her present state, she was aware of how attractive he was.

"I have a lot to offer a woman," Ryan said. "We could travel if you want, see the world together. I'll be patient. I won't rush you. But we were fated, Sara. From the very beginning, this was meant to be —"

"Ryan, you assume too much."

"Yes, I suppose I do. And I know this is an idiotic way to approach you, but suddenly I knew how much of my life I was wasting. I felt impelled to reach out again, as quickly as possible, to make up for all that lost time —"

Sara was aware of the train stopping at stations along the line, of people getting on and off. She tried vainly to keep an eye on her things above her head, but it was difficult. Ryan kept talking about making plans, and she suddenly realized she had a new problem to add to all the others. Once they reached Pennsylvania Station, how on earth would she get rid of him?

The train rumbled on, Ryan kept talking, persuading, being very charming, a different man than she had ever seen before. In another time, another place —

But it was now, today, D-Day, and in a few minutes she would reach New York. The briefcase would have to be handed over to the right man — she felt physically ill and pressed her forehead to the cool glass of the window.

"Darling, are you all right?"

"Yes, yes. Of course!"

"I've upset you."

He squeezed her hand and then held it to his lips. She was dumbfounded, searching vainly for a way to shake him once they reached the station.

At last, they were arriving. People began to stir, anxious to get off, gathering their belongings.

"My things —" she said.

Ryan got up in the aisle and took down her overnight bag and the briefcase, giving her a smile.

"I'll carry them for you —"

"No, I mean —"

Chadwick had told her there was a traitor at Windmere. He did not know who. She stared at Ryan. Could all of this have been an act? She ran her tongue over her dry lips. Whatever she did, she *had* to get away from him, her things intact.

They filed off the train with all the other passengers, and Ryan was talking about lunch.

"Could you meet me? Will you be tied up at the office all day?"

"More than likely."

She reached out for her things, but he shook his head. "I'll take them. We can share a cab. I'll go to my club and I'll drop you off on the way —"

"Ryan, I don't want to go in the cab with you."

He stared at her. "But why not?"

She took the things from his hands with a cool smile. "My dear Ryan, do you have any idea what you've done to me? You have my head spinning and my heart as well. I need time — away from you — don't you see —"

He was a long time replying, and she was aware of the pulse pounding in her throat. Then he smiled and leaned toward her. He kissed her for a long moment and then drew away.

"All right, darling. But when do I see you —"

"At Windmere in a few days. Give me that much time —"

Then she walked away from him. She did not dare look back to see if he was following her. The thing to do was make straight for the ladies' lounge. He could not follow her there.

She lingered in the lounge more than ten minutes. When she went back out, she looked about carefully, but she did not see Ryan anywhere. She was glad the station was so busy at this time of day, for she looked less conspicuous. Then, walking briskly, she made her way to the information booth, looking about her furtively, wondering which man it was who would contact her.

There was a line at the booth and she joined it. It inched along, and by now her fingers were frozen around the handle of the briefcase, her face stiff and her eyes stinging as she darted glances rapidly from this face to that one.

No one approached her. *No one* paid the least bit of attention to her! Where was her contact? What if he didn't come? What did she do then?

She knew that she had not asked Chadwick nearly enough questions. She was like a lamb being led to slaughter, dumb and trusting!

At last, she found herself at the window of the information booth. She asked for train times and the fare to Cleveland. Then having dallied as long as she could, she moved away. She sat down on a bench and in a notebook wrote down the information she'd been given, checking her watch.

Still no one came. Her heart was in her mouth everytime she saw a man with a raincoat over his arm, but no one gave her a second look. She had never realized before how many men carried raincoats and briefcases. Scarcely a man was without either, it seemed.

She kept waiting, trying to keep calm, telling herself this was just another bridge to cross.

Then Sara saw him. Her nerves tightened up and she felt every muscle snap to attention. The man was short and dark and coming straight for her. Her heart turned over. If she wasn't mistaken, this was the very man who had followed her to Denver, the man she thought possibly might be aboard the *Marybelle* in the cove, a Mr. Thornton, Tom had said. Could this mean he was working *for* the government?

Sara froze. She could not move. Then he was standing in front of her. He gave her a smile and a tip of his hat. "Excuse me, miss, but this is my first time here. Where do I find a taxi?"

She pointed nervously. "Over there."

"You're a native New Yorker?" he asked with a kind of lisp to his voice.

"No. Afraid not."

"What part of the country do you hail from?"

She forced herself to meet his dark, brooding eyes

and needles were pricking her nerves, sending them dancing. So far, everything had been according to plan.

"The South."

"Ah, The south. A Southern belle! Let me guess. You're from Mississippi, or is it Alabama? Maybe South Carolina, or is it Georgia —"

Her ears were ringing. The sequence was wrong! Georgia was to have been the second state named. A dozen thoughts flooded through her head. Had he simply made a mistake or could it be that this was *not* the right man?

Then Thornton was fumbling in his pocket and producing a map of New York. "Would you mind telling me a few things — I'm sure I'll get lost —"

He pointed to this and that and pretended to be asking questions. The two briefcases, his and hers, sat on the floor between them side by side. Then he refolded the map, put it in his pocket and smiled at her.

"You've been a great help, young lady. Good day."

Then he had gone, taking her case with him and leaving his. She watched him walk swiftly away, perhaps to the men's room, or to a car waiting outside. There would be precious little time wasted in opening the case, she was certain of that.

She moved swiftly herself, going in the opposite direction, stopping long enough to thrust her overnight bag and Thornton's briefcase into a coin-operated locker. She took another moment at a mailbox and then she went to find a cab, rode it for several blocks, got out, caught another and continued doing this until she had changed four times. If anyone was following her, she could not spot them.

She had decided against going back to Windmere on either a train, plane or bus. They might be watching those. A car seemed the safest.

Half an hour later, she was driving out of New York in a rented Ford, joining the streams of traffic. She watched in the mirror for a long time, but nothing seemed abnormal. Did she dare relax?

She didn't stop but kept driving steadily until she was well away from New York. Then she stopped long enough for gas and a quick lunch, watching everyone who came and went. No one seemed suspicious or interested in her.

She was nearly home free! When she reached Vincent, she considered swapping the rented car for her own at the station, but decided against it. She was desperate for the sight of Windmere.

As she drove through the town she wondered about Chadwick and if he had reached Washington safely.

Sara had just turned to one of the narrow, lonely roads that led back to Windmere when a car emerged out of nowhere and began following her. It was the blue car — the very one that she had seen nearly run down Ryan, the one they had chased that Sunday afternoon, the one Tom had found hidden!

She pressed down the accelerator, taking the curves at a dangerous rate of speed. The small blue car followed, gaining on her recklessly. Her heart was in her throat, her nerves jumping.

The blue car zoomed around her now and in a moment had drawn even with her. She saw at once that they intended to run her off the road, and she fought for control, but the wheels skidded off into the ditch. She shoved on the brakes, riding it out, being jostled and bounced about. Finally, she managed to come to a stop, but there was no hope for escape.

The blue car carried two occupants, men she had never seen before. They yanked open the door and pulled her out.

"Inside the car. Move it!"

They pushed her inside the blue car and searched her rented car thoroughly. But when they found nothing, they came back to question her.

"Where's the briefcase?"

"I have no briefcase."

"What did you do with it?"

"I don't know what you're talking about."

The two men eyed her and talked between themselves in a foreign language she could not understand. Then they got in and sped off, taking Sara with them. In a little while, they had gone down a road Sara had never seen before. They pulled the car into the brush and ordered her out.

"We'd better camouflage the car," one of them said.

"No time," the other replied. "Let's get her aboard."

Sara was taken at the point of a snub-nosed pistol to a small motorboat that had been beached and hidden. She knew now her destination was the *Marybelle* in the cove. Her luck was running out fast!

Never before had she realized how quiet and uninhabited it was here. She could see the turrets of Windmere, and her heart throbbed at the sight of them. Only this morning, she had been safe under the cottage roof and now —

They sped out to the yacht and in a few minutes she was aboard. She was met by a woman with red hair, parted in the middle, the same woman who had followed her back from Denver, the woman who called herself Mrs. Thornton.

"Where's the briefcase?" she asked harshly.

The two men looked pale and anxious. "We don't know, Natalie. She pulled a switch some way and she won't tell what she's done."

"We have ways of making people talk," Natalie said. "Many ways!"

Sara was shoved roughly down the steps to the quarters below. She caught sight of someone else there half-hidden in the shadowy room. Then he stood up, a tall, slim, nattily dressed man. She stared with surprise.

"Hello, my dear —"

"Wally!"

28

AFTER MIDGE'S BIRTHDAY PARTY, Tom had rushed away down the beach and caught up with Lee and Jan just as they were leaving Midge at the steps to her house.

"Have you got a minute, birthday kid?" Tom asked.

Midge laughed. She was bubbling over with good spirits now and it was a joy to see. "I have a great idea," Tom said. "Why don't you come home to dinner with me tonight?"

"Will Sara be there?"

"I thought we'd keep it private," he said with a wink. "Just you and me."

Lee and Jan were pleased with the idea. Tom suspected that while they wanted to do all they could for Midge, right now they wanted to be alone. He had seen the looks they had exchanged during the party.

"I'd have to go and tell Mother," Midge said.

"Okay. I'll wait right here."

Jan and Lee walked on with a wave and Tom waited impatiently while Midge raced up the steps to the house. She was gone nearly ten minutes, and he was afraid permission had been denied. He was about ready to go and find her, when she came tearing down the steps.

"It's okay."

They walked hand in hand, and Tom moved along swiftly.

"It was a keen party, Tom," Midge said.

"I rather liked it myself," Tom said with a smile. "It might have been better if we could have stayed on the beach. You seemed to make a hit with Lorna Cellman."

"I don't like her," Midge said.

"Oh, why's that?"

"She's nosey. Asks too many questions. She wanted to know where I got my locket."

Tom's nerves tensed. "She was admiring it, I'm sure. Matter of fact, I like it too. Where did you get it? Was it a present?"

Midge twisted her head up to look at him, and he was startled by the wisdom shining out of her eyes.

"You want to know about it, like Lorna, don't you?"

Tom squeezed her hand gently. "I know it's not yours, Midge. You found it somewhere, didn't you?"

"Sure, in the rocks below Windmere. Last spring vacation. After Tania died — I found it there — we were friends; did you know that, Tom?"

Tom shook his head. "No. I didn't."

"She used to wear the locket all the time and I thought it was pretty. I asked to see inside it once and she said it didn't open. That's a funny kind of locket."

Tom's heart was pounding harder now. "Did you ever get it open?"

Midge shook her head. "No. I guess she was right. It

just doesn't work that way. Anyway, I found it and kept it. Was that a bad thing to do?"

Tom shook his head. "No, honey, it wasn't. I think Tania would have liked for you to have it, since you were friends."

When they reached the house on Widow's Point, Tom fixed them a meal that he knew Midge would like, leaning heavily to the hot dogs and potato chips. For dessert there was ice cream from the freezer.

The locket swung enticingly golden around Midge's neck and Tom tried not to stare at it. He fed Midge until she couldn't hold another bite. Then he showed her the pictures he had amassed for his book. After she'd looked at the pictures all she wanted, he suggested a movie on TV and made her comfortable on the couch.

As he had hoped, Midge grew drowsy. It had been a long and exciting day for her. When he was certain she was sound asleep, he carefully unfastened the locket from around her neck and carried it to his desk.

There was a certain little spring that would release the lock and in a moment, the locket had popped open. Behind the two old photographs inside, he found what he had hoped would be there. He put the small piece of microfilm in an envelope and thrust it quickly inside his desk. Then he replaced the locket around Midge's neck and fingered it for a moment, liking it there. Tania would have wanted Midge to have it, he knew.

The phone was ringing, and he was surprised to be

told it was Dorothy Hanson calling. She was concerned about Midge, as it was growing late.

"She's fallen asleep," Tom said. "But I'll bring her home in the car in just a few minutes."

"We were afraid she'd decided to walk home alone, and it looks stormy again."

"No, Mrs. Hanson. She's safe and sound. We'll be there shortly."

He was surprised to find that Dorothy Hanson had sounded rather pleasant, and there had been genuine concern in her voice. Tom drove Midge home and she stirred sleepily as he carried her to the house and gave her over to Carl Hanson.

"She's getting pretty big for this," Hanson said.

"An armful," Tom said. "A very sweet armful, I might add. I wonder if you know how fond we all are of her. We'll miss seeing her on the beach."

The Hansons exchanged an embarrassed look, said goodnight and carried Midge away. Tom drove back home and went straight to the desk. He took the piece of film down to his darkroom and with the use of his enlarger, he managed to blow up the microfilm until the typed words there were legible. He sat for a long time, chin in hand, contemplating them.

It was late when he decided to phone his father. This news couldn't keep.

"Dad!"

"Tom, what's wrong? Why are you calling at this hour?"

"News, at last. Good news."

He explained quickly and in a moment, he heard his father's relieved sigh on the phone.

"Then you were right, Tom. Thank God. I hope you forgive me for my doubts."

"It's okay, Dad. I'll be in touch again, soon. I think things are coming to a head fast."

They said goodbye and hung up. Tom wondered what to do with the microfilm. Finally, he took his cigarette case, removed an inner lining and tucked the film beneath it. It was as good a place as any. Tomorrow he would take steps to give it to the right people.

It was about nine the next morning when Tom had a visitor. He answered the knock to find Wally Chadwick.

"Well, what a surprise," Tom said. "Come in. I was just having some coffee."

Wally stepped in, natty as ever, took a chair but refused the coffee. He seemed nervous and finally jumped to his feet and went to stare out at the *Marybelle*.

"You got your hands on the locket, didn't you?" Wally asked.

Tom felt his nerves tighten up. Wally gave him a thin smile. "It's all right, Tom. I watched you after you left the party, I saw you lure Midge down to your house. I guessed your purpose. What did you find inside it?"

Tom swallowed hard. "Wally, I don't know what you're talking about —"

Wally reached inside his pocket and brought out a small leather case. From it, he extracted another piece of film from a slit in the lining and gave it to him.

Tom's eyes widened.

"You can blow it up and have a look if you want, but I'll tell you what it says. It's my I.D. as a federal agent. My brother is involved in an important device vital to this country's defense. I was approached by our government and asked to keep an eye on things — they needed a man inside, is the way they put it."

"I see."

"What was Tania to you?"

Tom drew a deep breath. It would be a relief to get it all out in the open at last.

"Tania was my sister. We knew she was involved in some kind of secret affair for the government. When she died, we were told very little. My father wouldn't rest until we knew the full truth. He had this crazy idea that perhaps Tania had swung to the other side. You have to understand that my father is ill, otherwise, he would never have doubted Tania. I never did for a moment. But I came here for some kind of proof, to learn more about the events that led up to her death —"

"When she died, I was asked to fill in for her," Wally said. "I don't mind telling you, it didn't rest easy with me."

"What is it you want of me, Wally?"

"Sara's taking the plans to New York — Eldridge pulled a switch, as a precaution. I overheard them talking last night."

"Wouldn't it have been simpler if you had just made yourself known —"

"I can't. Not yet. It's too soon to blow my cover. I'm trusting you, Tom, because I need help. As long as that yacht stays in the cove and the foreign agents are aboard, Sara's safe — they won't go until they have what they came for."

By now Tom's heart was knocking against his ribs in quick protest.

"Sara's in danger?"

"She might be able to pull it off. Eldridge will go to Washington as originally planned, try to decoy them away from Sara. But they're smart. I don't think they'll fall for it."

"Can't you *do* something?"

"We want to catch them red-handed, with the goods —"

"But Sara! What about Sara?"

"We'll do all we can to protect her."

"Why has Chadwick let this happen? Why —"

"He's a fool to begin with. And rather naïve. He thinks he has handled it very well, and to a point he has. He doesn't know that —"

"That he has a traitor in his house?" Tom said quietly.

Wally lifted his brows. "So you know?"

"There were three names on Tania's microfilm. I suspect two of them belong to the so-called Thornton couple on the yacht. The other —"

Wally nodded. "Poor Eldridge. I'm afraid he's in for quite a shock."

"But what do we do? We can't just sit here —"

"I want you to watch the *Marybelle*. Every second!

I'm off to Vincent to get some help. It's too risky to use a phone here. I suspect the phones have all been tapped, even yours —"

"My God —"

"I told you, they're very clever people and they have ways of doing things the average person would never dream of. Now, I'm off — wish me luck —"

Then Wally was gone, and Tom stood there with his head spinning. He went to the window and took up his binoculars, training them on the yacht. He watched all morning, skipped his lunch and continued his surveillance. The perspiration poured off his face. Nothing was stirring out there. Maybe Wally had been wrong. And Sara — dear God, what about Sara?

It was in the middle of the afternoon when he saw a small boat go out to the yacht. It was the first time he had ever seen this happen in the daylight, although he suspected it happened under cover of darkness. He focused in with his glasses and his mouth fell open. Wally was going aboard! At first Tom thought Wally had told him a pack of lies until he caught a bare glimpse of a pistol being held to Wally's back.

Tom's hands began to shake. What could he do now? What *must* he do? Wally had been suspected, apprehended and captured. It meant he had not been able to get word to anyone for help! Tom rushed to the phone and then remembered what Wally had told him. It might be bugged. He couldn't risk it. He left the house and ran down the beach to the Windmere house. Lee. He could trust Lee! By the time he had covered the steps up to the patio, he was winded. He went to the cottage first and found it empty. Then he heard Lee in the garage and ran there.

"Lee, I have to talk to you!" Tom gasped out.

"What's with you?" Lee asked. "You look like you've seen a ghost."

"Come with me, away from here. I'll explain then."

"Have you gone nuts, man?"

Tom gripped Lee's arm in a tight vise. "Come with me!"

Lee decided not to argue. They left the garage and went down on the beach. There, Tom told him all he knew, and Lee's face went white.

"You mean Sara —"

"They already have Wally. God knows, they may have Sara too by now. We have to stop that yacht from leaving."

"Got any ideas?" Lee asked.

"Once I took the boat from Widow's Point out there and managed to get aboard, pleading engine trouble. I think I convinced them the boat was on its last legs. I might try it again —"

"Risky."

"What else can we do? I don't know how many people are involved. If we drive to Vincent — even if we could get there — we might be too late! I have a hunch everyone here is being watched very closely."

"I could hide aboard your boat under a piece of canvas."

Tom sighed. "Midge did that once — the little imp — I thought she was going to blow the whistle on me."

"If you could get up to the yacht, distract them, and give me about five minutes —"

"To do what?"

"A piece of wire wrapped around their propeller will foul them for awhile."

"That's risky, too," Tom said.

"It's our only chance."

29

THE CABIN BELOW on the *Marybelle* was not well lighted, but Sara's eyes were not deceiving her. Wally was there! Her head was reeling with the implication of it as he took a step toward her.

Then the red-haired woman called Natalie spoke harshly to Wally.

"Keep your distance, Chadwick!"

"I don't understand," Sara said. "Wally —"

"I got caught," he said. "I tried to get help, but they were onto me. I was hoping you were safe. I'm truly sorry, my dear."

"Then you're not one of these people?"

"Scarcely!" Natalie scoffed.

"You won't succeed, you know. There are federal agents all over. By the way, how did I blow my cover? I was very careful," Wally said.

"We have our ways of learning things!" Natalie retorted. Then she spun about to give Sara a glowering look. "Now, where is the briefcase, Miss Denning?"

"I have no briefcase!" Sara insisted. "I made the swap as I was told to do — with your man — I know it was your man now. The briefcase he left me was worthless, so I tossed it in a wastebasket at the station

— I didn't want to carry it around with me. Then I rented a car and came home — you know the rest."

"There was *nothing* in the briefcase!" Natalie said shrilly. "As you very well know!"

At that, Wally slapped his knee and began to laugh. They all stared at him. "So, my brother pulled a double switch and took the real stuff himself, after all. Well, I never thought Eldridge would be that clever. I never once dreamed he'd have the nerve to do anything like that —"

Sara saw Natalie straighten and flick a glance at her two accomplices. "Is it possible?"

The two men shrugged. "We only did as you told us!"

"Someone was watching Chadwick! Why haven't we had a report? Why is everything going wrong!"

"Has there been nothing on the radio?"

"Absolute silence. We feared we were being monitored. The radio is no longer safe!"

"No signal from the house?"

Natalie shook her head. "None. It's too risky in the daytime."

"When will she join us?"

"Later tonight. We'll pick her up as arranged, but we have to get those plans, and quickly. We're cutting this much too fine. Go ashore! Make contact with our people. See what is going on!"

Natalie's voice was shrill and frightened. Sara dared another glance at Wally, but he was looking carefully at his hands, as if he had never seen them before, inspecting them nail by nail. The two men started up the steps to the deck, Natalie still shouting instructions to them, and in that moment, Wally quickly turned his head and gave Sara a wink.

She understood! Eldridge had *not* made a double switch — she had been carrying the real thing. How long would it take them to figure out what she had done? Not for a while, at any rate, and it would give them time. Every minute was precious now.

"What's that?" Natalie asked, stiffening with nervousness.

"I didn't hear anything," Wally said calmly.

Natalie was poised and angry. "Something's gone wrong —"

Natalie started for the steps to the upper deck. Wally sprang faster than Sara dreamed he could move. He got a wrestler's hold around Natalie, her arm twisted behind her back, his own arm tight against her throat.

"Sara, look for a gun, a weapon — anything —"

There were scuffling noises overhead now, angry shouts, and a shot rang out. Sara's trembling hands searched for a weapon and found one. Wally had his hands full trying to handle Natalie, who had been well trained in judo.

"Who's up there, Wally?" Sara asked.

"I hope it's some of my colleagues. They were expecting a report from me today, and when they didn't get it — I'm sure they came to investigate."

There were steps on the stairs now, and the pair shrank back, waiting. Sara clutched the pistol, and it wavered uncertainly in her hand. Her finger was moist on the trigger. She had fired a gun only once in her life, and even then with Lee standing beside her, telling her how, she had been afraid and repelled by it. Now — any moment, she might actually have to fire to protect them —

"Sara!"

She dropped the gun in surprise as Tom came down the steps. She ran to him, and he put his arms around her in a quick moment of relief.

"You're safe!" Tom said. "Thank God, you're safe!"

"What about the others?" Wally asked briskly.

"Lee's trussing them up. Do you need some help with her?"

Wally grinned and tightened his hold on Natalie. "I haven't enjoyed myself so much in a long time. Can you operate the radio?"

"No need. I saw a Coast Guard boat coming in our direction."

"That will be my friends. You did as I asked and watched with the binoculars?"

"Yes."

"Good boy! We'd be dead ducks if you hadn't. But I didn't expect you to play the hero."

"When I saw them bring you aboard, it was bad enough," Tom said. "Then before Lee and I could get out here, we saw them bring Sara too. We sort of lost our heads — we were ready to try anything."

By now they could hear the siren of the Coast Guard boat, and Sara knew the nightmare was nearly over.

"Let's go topside now," Tom said.

"There's going to be some questions asked," Wally warned them. "And there's still one important matter to be taken care of."

Tom nodded. "Lorna Cellman?"

"Lorna!" Sara exclaimed.

"She was the brains of this outfit," Wally explained. "Frankly, they behaved like rank amateurs at times. It seems this whole outfit is not on the best footing with their own country and they wanted to do something big to get back in their good graces."

"You mean Lorna —" Sara could not believe it even yet. "Your brother's trusted associate?"

"Lorna is waiting for a signal from the *Marybelle* that all is ready. They were planning to pick her up tonight, and together the whole nest of them was going to rendezvous with a larger boat, from there — where, my dear?" Wally asked Natalie. "To your homeland?"

Natalie would only glower at him, but Sara was certain Wally had guessed the truth.

An hour later, Sara was back safely at the cottage. Lorna had been watching the *Marybelle* from the house and sought to escape. But she was stopped just beyond the Windmere gates and taken into custody.

Eldridge Chadwick returned to Windmere that day on the four o'clock train. Lee met him at the station and drove him home, but did not tell him what had happened. When they reached the garage, Sara and Wally were waiting for him.

Chadwick took one look at them and knew something was up.

"What's happened?" he asked anxiously.

"Lorna's under arrest," Wally said gently. "Sorry. She was a plant from the beginning."

"How do you know this?" Chadwick asked hoarsely, going white.

Wally explained his part in the affair, and Chadwick looked sick and exhausted, defeated.

"And the plans?" he asked. "Core Red has been lost, hasn't it?"

Sara shook her head. "Tomorrow morning in the mail, you should receive a key to a locker in Penn Station. There you will find my overnight bag and inside it is your briefcase, the plans intact."

Chadwick stared at her. "I don't understand — how —"

"I was afraid something would go wrong, so I took my own precautions. The contact made a mistake when he approached me, and I knew it was not your man. I own a briefcase very much like yours. I carried it, and when we made the swap, that was the one I let him have. After I'd left the overnight bag in the locker and mailed the key, I ran for my life!"

"If they hadn't been so flustered, so greedy, they might not have been so easily fooled," Wally said. "The fact is, they took the bait you put out, Eldridge, and started following you, certain you had the plans. But they had been watching Penn Station, too, as a double check. When they spotted your man they knew the transaction was going through as originally planned."

"Of course, they stopped him," Eldridge said.

"And forced him to reveal the details of the meeting with Sara, but he was clever enough to rearrange the names of the southern states so that Sara would realize she was being contacted by the wrong man — not that there was much hope she could do anything about it."

Chadwick shuddered and covered his face for a moment with trembling hands. "You've no idea how glad I am it's over. I know that I'll never again attempt anything like this on my own. I was such a fool to think —"

"Forget it now, Eldridge," Wally said. "I'm glad it's over, too. I don't play spy very well, even for the sake of my own brother!"

It was evening now, and Chadwick had stepped out to the patio. The *Marybelle* had been taken in by the Coast Guard, and the cove seemed unusually empty and quiet. Chadwick leaned against the railing and looked down to the rocks where Tania had fallen.

He was surprised when Ryan appeared beside him.

"Elsa told me you had gone to New York," he said.

Ryan nodded. "Yes. But I'm back. Wally told me what has been happening here." He looked down to the rocks. "Well, at least I know the full story about Tania now."

Chadwick put a hand on his son's shoulder. "We've not been very lucky with our women, have we?"

"Tania was planted, of course, to get information through me about your dealings with Barstow. Wally tells me that it's highly likely that Lorna got onto her and in a quarrel, either pushed or accidentally caused Tania to fall — that's yet to be determined."

"Lorna has steel in her; it will be hard to break her," Chadwick said with a sigh. Lorna also had a softness about her — a guilelessness that had tricked him. It would take awhile to forget her and to live with the fact that she had made such a fool out of him.

"And when they ran me down —"

"I think that *was* an accident," Chadwick said.

"It seems Lee and Tom Barclay played the hero bit," Ryan said.

"Thank God they did," Chadwick replied.

"I'm the biggest fool of all," Ryan said. "I thought for a while today that perhaps Sara and I —"

He clamped his lips shut and Chadwick gave his son a long look.

"You care for Sara?"

"I could very easily. I think she could make me forget Tania. But I'm afraid —"

"We're a sorry lot," Chadwick decided. "The three of us. You, Marcia and myself. Only that scoundrel Wally seems to be unscathed."

"Dad —"

"Yes, son?"

"You mentioned a trip to Europe once. Remember?"

"I certainly do."

"Marcia's champing at the bit about going over there on some kind of crazy biking trip. But if we were all to go — maybe she'd come to her senses.

Maybe I could come to mine and maybe you —"

Chadwick took a deep breath. The nightmare of Core Red was over and he wanted to forget it. He had missed his family, for lately they had grown far apart.

"We'll make plans for next week and if we can get bookings, let's take a long, leisurely cruise."

30

Lee had never been so tired as he was that night. The ordeal of the day had exhausted him, and when he thought of the close call Sara had, he thanked the stars that she was safe. But despite his fatigue, he knew he could not go to bed that night until he had seen Jan. When he had crawled aboard the *Marybelle* and stared at possible death by the hands of the two spies, he had met truth face to face.

If he had not been sure what he felt for Jan then, he knew now.

He walked down to the lighthouse just before dusk and was surprised to see Midge come racing toward him. By now the entire neighborhood had no doubt heard about the spies that had been caught, and he expected a barrage of questions from Midge. But she seemed to have other things on her mind.

"Guess what! Guess what!" she shouted to him.

"I couldn't guess in a million years. What is it?"

She was as radiant as a rainbow. "They're not getting a divorce. They're going to stay here the rest of the summer till school starts and have a vacation together. They're not getting a divorce —"

"You mean the Hansons?"

"I'm not going back to that dumb old orphanage! I'm staying with my folks — like I wanted."

Lee looked into her merry eyes with surprise.

"Wait a minute. Let me get this straight; do you mean you're happy with the Hansons? I got the idea that you weren't — ever —"

Midge hung her head for a moment, digging the toe of her sneaker into the sand. "Just when they're fighting, I don't like it, but when they're not, they're super!"

Lee knelt down so that he was looking her square in the eye. "You're telling me the truth?"

Midge nodded. "But I love you too, Lee, and Jan and everybody!"

Lee laughed. "You mean all this time we've been thinking bad thoughts about the Hansons —"

"I guess it was my fault," Midge admitted. "Are you mad at me?"

Lee drew her close in a hug. "Of course not. I just want you happy — that's all. Does Jan know about this?"

Midge nodded, eyes shining. "She was going to call you and tell you —"

"I'm on my way there now."

"Can I come?"

"Not this time, honey. This time, I have to have Jan all to myself. Because I have some things to say to that girl —"

He left Midge and walked swiftly away, rounded the rocks at the point and jogged toward the lighthouse.

Jan saw him coming and ran to meet him. They

paused to look at each other and then Jan was in Lee's arms, clinging to him.

"I heard the news. Oh, Lee, you could have been killed!"

"Sh! That's all past now. We've other things to think about."

She leaned back in his arms, a flush on her cheeks. "Do we?" she asked.

"I love you, Jan. I never knew how much until today."

"Oh, Lee, how I've wanted to hear you say that!"

He pulled her close and kissed her for a long, tender moment, and then she was smiling up at him, her cool hand against his cheek.

"I want to make plans," he said. "I want to buy out Mark Williams. I don't know how I'll do it, but I will. Will you stay, will you take that teaching job that was offered to you?"

"I already have," she said, nestling deeper into his arms. "I could help with the garage payments. We could do it together, Lee —"

"How can everything be so right, so good? You know about Midge —"

"Yes. Dorothy Hanson came to see me this afternoon. She's really very different than I thought and nice, too. They love Midge. We were wrong about that. I think Midge has twisted the truth just a little."

"The imp!" Lee laughed.

"Dorothy told me that the only reason they were going to take Midge back to the orphanage was because they felt it best. Knowing how Midge felt about both of them, they knew it was hard on her to see them quarreling, at odds with each other, and going separate ways — I don't happen to agree, but their intentions were good ones, Lee, and right in their own minds."

"I just want her happy," Lee said.

"So do I. I had fancied myself taking Midge, but I'm glad it has worked out for her."

"We can have our own little Midge," he said. "A whole houseful if you want."

"And to think I almost didn't come to visit this summer," Jan sighed.

"It was meant to be," Lee said. "How else can you explain it?"

She laughed happily and grasped his hand in hers. "Come on, Lee. Let's go tell Grandpa!"

Her eyes were bright and happy, her sunshine smile warm and sweet. He put his arm around her and they walked back toward the lighthouse, anticipating the happiness they would see on Herb's weathered face when they told him the news.

Sara noticed, too, that the cove seemed quiet this evening. It was a good omen, she thought. The surf kissed the shore, rushing back and forth with its love messages. Tom was waiting for her, and Sara walked along the beach with anxious strides.

Tom saw her coming but waited for her at the top of the steps at Widow's Point, a tall man with black hair and a nice smile, wearing swimming trunks, a towel tied around his waist. He looked exactly as she had seen him the first day on the beach. Then he had been an attractive stranger. Now, he was her beloved. The sight of him sent off little stirrings deep inside, impatient rustlings, the terrible need to be held in his arms.

"Tom —"

He reached his hands for her. He pulled her to him and she stood happily in the shelter of his arms.

"It's good to be home," she said with a sigh.

"Does that mean —"

"I'll phone Bob Waterman tomorrow and tell him that unless I can work on Cloud Nine here, I don't want the assignment."

"I've already called Dad. I told him I wanted to stay here. He said he'd be happy to move to Vincent and be close by. That takes care of everyone else, Sara, but what about us? You've never said you'd marry me, that you'd stay with me by the sea and be my love —"

There was one more bridge to cross. She stood there now, and saw that it spanned the way to the road that would stretch out through all the rest of the days of her life. It was the most important bridge of all.

She smiled up into Tom's eyes.

"Consider it settled."

She kissed him tenderly, deeply, fervently, and the bridge was crossed at last.